D0250777

A Christmas Bride in Pinecraft

By Shelley Shepard Gray

Sisters of the Heart series
Hidden • *Wanted*
Forgiven • *Grace*

Seasons of Sugarcreek series
Winter's Awakening • *Spring's Renewal*
Autumn's Promise • *Christmas in Sugarcreek*

Families of Honor series
The Caregiver • *The Protector*
The Survivor • *A Christmas for Katie* (novella)

The Secrets of Crittenden County series
Missing • *The Search*
Found • *Peace*

The Days of Redemption series
Daybreak • *Ray of Light*
Eventide • *Snowfall*

Return to Sugarcreek series
Hopeful • *Thankful* • *Joyful*

Amish Brides of Pinecraft series
The Promise of Palm Grove • *The Proposal at Siesta Key*
A Wedding at the Orange Blossom Inn
A Wish on Gardenia Street (novella)

Other books
Redemption

A Christmas Bride *in* Pinecraft

An Amish Brides of Pinecraft Christmas Novel

Shelley Shepard Gray

INSPIRE
An Imprint of HarperCollins*Publishers*

"Golatschen Christmas Cookies" recipe from *Simply Delicious Amish Cooking* by Sherry Gore (Zondervan, 2012) reprinted with permission.

This book is a work of fiction. The characters, incidents, and dialogue are drawn from the author's imagination and are not to be construed as real. Any resemblance to actual events or persons, living or dead, is entirely coincidental.

HarperCollins books may be purchased for educational, business, or sales promotional use. For information please e-mail the Special Markets Department at SPsales@harpercollins.com.

FIRST EDITION

Designed by Diahann Sturge

Illustrated map copyright © by Laura Hartman Maestro
Chapter opener photograph © by Lost Mountain Studio/Shutterstock, Inc.
Photographs courtesy of Katie Troyer, Sarasota, Florida

Library of Congress Cataloging-in-Publication Data has been applied for.

ISBN 978-0-06-233777-1

15 16 17 18 19 OV/RRD 10 9 8 7 6 5 4 3 2 1

To Tom, Arthur, and Lesley

And Mary said:
"My soul glorifies the Lord and my spirit rejoices in God my Savior,
For he has been mindful of the humble state of his servant.
From now on all generations will call me blessed,
For the Mighty One has done great things for me.
Holy is His Name.
His mercy extends to those who fear him,
from generation to generation.
He has performed mighty deeds with his arm;
He has scattered those who are proud in their inmost thoughts.
He has brought down rulers from their thrones but has lifted the humble.
He has filled the hungry with good things but has sent the rich away empty.
He has helped his servant Israel,
Remembering to be merciful to Abraham and his descendants forever,
Even as he said to our fathers."

Mary's Song, Luke 1:46–55 (KJV)

Sometimes the dreams that come true
are the dreams you never knew you had.

Amish proverb

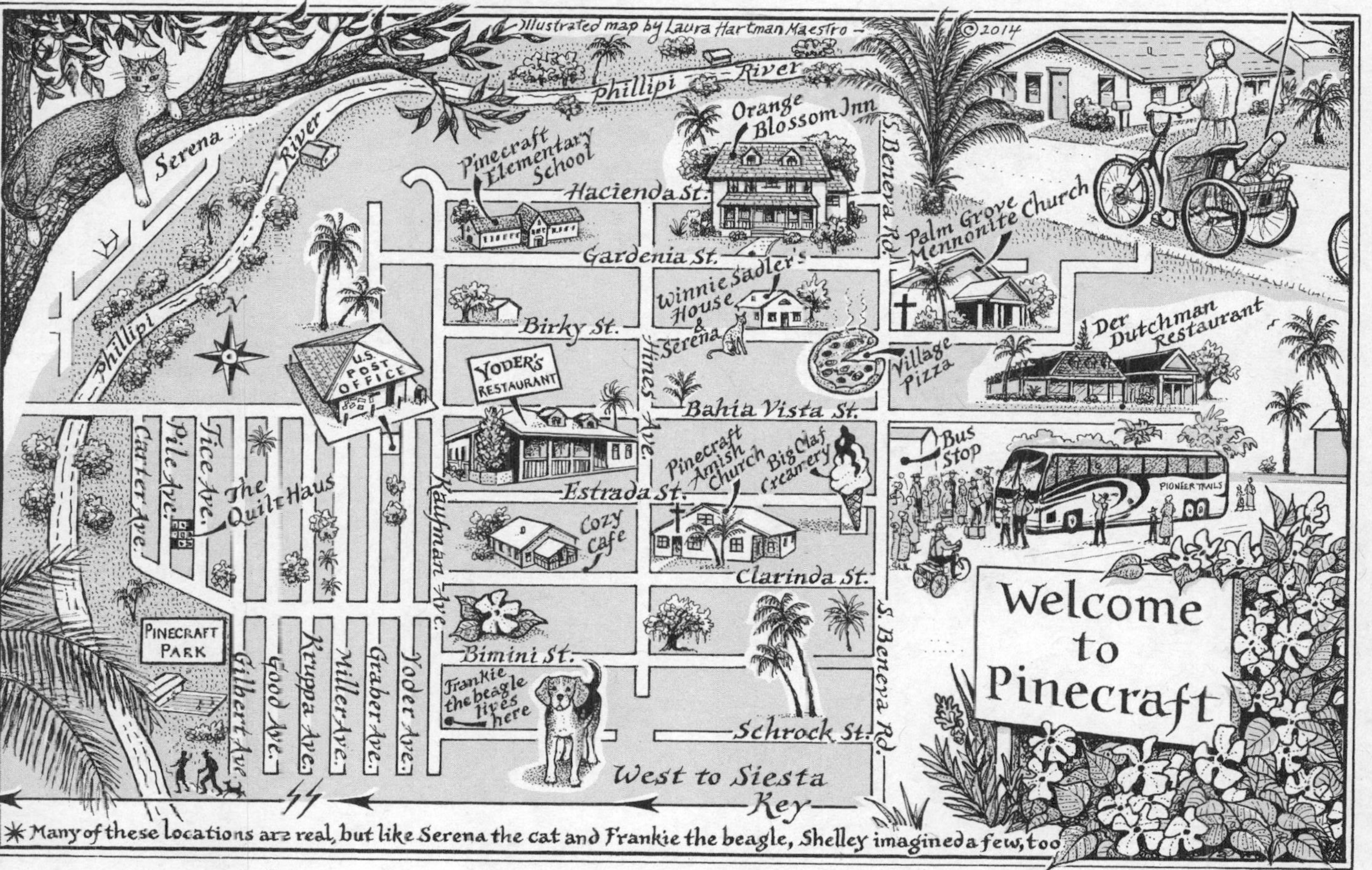
Illustrated map by Laura Hartman Maestro
© 2014
Serena River
Phillipi River
Orange Blossom Inn
Pinecraft Elementary School
Hacienda St.
Gardenia St.
S. Beneva Rd.
Palm Grove Mennonite Church
Winnie Sadler's House & Serena
Birky St.
Der Dutchman Restaurant
Village Pizza
U.S. POST OFFICE
YODER'S RESTAURANT
Hines Ave.
Bahia Vista St.
Bus Stop
PIONEER TRAILS
Pinecraft Amish Church
Big Olaf Creamery
Estrada St.
Cozy Cafe
The Quilt Haus
Tice Ave.
Pile Ave.
Carter Ave.
Kaufman Ave.
Clarinda St.
Bimini St.
Frankie the beagle lives here
Schrock St.
West to Siesta Key
PINECRAFT PARK
Gilbert Ave.
Good Ave.
Kruppa Ave.
Miller Ave.
Graber Ave.
Yoder Ave.
Welcome to Pinecraft
* Many of these locations are real, but like Serena the cat and Frankie the beagle, Shelley imagined a few, too

Chapter 1

December 2

Beverly Overholt froze in shock the moment she turned the corner onto her street and spotted a group of flashing red and blue lights in front of her inn. She blinked, sure that her eyes were deceiving her. Surely she was simply imagining that the lights were located right in front of the Orange Blossom Inn! Perhaps they were merely the reflection of one of her neighbors' Christmas lights? Some neighbors had strung lights over every tree and shrub in their front yard.

Then reality set in. The lights weren't Christmas decorations. They were coming from the three police cars parked at the curb.

Immediately, instinctually, Beverly started praying.

The prayers continued as she started forward on the sidewalk, asking the Lord to give her the strength to handle whatever had just happened to the lovely three-story Victorian house that was not only her place of business, but her home, too. And although those prayers were undoubtedly giving her some strength, one thing was becoming very apparent: Even the Lord's help wasn't going to make Beverly calm, cool, or collected.

No. She was on the verge of becoming a nervous wreck. Panic set in as a dozen scenarios clouded her mind. Had someone gotten hurt? Was the inn on fire? A line of sweat trickled down her back, the perspiration having nothing to do with the heat and everything to do with the fears taking hold of her.

Unable to tear her gaze from the large crowd gathered in front of the inn, she picked up her pace, racing past her neighbors' houses without a scant look at their merry decorations. She was quickly winded as the canvas bag on her shoulder began to feel like it weighed a hundred pounds. All the Christmas gifts she'd bought that morning now felt like heavy burdens. To make matters worse, the tote kept thumping painfully against her hip with each step. And when it wasn't, it felt as if it might pull her arm from her shoulder. She was tempted to drop it on the ground and simply pick it up later.

Just as she was about to divest herself of that bag, her best friend appeared out of the crowd and snatched it from her hands. "I've got this, Beverly," Sadie said in that forthright way of hers.

"*Danke*," she murmured, reverting to the Pennsylvania Dutch of her childhood, as was her way when she was anxious. "Do you know what's happened?"

"*Nee*. I just noticed the police lights a moment ago. You go on ahead. I'll hold on to your tote and bring it by later." She reached out and grabbed Beverly's arm as she started forward. "Oh, and do try not to panic, dear. Just because a couple of police cars are parked in front of the inn, it don't necessarily mean that there's something wrong."

If her heart hadn't felt like it was permanently lodged in her windpipe, Beverly would have stopped and given her best friend a look of pure disbelief. Of course something was wrong! She felt it as surely as if there were loudspeakers lining the street, proclaiming to one and all that very thing.

In the three years that she'd lived in Pinecraft, Beverly had never seen such a police presence. This was a safe community. Peaceful.

Well, until now.

Though puzzling, her friend's well-meaning words enabled her to refocus. Falling apart now wouldn't help anything and would only serve to make things worse. She had to be strong. Picking up her stride, she walked into the gathered crowd, then stopped abruptly when the inn finally came into full view.

What a sight it was!

One of the parlor windows was broken, the front door hung wide open, and uniformed officers stood scattered around the lot as yellow police tape kept the onlookers at bay.

As she looked from one officer to another, panic set in again. She couldn't determine who to approach.

So she scanned the crowd for familiar faces, for anyone who might be able to give her some indication about what had happened. But most folks, unfortunately, simply looked shocked.

Then she spied Zack Kaufmann. She'd gotten to know him and his family well a couple of months ago when he'd been courting one of her guests.

"Zack?" she called out as she made her way over to him.

He stepped forward, waving a tan arm above his straw hat. "There you are!" he exclaimed as he looked her over. His usually bright blue eyes were shadowed with worry. "The police have been waiting for you."

She pressed her lips together to keep them from trembling and drew in a shaky breath. "Zack, what happened? Do you know anything?"

"As far as I can tell, it looks like you've had a break-in."

"A break-in?" It didn't even make sense. She'd never heard of any sort of crime happening in Pinecraft. Why, some people even left their doors and windows unlocked! Not her, though. This inn meant everything to her.

Zack looked as if he was attempting to figure out a way to reassure her when his eyes lit up on someone approaching her from behind. "Oh, *gut*," he murmured. "Officer Roberts, this here is Beverly Overholt. She owns the inn."

"Runs," Beverly corrected absently. Until earlier this year, she'd believed she'd owned the inn, having inherited it after her aunt's passing. Now she knew that Eric Wagler was the actual owner. Her aunt had merely been renting the property and now Beverly just managed it for him.

Immediately, a new dread coursed through her. Oh, how was she going to tell Eric what had happened? And when she did, what was he going to say? Would he blame her for this mess? Though she had no guests this week, she certainly hoped no one had been nearby and gotten hurt. Staring at the building, she bit her lip so hard she drew blood. What had actually happened?

"Miss Overholt, are you all right?" Officer Roberts asked. His light brown eyes filled with concern. "You're looking a bit pale."

With a shake of her head, Beverly made herself focus on the scene in front of her. Pulling her shoulders back, she strengthened her resolve. "I'm all right, Officer. *Danke.*" But her voice sounded faint and distracted, even to her ears.

"Sure?" He held out one hand, as if he feared that she might collapse at his feet.

She didn't blame him. She felt foggy and out of sorts. "Positive. However, I will admit to feeling mighty confused. What in the world has happened?"

"You had a break-in, ma'am."

"I see." She'd been hoping Zack was wrong, but now that the officer had confirmed it, she began to feel slightly ill as visions of what that meant flooded her brain. Someone uninvited had entered her home. Most likely stolen from her. And if the window was any indication, they had obviously damaged the place.

Zack grabbed her arm when she began to sway on her feet. "Easy now, Miss Beverly."

"Yes. Let's go sit down," Officer Roberts said. Snapping his fingers, he called out, "Hey, Morris? Is the front room clear?"

"Yep, we're good," another policeman replied.

Officer Roberts rested a hand on her shoulder lightly. "Come with me, Miss Overholt. We'll go sit inside and I'll fill you in on what we know."

When she hesitated, Zack said, "Are you going to be all right?"

"Would you mind coming in with me?" She was nervous about sitting alone with a police officer.

Zack nodded. "I'll be happy to. Give me a minute and I'll bring over my wife as well."

Beverly sighed with gratitude as Zack trotted off. She didn't particularly want to sit with the policeman by herself. And though Zack and Leona were only in their early twenties, almost ten years younger than herself, she considered them to be her good friends.

Zack paused. "Bev, want me to bring Miss Sadie in, too?"

Beverly saw Sadie chatting with others in the crowd. Though she loved her best friend, Sadie could be quite the gossip. The last thing she needed was for Sadie to relay her private conversation with the police to the rest of Pinecraft.

With all that in mind, Beverly shook her head. "*Nee.* She has my tote bag, but I, um, would rather it just be the four of us for now."

"Gotcha. I'll grab the bag from Sadie, then Leona and I will be right there."

"*Danke*, Zack."

Beverly followed Officer Roberts up the front stairs of the inn and for the first time in her memory, she wasn't looking at the pretty flower beds she'd spent hours tending or the colorful welcome mat. She wasn't feeling proud of the neat and attractive way she kept the inn. Instead, she was noticing the broken glass littering the porch and the scratches surrounding the front door.

But then, as she crossed the threshold, Beverly couldn't help but gasp. The main gathering room was in complete disarray: Furniture had been knocked over; her pretty framed prints were off the walls and lying in pieces on the floor; and one of her prized hurricane lamps had been shattered.

"Ack, but this is terrible." Tears pricked her eyes. "Who would do such a thing?"

Officer Roberts looked dismayed as they walked carefully through the pieces of broken glass. "I'm sorry, Miss Overholt, but I have no idea."

"It's Beverly, Officer. Please call me Beverly."

"Oh, my goodness," Zack's wife, Leona, whispered as she entered the room. Her brown eyes widened and she looked as shocked as Beverly felt. It was only after Zack whispered in her ear that she began to walk forward hesitantly. Once by Beverly's side, she reached for her hand. "I'm so sorry, Beverly."

"I am, too."

Leona straightened a couch cushion and said, "Let's sit down."

Beverly did as Leona suggested and squeezed her friend's hand as Officer Roberts perched on the edge of the chair across from her and fidgeted uncomfortably.

"Beverly, two hours ago, we got a call from a neighbor who noticed that one of your front windows was broken and things didn't look right. We drove by and saw the front door was cracked open. We checked things out, but whoever did this was long gone. I'm sorry to tell you that the majority of the main floor looks a lot like this room. The intruder caused extensive damage."

"In the guest rooms, too?" She was almost afraid to ask.

"No, luckily, it doesn't seem as if the culprit was interested in the guest rooms."

"I suppose that's something," she murmured, though she wasn't sure the knowledge really helped her all that much. As she looked around, she shook her head at the wreckage. The destruction all seemed so unnecessary.

"Do you have any current guests?"

"*Nee.* I don't have any guests right now."

At Eric's urging, she'd given herself a week's vacation. She'd wanted a little time to sleep late, shop, and relax before the next round of guests arrived for Christmas. Taking a week off had sounded like a wonderful idea, especially since she knew how full the inn would be the rest of the month. But now she wondered why it had ever sounded good at all.

Why had she ever thought she needed a break in the first place? If she'd had guests, no one would have dared to come inside. Her mind continued to race. Or had someone been watching the inn? Had they known it was empty? It was such a disconcerting thought that she couldn't bear to dwell on it.

"Good to know." Officer Roberts punched something into his phone. "We'll do our best to find those responsible, ma'am. But in the meantime, when you're ready, we'll need you to walk through the inn and tell us what's missing."

He continued on about fingerprints and motives, police reports and pawnshops, but none of what he said made much sense to her. Not that it mattered. Beverly was done listening. She really couldn't take anymore. Someone had ruined her livelihood. She felt as betrayed as she had when she'd discovered her fiancé had fallen in love with her best friend all those years ago.

Taking a deep breath, she tried to push those thoughts away. This wasn't the time to revisit those painful wounds.

"Are you going to be all right?" Zack asked. "Do you want me to get you a glass of water or something?"

"I'm fine," she said at last and tried to mean it.

Because she had no choice.

"Your insurance should cover the damage," Zack said quickly, as though not having to worry about the financial repercussions would ease her mind. It didn't. Insurance money could not replace the most valuable thing stolen from her today: her sense of security.

But Beverly nodded anyway. "*Jah*. I imagine it will."

"Do you want me to call Eric for ya?" Leona offered. "I don't mind."

She looked at Leona and shook her head. "*Nee*. I'll do it."

"Who's Eric?" the officer asked.

Beverly said, "He's the owner of the inn." But in truth, he was more than that. During the last few months, he'd also somehow become the best friend she'd ever had.

She only hoped when he heard her news that that would still be the case.

Chapter 2

December 2

"It's going to be all right, Beverly," Eric said into the phone for at least the fourth time in fifteen minutes. When he heard no immediate reply, he walked to his window, stared out at the gray Philadelphia sky, and explained himself. Again. "I know this is a shock, but you'll get through it," he said gently. "What matters is that you weren't hurt." He closed his eyes as he imagined how much worse things could have been for her. He wasn't sure how he would have handled it if she'd been calling from the hospital.

"But . . . but, Eric, it's terrible. It's so terrible," Beverly sputtered. Her voice had a definite Pennsylvania Dutch accent, a sure sign that she was extremely distressed.

He had to get there as soon as possible.

He ached to comfort her and wished he were sitting across the kitchen table from her so he could see her pretty green eyes and ascertain just how flustered she was. Instead, he was reduced to sitting in his office with a phone to his ear, trying to do his best to reassure her. Outside, Eric noticed that snow had started to fall, adding to the seven inches that had accumulated the evening before. He wandered back to his desk and clicked on his laptop. Hopefully flights weren't grounded. He needed to get on one headed south and fast. "I know, dear. But—"

"But what?" She hiccupped. "Ach! Eric, all the money in the lockbox was taken. And the lockbox itself! I'm so very sorry."

"You have nothing to apologize for."

"But still . . ."

But still she was going to apologize.

While the search engine on his computer looked for flights, Eric leaned back in his chair and propped his slippered feet up on his desk, hoping and praying that eventually some of his words would penetrate her fog. "We can get you another lockbox," he soothed. "The cash may be gone, but it was just five hundred dollars."

"That's a lot of money."

"It is, but it's not your life savings, Bev."

She ignored him. "And the gathering room? It's a terrible mess. A horrible, terrible mess. Lamps are broken! Glass is everywhere. I don't know how I'm going to get everything to rights in time for the next guests."

"You will. You always do." He couldn't resist smiling as he remembered the first time he'd visited the inn after inheriting it from his neighbor. Beverly had been cool and distant. But she'd also carried an air of supreme competency. He'd realized right then and there that she was a born innkeeper. She could juggle multiple problems with ease. And in the months since their first meeting, she'd proven that his first impression had been right on the money. It was one of the reasons he hadn't felt too guilty about returning to Philly until his house sold and he could relocate to Pinecraft for good.

She could handle anything. Now he just needed to make sure she remembered that.

"You sound so confident, Eric."

"I'm confident in you." Hating that he wasn't standing right by her side so she could see how sincere he was, he continued to coax and cajole her as best he could. "Look, why don't you take a deep breath and just ignore the mess for now. I don't want you to get cut or hurt."

After sighing, she said quietly, "Eric, I can't just sit here and stare at everything. My mind is such a blur."

"That's because you need to calm down. Everything will look better in the morning." Especially because, by then, he would be headed her way.

"I doubt that. All the glass and debris will still be on the floor." Her voice turned weepy again. "I know I'm not making a lick of sense, but I really am at a loss of what to do first."

At last, it seemed she was asking for suggestions. Though she couldn't see him, Eric smiled. "I know. Go make yourself a cup of tea, honey." He winced as the endearment slipped through. "You should eat a couple of cookies if you have them, too."

"Cookies?"

"The shortbread. Those are still your favorite, right?" he murmured as he clicked on a one-way flight and pulled out his credit card.

"Eric, I'm not *hungahrich*—"

And here came the actual Amish words.

"Honey," he began just as he realized what he was saying again and quickly amended it. "I mean, *Beverly*, please listen to me. Please, go get some hot tea and sit down. Then I want you to try to relax. I'll be there tomorrow."

"Eric, tea won't help. And while shortbread cookies might actually taste good, I don't think I have any butter— Really?" She gasped suddenly. "You will?"

"Really." Glancing at his laptop, which showed his flight confirmation, he said, "I'm getting on the first flight out to Sarasota. I'll be with you around lunchtime tomorrow. And I'll even bring you cookies." He looked at his watch. "That's just a little more than twelve hours. Just hold on until then, okay?"

At last, he heard her sigh and relax. "You don't mind coming down here to help me? I mean, I know it's your inn and all. But truly, you don't mind coming on the spur of the moment like this?"

"If you knew me better, you wouldn't ask."

She hiccupped again. "I thought I did know you well. What don't I know?"

It was time to evade and redirect. "You know me as well as anyone. The best parts of me, anyway."

She sniffled into the phone. "We can talk about your past, if you'd like."

"Don't worry about me right now."

He was starting to realize that he'd kept too much of himself hidden from her before now. But he hadn't wanted to shock her about his past and so he'd kept it firmly locked away whenever he'd been around her. It hadn't been a difficult undertaking. Beverly had been raised Amish and now was a conservative Mennonite living in the middle of a quaint Floridian Amish community. She spent her days baking and looking after guests and visiting with her neighbors. She worried about how much flour and sugar were in her pantry. She knew how to fold a napkin into a work of art.

In short, her life was pretty much the exact opposite of his, and he was glad of that.

But now he couldn't help but feel that if she'd known a little bit more about his past, about the things he'd experienced, she would have had far more confidence in him. She would have realized that a simple burglary wouldn't faze him.

Not in the slightest.

"There's more to me than what you've seen, Beverly."

"That sounds rather ominous."

He felt a bit ominous, actually. Chances were good that Beverly wasn't going to like some things she found out about him—if he ever really opened up to her. He cleared his throat, hating how awkward he sounded and felt. "All I'm trying to say is that you can count on me to handle just about anything."

"This robbery might put you to the test."

"I can handle it," he repeated. Knowing it was time to change the topic, he said, "So, are you going to sleep at your friend Sadie's tonight?"

"At Sadie's? Oh, *nee*."

Perturbed, he dropped his feet back down to the tan Oriental carpet covering his cherry floors. Frowning, he asked, "If not Sadie's, where do you plan to sleep?"

"Here, of course."

He didn't have to be standing in the same room as she to hear the slight tremor in her voice. Once again, he tried to be the voice of reason from much too far away. "Beverly, I'm sure Sadie won't mind if you sleep in her guest room. I think you should go over there as soon as we hang up. You'll rest better."

"I couldn't."

"Bev, I don't want you to be by yourself." Surely if she stayed the night alone at the inn she wouldn't get a single moment's sleep. Every creak and groan would keep her on edge. And understandably so. Thinking of her scared and frightened made Eric feel worse than helpless. "Just grab your toothbrush and walk over to Sadie's house. We'll deal with everything when I arrive. You said the police helped you board up the window?"

"*Jah.* The *fenshtah* is boarded up."

"Then the inn will be safe enough. Simply lock the doors and walk next door. The break will do you good."

"I can't go next door. Sadie was almost as upset as I was. And, well, you know how she talks. If I stay any length of time around her, she's going to only make me more distressed."

She probably had a point. Her friend Sadie did talk nonstop and seemed to believe only in extreme emotions. Eric could just imagine what doom and gloom Sadie might invent and share with Beverly. She'd probably get Beverly so wound up, neither one of them would get a bit of sleep. "Perhaps you are right. But still, I don't like the idea of you staying there alone tonight. Would you like me to make some calls?"

"Don't worry about me, Eric. Now that I know you'll be coming here tomorrow, I'll be fine."

She wasn't going to be fine but he decided not to argue with her. The minute they got off the phone he was going to take matters into his own hands. It was better that way. Then she wouldn't be able to argue with him.

"All right, then. Try to get some rest, and I'll see you tomorrow."

"*Jah. Meiya.*"

Though he could only hope *meiya* meant tomorrow, he thought he heard a hint of relief in her voice. "Okay. I'm going to go, but I'll get there as soon as I can. Look for me around lunchtime."

"I—I will do that."

"I'm going to let you go now so I can get packed."

"*Jah*, that is a mighty *gut* idea. *Danke*, Eric." She sounded forlorn. And so very Amish. And so alone. He would give just about anything to wrap his arms around her and hold her close, but until he got to Florida, all he could do was attempt to soothe her with words. "You're welcome, Bev. Now, please don't worry anymore. We'll figure out everything when I get there. All you should think about is resting. Okay?"

"Okay. But maybe I should sweep a bit. Eric, the mess—"

"We'll deal with that tomorrow," he said more firmly. "I promise, I don't care about anything besides the fact that you are all right. Now, please, just take care of yourself. We'll get everything sorted out when we're together tomorrow."

"I think you might be right," she said, her voice holding a bit of hope in it for the first time. "It might be easier to tackle all this together . . ."

"I know it will be."

"I'm mighty glad you're comin' out."

"I am, too." Hoping to lighten things up, he teased, "Now, let's hang up so I can pack, okay?"

She giggled. "All right. Good-bye, Eric."

"Good-bye. I'll see you tomorrow." He hung up with a grin. That small little chuckle in her voice had made him feel like he was the king of the world. She was going to be okay.

Now all he had to do was make sure she wasn't alone until he got there. He ran his thumb across his cell phone's screen until he came across the Kaufmanns' house number. Even though the Kaufmanns were Amish, they were New Order, which meant they had a phone in their kitchen. Thank goodness.

To his surprise and relief, Zack answered on the second ring. After learning that Zack and his bride had been over at his parents' house playing cards and talking about the break-in, Eric got down to business.

"Hey, I know it's late but I need a favor," Eric said.

"Of course. What may I do?"

"Is there any way you could ask your parents to let Beverly stay at their house tonight? She's alone at the inn and though I know she's scared to death, she's refusing to impose on anyone. I know your mom will make her feel more at ease."

"Of course we'll do that."

Eric closed his eyes in relief. "I owe you. Thanks a lot."

"*Nee*, thank you for calling. We should have done that already. Actually, I shouldn't have taken Leona home and left Beverly there by herself."

"You needed to see to your wife, Zack. I understand that." Eric was starting to realize that he felt just as responsible for Beverly. Because she had such a confident air about her, most people forgot she was only in her thirties and running a business by herself. She needed someone to have her back, to make sure she took care of herself. He was now happy to be fulfilling that role. "Now, are you sure your parents won't mind having her stay the night?"

"They won't mind at all. I bet we'll have her safely nestled in my parents' guest bedroom in no time."

"Thanks. Listen, if your mom has time, you might ask her to go with you to get Beverly."

Zack chuckled softly. "You think I'm going to need some help, do ya?"

"Maybe. She can be pretty stubborn." Thinking of all Beverly's protesting, he added, "She was actually thinking about sweeping the floors tonight."

Zack whistled low. "Sounds like I better get going, the sooner the better."

"I'd really appreciate it if you could get over there as soon as possible." For a moment, he considered even asking Zack to call him after he got Beverly situated, but he didn't want to impose on the man's time even more.

"We got this. And don't worry. You know my *mamm*. She'll be eager to help. As will Leona. Between the three of us, we will get Beverly settled in without a problem."

"Thanks. And try to get her to rest in the morning if you can, would you? My flight doesn't land until noon or so and I don't want her going back to the inn at seven in the morning."

"We'll do our best to keep her occupied until you arrive."

Eric was starting to feel like he was asking too much. "Um, are you sure you have time? I could try to call Penny and Michael Knoxx . . ."

"I'll call them if we need to, but I think for now we'll be okay. We'll take Beverly out for a long breakfast tomorrow. We'll go stand in line at Yoder's!"

"Perfect." He knew Beverly loved eating there but never could spare the time, since she was usually making breakfast for others. The novelty of letting someone else look after her should keep her occupied until he arrived.

"Don't worry about a thing."

"I won't worry now. Thanks again for everything, and I'll see you tomorrow." After finally passing on his flight information, Eric hung up. With a sigh, he leaned his head against the wall and finally allowed himself to focus on what was about to happen.

Early tomorrow morning, he was heading back to Florida. To Pinecraft. To Beverly. He would help her clean up and settle down. But most of all, he would be able to show her how much he cared about her. She would know she wasn't alone.

Maybe then, if she was willing to trust him, he wouldn't be alone anymore, either.

By the time Zack hung up the kitchen phone, the whole family was standing around him, waiting to hear about the unexpected phone call—Effie, too.

Even though they were New Order Amish and could have a telephone, phone calls were pretty rare. Actually, the only time Effie could recall the phone being used a lot was when her brother had been courting Leona last winter.

Leona had come to Pinecraft on a girls' weekend and met Zack her first night in town. After she'd gone back home to Ohio, Zack had called her almost every day. Before long, Leona returned, and Zack proposed. Now they were married and living in a small house a few streets over.

Which was why it was so unusual for him to talk on their parents' phone for any length of time.

"Well, don't keep us in suspense any longer, son," Mamm said. "Who was on the phone?"

"It was Eric Wagler."

"Isn't he in Pennsylvania?" Leona asked.

"He is. He called here for a favor."

"What does he need?" Daed asked.

"He asked if Beverly Overholt could spend the night here."

"Tonight?" Effie's mother's voice had gone up two octaves.

Zack ran a hand through his dark hair. "*Jah*. Beverly's upset, of course. She called him and told him all about the break-in. Now he's coming down tomorrow. He thinks he'll be here around lunchtime."

His *daed* blinked in surprise. "So soon? That is a mighty long way. I wonder how much the plane ticket cost?"

"Probably more than we need to worry about."

"He must be terribly worried," his mother added. "Ain't so?"

"It is his inn, Mamm," Daed pointed out.

"It is also just a building."

Looking a bit bemused, Zack replied, "If you want to know the truth, I doubt Eric has even thought two seconds about the actual building. When we spoke, all of his concerns were centered on Beverly."

She smiled softly. "I knew that man's heart was in the right place. Beverly didn't think much of him becoming her boss, but this just goes to show ya that the Lord's plans are always in the right place. He really cares about her."

Zack nodded. "And that is why he asked for a couple of us to go to the inn and convince her to come over. He said she's trying to be brave but she's pretty shaken up about the day's events."

"I'm sure she is," Effie's sister Violet said as she walked to the kitchen and began putting away the few glasses that were drying on the wooden dish rack. "Anyone would be."

"So, who wants to go over to the inn with me?" Zack asked.

"I will," Leona said.

As always happened when he looked at his wife, Zack's expression softened. "*Danke*, Le, but I think Mamm or Daed should come, too."

His mother picked up a cloth and started wiping shelves. "Eric is sure Beverly needs to come here?"

"Uh, *jah*." Zack looked completely puzzled. "You don't mind, do you?" When she didn't reply right away, he glanced at Violet and then at Effie.

Effie shrugged. Their mother's reaction was as much a surprise to her. She'd never known their mother to ever be inhospitable to anyone in need.

"Ginny, what is wrong?" Daed asked.

"Nothing. I mean, of course I don't mind . . ."

"Then why are ya acting so upset, Mamm?" Effie asked.

"I'm not upset. It's just that we are going to need to rearrange things." She stared at them all, obviously reconfiguring sleeping arrangements in her head.

"What's there to rearrange?" Daed asked. "Beverly can have the guest room. That's what it's there for."

She nodded slowly. "That would work. But that also means that we're going to need to change sheets and clean bathrooms . . ."

Effie shook her head. "But everything's just fine." Looking around their spacious living room, Effie thought things looked rather neater than normal. Everything was picked up, the floor had been swept, and even her mother's favorite stack of *Better Homes and Gardens* magazines were neatly organized.

"Not for an innkeeper like Beverly to see, it's not."

"Violet and I can freshen up the bathrooms and change sheets," Leona said. "And Effie can help, too."

"I guess we have a plan then," their *mamm* said.

"We do, but it can't take all night," Zack said. "I promised Eric I'd get over there as soon as possible. He was really worried about Beverly being alone."

"I agree," their father said with a look of understanding. "Dear, we'd better go over to the inn within the hour."

That apparently spurred Mamm on. "That gives me just enough time to whip up some pumpkin-and-chocolate-chip bread."

Violet groaned. "Mamm, we don't need bread . . ."

"Oh, yes we do." Her voice turned sharp. "This is Beverly

Overholt, remember. She bakes fresh goodies for dozens of people every day. Every single day." After letting that announcement percolate for a few seconds, she added, in a more panicked tone, "She also offers complete strangers a clean, beautiful place to stay."

"That's her job," Violet said impatiently. "She runs an inn. She would never expect us to go to so much trouble or to act so formally."

"That is true, but she still has eyes and a nose."

Effie wrinkled her nose. "What does that mean?"

"Everything. I don't want her going around thinking that I have a dirty house with nothing good to eat."

Zack looked as if he was about to lose his patience. "Beverly is coming over because she's upset, not because she wants fresh bread."

Leona reached out and squeezed Zack's hand. "If we get started, we'll be done in no time," she said in her usual soft manner.

"I agree with Leona," Violet said. "I bet together we can make everything perfect in an hour or less."

It was as if that reminder about time was all she needed. Their mother took a deep breath, steeled her shoulders, and nodded. "You are right, *kinner*. One hour is more than enough time to make this house shine." And with that, she started barking out orders ruthlessly, adding a generous amount of pointing as she did so.

Before heading to her room, Effie walked to her brother's side. "You'd best get out the egg timer, Zack."

"You think?"

"Otherwise, Mamm is going to have us cleaning all night and you'll be late to get Beverly."

Zack winced. "And then Eric will never let me hear the end of it." Turning to Violet, he said, "Hurry and go set the timer for fifty minutes. We've got to get out of here and get Beverly before it gets too late."

"I'll do one better," Violet said with a wink. "I'll set it for forty-five."

Staring at the three siblings, Leona frowned. "But your *mamm* said an hour."

"Don't worry, Le. We do this all the time."

"It's true," Zack said with a grin. "Otherwise nothing would ever get done."

Chapter 3

December 3

Beverly appreciated the Kaufmanns' hospitality. She really did. And she was also grateful for their offer to take her to Yoder's for breakfast. The food would be wonderful, but there was no way she was going to be able to handle standing in that long line with half the community. Chances were very good that she would see several people she knew. Chances were even better that someone would ask her about the robbery and how she was feeling.

Just the thought of coming up with a reply made her cringe.

Besides, now that a little bit of time had passed, she was feeling less rattled and more focused. She needed to take some time to pray, to clear her head, and begin to make plans.

Eric's arrival was also on her mind. She wanted to be by his side when he first walked through the inn's doors. Though it might be silly, she thought he might need her when he first saw the damage. She would love to be the one offering support for a change.

All of those reasons were good ones. They were the reasons she'd simply had a bowl of cereal and a cup of coffee at the Kaufmann house before taking her leave. But once she'd stood on the front walkway of the Orange Blossom Inn and spied the boarded-up front window, all her good intentions left in a flash. She simply wasn't up to the task of confronting the disarray by herself. Thinking of the broken glass and the damaged lamps on the floor made her stomach clench tightly.

Instead, she'd turned around and gone to the library to use their computers. There, she contacted the guests who had booked a room for the following week and cancelled their reservations. Then she'd wandered around, absently looking at books and magazines. But when she realized not even the new issue of *Southern Living* could hold her attention, she returned to the inn and sat on the stoop.

And that was why she was sitting outside when Eric pulled up in his rental car two hours later.

The moment he saw her, he raised a hand and waved through the windshield. She waved back, and sat patiently while he parked, pulled out a backpack, heavy coat, and duffel, then crossed the street toward her. As usual, he was dressed in faded jeans and a plain, snug-fitting T-shirt. What was unusual were the thick boots on his feet. Those boots made him seem even taller than his six feet and, somehow, even more rugged than ever.

"You are quite the welcome party, Bev," he teased.

Beverly got to her feet and held out a hand for his backpack. "Hardly that."

He ignored her offer of help. Instead, he set his bags down on the porch and took her hands in his. "It's good to see you," he said quietly.

Looking into his dark brown eyes, now filled with warmth and compassion, Beverly felt the same way. She sighed in relief as his warmth permeated the cold feeling that had settled deep inside her since the break-in. He squeezed her hands gently, bringing with his touch the reminder that she was no longer alone. She felt the muscles in her neck and shoulders ease, lessening some of the stress she'd been holding on to—stress she hadn't even realized existed until it dissipated.

He studied her, his gaze skimming her features. "You okay?"

Though she'd wanted to at least act brave, she found she couldn't do it. "Nope," she admitted with a shrug and an embarrassed smile. "Even though the police have assured me that there was most likely nothing personal about the robbery, I still can't help but feel that I've been violated."

"I know."

"I keep thinking that I shouldn't have left the house. And definitely not because I wanted to do a little early Christmas shopping."

"There was nothing wrong with taking the day off."

She knew he was right, but it still didn't sit well with her. "But, still . . ."

"Bev, if you hadn't left, there's the possibility that you could have been injured. The thieves might have decided to rob the Orange Blossom Inn no matter what."

Just imagining that made her shiver. "You're right. I need to stop worrying about what I could have done to prevent it and continue to count my blessings. It could have been much worse."

Respect lit his eyes. "Good girl. So only your lockbox, television, and DVD player were stolen?"

"Other things were rummaged through, Eric. Someone went through my drawers." She shivered. "The police think they walked in my closets, too. Why were they looking through my clothes?"

"I imagine they were searching for jewelry and such."

"I bet if I'd had more items of worth, they would have taken those things, too."

To her amazement, he looked like he was trying not to smile. "I imagine that is true."

Hurt, she let go of his hands. "Are you laughing at me?"

"Of course not."

"Eric, you look amused." Though he looked concerned about her, there was something in his eyes that told her he thought she was being a bit overdramatic.

"I promise, I'm not amused," he said quickly. Stepping closer, he lowered his voice. "You know how worried I've been about you."

"But?"

"But I, um, well, I'm kind of surprised that you're taking all of this so personally. Sometimes robberies are just robberies, you know?"

She shook her head. "*Nee,* I do not."

"All I'm saying is that someone might have robbed you simply because they needed the money."

"If that is the case, I have to say that they are going about things the wrong way. They should go get a job."

His expression turned serious. "Of course. Of course you are right. It's just that sometimes desperate people do desperate things."

She was about to reiterate that breaking into her inn was the wrong way to handle one's problems when something occurred to her. Eric sounded like he knew what he was talking about. "How do you know so much about this?"

For the first time since they'd started talking, he looked uncomfortable. "I don't. Aren't you ready to go inside?"

She wasn't. Instead, she chose to concentrate on his very un-Eric-like response. He also looked a little embarrassed, but she couldn't ever remember him acting embarrassed about anything.

She decided to give him a way out. "Do you know so much about crime because you live in a big city?"

"Philadelphia is a big city," he said slowly, "and it can be dangerous. I think most everyone in big cities knows someone who has been a victim of a crime at one time or another."

"Well, I'm glad I don't live in a big city, then. I hate that this crime has happened to me. It's made me rattled and scared. I wouldn't wish this on anyone."

"I hate that the inn was robbed, Beverly. I hate that you've been so rattled, too. That's why I came here right away." His voice was soothing now. "Do you have your key? Let's go inside and see how everything looks."

She still didn't want to go in, but she felt better with him by her side. Beverly handed him the key and found herself holding her breath when he slid it inside and jiggled it to the right—the way you had to because it always stuck—then at last turned the knob.

She found herself still holding her breath when they stepped inside.

"Breathe, Bev."

Immediately, she exhaled and then realized she was having to remind herself to continue to breathe as she looked around the space.

Everything looked just as bad as it had the day before. Glass was still sprinkled on every surface, couch cushions were on the floor, a photo had been knocked over on its side. The glass protecting the picture was shattered.

"Oh, Eric." And though she'd hoped to be far stronger for him, tears filled her eyes.

"Come here, Beverly," he coaxed.

But she didn't need any coaxing. Instead of fighting off more tears or pretending that she was going to be fine, *just fine*, by herself, Beverly gave in to temptation and walked to him. She leaned close when he wrapped his arms around her. Slipped her hands around his waist and held on tight. Smelled his fresh cologne.

And almost believed him when he said everything was going to be okay.

December 3

"Hey, Effie," Josiah said as Effie was walking by his seat in the library.

Feeling as flustered as she always did whenever he was around, she stumbled over her response. "Oh! Hey, Josiah. I almost didn't see you there." Of course that was a lie. He was sitting in one of the study cubbies near the back of the room. He'd gone there the moment their history class had walked into the media center. Effie knew this because no matter how much she tried, she couldn't seem to end her infatuation with the cutest boy in the seventh grade.

He gestured to an empty chair nearby. "Want to sit down?"

"Sit?"

"Uh, yeah." He looked at her strangely.

Which, of course, made her feel even more foolish. She really needed to stop always assuming that he was thinking about the braces she wore on her legs. It was obvious that he was simply trying to be nice. Quickly, she sat down. Then, of course, she couldn't think of much to say. Her cheeks started heating up, no doubt staining her cheeks and neck pink, too.

It was beyond embarrassing.

"I wasn't sure if you were going to be here today. I didn't see you on the front lawn this morning."

All the kids congregated on the school's front lawn until the first bell rang. Though they didn't hang out together, he usually smiled at her whenever their glances met. "I was late."

"What? Your *mamm* let you sleep in?"

"Kind of. We had a guest stay at our house last night. Miss Overholt came over."

"Who's that?"

"Beverly Overholt runs the Orange Blossom Inn. My *daed* has done some work at her bed-and-breakfast, and over the last year, my family has gotten to know her better."

He looked at her curiously. "If she runs the inn, how come she had to stay at your *haus*?"

"Oh! Josiah, it's so sad. Someone broke into her inn yesterday. She was robbed!"

A variety of emotions crossed his face. First he looked stunned, then upset, then kind of distant, almost as if he didn't care. "Is she all right?" he finally asked.

"I think so but she was afraid to be there by herself. So Eric, the owner of the inn, asked my parents to have her stay with them for a night." As soon as she finished her lengthy, rather convoluted explanation, she noticed that he looked uncomfortable all over again. And no wonder; she'd just given him way more information than he'd asked for. "Sorry. I didn't mean to bore you."

"You didn't bore me."

Peering at him more closely, she noticed that his eyes looked a little glassy. Like he was really tired. Or maybe really upset about something. "Hey, are you okay?"

"Yeah." His voice turned cold. "Why are you asking?"

Until recently, a question like that would've made her want to apologize about five times and then get up and leave. However, things were different between her and Josiah. They'd grown closer over the last year. Not really close—it wasn't like they saw each other outside school or anything—but they now talked enough at school that she felt comfortable around him.

Comfortable enough for her to act like a real friend.

Almost a year ago, her parents had hosted a party for Zack and Leona. In the middle of it, she'd tripped in her front yard and broken her leg. Josiah had been right there, and had even visited her at home a couple of times. Then, when she'd been on crutches, he'd offered to carry her books when she had to catch the bus.

Now, here they were in seventh grade, and most people thought they were the oddest pair of friends in the school.

She didn't blame everyone for thinking that. Josiah Yoder was really good-looking. With dark brown hair, light blue eyes, and a perpetual tan, he was just about perfect. He was also pretty much the coolest boy in their class. Everyone liked him, kids who were Amish, Mennonite, and English. She knew it was because he didn't try to be anyone other than who he was. And he seemed to accept everyone.

Even her.

She knew she was seen as the opposite of him. She was shy and awkward around most people. And while pretty much everyone thought he was handsome, she was, well, ordinary. She had long, thick, dark blond hair that was always pinned up under her *kapp*. Violet said Effie's best feature was her dark blue eyes. Effie had to agree, though she was starting to think that maybe her best feature were her hands. She had pretty, slim hands with long fingers. They were in direct contrast to her legs, which were rather spindly and still weak, as a result of her Perthes disease.

Since having broken her leg last year, she'd been wearing braces on her legs again. The braces chafed after several hours, and even though that was a pain, it was nothing compared to the worst consequence: the return of her halting, Frankenstein-like gait. Thankfully, her brothers and mother had been taking her to physical therapy to help her walk more normally. She spent hours doing exercises and sweating through the pain but was now almost back to where she'd been before the accident.

Still, she hated that her stilted walk was the first thing people noticed about her. Kids her age usually commented on her awkwardness, which was the reason she was shy around most people except for her family.

And except for Josiah Yoder.

With him, Effie was an odd mixture of chatty and bumbling. For some reason, Josiah thought she was funny. He said he liked to talk to her because she didn't expect anything from him. She didn't want to suddenly become popular. She didn't flirt and try to be his girlfriend. Of course she didn't; he was Josiah! She was happy to simply be his friend.

He seemed to feel that way, too. He often told her how much he liked hanging out with her. And one time last summer he'd even said that she was pretty.

Because of all this, Effie ignored his gruff tone of voice and concentrated on how troubled he looked. She leaned closer and lowered her voice. "You seem kind of upset. Are you? Or, um, are you sick or something?"

The shadow that had been lurking in his eyes became more pronounced. "Something is wrong, but I'm all right."

"If something is wrong, you probably aren't all right," she said with a small smile. "Believe me, I know all about things like that."

His gaze skimmed over her body, stopping on her legs. Though her dress covered her braces, she felt exposed.

"*Jah*, I guess you would," he said at last.

She knew he didn't mean it in a cruel way. He was no doubt referring to her braces. "So, what's wrong?"

A thread of vulnerability slid into his eyes before he blinked and his expression hardened. "Why are you even asking?"

"Well, um . . ."

"You think you can solve all of my problems while sitting here in the library?"

She flinched at this new tone. His words felt as harsh as if he had been making fun of her in front of the whole school. He was probably right, anyway. He had a lot of friends. If he had a problem, he'd pick one of them to tell, not her. "Sorry. I . . . I, um, didn't mean anything." Bracing her hands on her chair, she pulled herself up.

Immediately, pain crossed his features. Reaching out, he grabbed her arm. "Hey, Eff . . . wait."

Still unable to look at him, she paused, hating that she did so. She'd thought she had more self-respect than that. "What?"

"I'm sorry I spoke to you that way. I didn't mean it. Sit back down, would you?" After looking around the room, he lowered his voice. "Please?"

Though she felt more than a couple curious gazes focused on them, Effie sank back into her seat. "Josiah, I don't know what you want me to do."

From the way he was staring at her, she wondered if he didn't know, either. Seconds passed. A couple of his friends walked by. He kind of lifted his chin at them but remained silent.

By now, she was really uncomfortable. "Maybe we can talk later."

"Do I really look messed up?"

"You don't look messed up. Um, just a little worried." Thinking she needed to be completely honest, she patted the skin around her eye, too. "And, um, your eyes look kind of weird. Like you're really tired. Or something."

He ran a hand over his face. "Huh. I thought I'd gotten pretty good at hiding things."

What in the world did that mean? "Most people wouldn't notice anything was wrong," she hastened to reassure him. Because, well, most people probably weren't looking at him constantly, the way she was.

Not wanting to make things worse, she added, "Listen, I'm sorry I said anything."

"*Nee*. It's not you, it's me." He exhaled again. "So, are you looking forward to break?"

"*Jah*. Only a couple more weeks to go. I hope it goes by fast."

"Me, too." He smiled weakly, but she noticed that he didn't sound all that excited about the upcoming winter vacation. The tension pulled tighter between them and made her feel even more awkward.

"Hey, my *mamm* said she was taking today off to bake."

"Why is she doing that?"

Sometimes Josiah said the oddest things. "Because she is doing her Christmas baking," she replied. "Isn't your *mamm* baking nonstop right now?" Nearly every one of her Amish friends were either complaining or celebrating that their mothers were all baking up a storm.

"Ah, *nee*."

"Really?" She was about to ask what his mother was creating for all the gift exchanges and charity auctions that were on everyone's social calendar, but something in his manner stopped her. Almost as if he was embarrassed about something.

Suddenly Effie realized that she'd never seen Josiah's mother at any of the usual bazaars or bake sales. Maybe his *mamm* was a shut-in or something? Not wanting him to feel self-conscious—after all, he bent over backward to avoid mentioning her bad legs—she smiled brightly. "Hey, do you want to come over after school and have a piece of cake?"

His eyebrows rose. Which, she realized, they probably should. Because she'd just invited the most popular boy in the seventh grade over for cake. Who invited boys over for desserts, anyway?

"Sorry. I guess that was stupid of me to ask."

"What was?"

"You know, me asking if you wanted to come over."

He looked down but shook his head. *"Nee . . ."*

There was her answer. "Okay."

"*Nee*, Effie. It weren't stupid. What I'm trying to say is *jah*. *Danke*. Some cake sounds great," he said quietly.

Belatedly, she added, "My sister usually picks me up from school."

"Okay. I'll wait for you outside your classroom."

"Okay. I'm in the art—"

"I know where your last class is," he said as he got up. "I'll be there." He looked at her for what felt like a solid minute before he turned and walked over to a group of boys by the reference books.

Two minutes later, Jennifer C. stopped by Effie's seat. "Is Josiah being weird again? Don't worry about it, Effie. He's been that way with everyone lately."

Effie didn't respond, but inside she was secretly smiling. Josiah might be "that way" with everyone lately, but not with her. Instead, he was going home with her.

And she could already guess what people would say when that news got out.

Chapter 4

December 3

"What we need is a list," Eric pronounced. "Go get a pad of paper and a pencil, Bev."

After Beverly had first shown him inside, he'd asked her to walk through the rest of the inn with him. At first she'd been fighting an awful lump in her throat—unable to see anything but the destruction—but Eric's response had been far more optimistic. Every time she'd noticed something out of place, he'd noticed something positive.

And now that they'd reached the end of their tour in the kitchen, she had calmed enough to not feel completely out of sorts.

When she was holding both paper and a pencil, she raised a brow. "I've got them. Now what?"

"Now we figure out what to do next." Pulling out one of the kitchen chairs, he motioned for her to sit.

Again, she did as he bid. But as she looked at the blank page on the table, a new bubble of insecurity flooded through her. There was too much to do, too much to think about. She honestly had no idea how to begin to fix things. "Eric, I don't even know where to start."

"That's why you've got me," he said as he took the chair next to her. "Look, I know you're upset. I know you're hurting, too. But I think your worries will ease if we concentrate on something else for a while. Let's make a list of everything that we can do now so you can open the doors again."

"Oh, I don't want to do that." When he stared at her in confusion, she clarified. "I mean, don't you think we should wait awhile? I was thinking the inn could remain closed for the rest of the month."

"But you told me yourself that December is always a busy month for the inn. You said you were almost completely booked."

"That is true. But I emailed some guests this morning and cancelled reservations."

"All of them?"

"Just the ones for next week." She bit her lip. "Eric, I was thinking I'd call the following week's guests, too."

"Are you sure that's the right thing to do?"

She nodded. "The window is broken and the gathering room is a mess."

"We can clean all that up." He paused, then continued, speaking slowly, as if he was being very careful about how he phrased things. "I know this is hard but I really think you'll feel better if we get you back into your normal routine."

"But, Eric, I just don't know. I mean, so much is a mess. Why, even the lamps were broken."

"What happened was scary. I know that. But nothing happened that can't be fixed or replaced. I'll buy some new lamps. Everything is going to be all right. I promise. Try to keep that in mind."

His words made sense, but they didn't ease her fears. "I'll try," she said weakly.

He frowned. "Beverly, what is really upsetting you?"

At last, she shared her greatest concern, the one that had kept her up most of the night in the Kaufmanns' guest bedroom. "I'm worried that the robbers will come back. I don't know what I'll do if that happens."

"If they come back, I'll take care of them." Reaching out, he snagged the pad of paper and pen out of her hands. "Now, what should we do first?"

She wasn't about to let him brush off her fears like they were foolish concerns. In fact, his confidence was actually beginning to grate on her. "How would you even know what to do, Eric? They could be dangerous. Rough."

He smiled. "I can be dangerous, too."

Eric was tall and he was strong. But she doubted he would be any match for a desperate thief. "You don't know what you're talking about. Why, you haven't even spoken to the police yet."

"I know enough."

Though she knew she was on the verge of sounding like a

shrew, she retorted, "No offense, but I don't think you're in the position to know what we're dealing with." She lifted her chin. "I talked to Officer Roberts."

"You're exactly right. I do need more information. I'll call him or stop by his office tomorrow and get the full report."

"*Gut.* But be prepared, he might tell you that I'm right and that the burglars might come back."

"We'll see, but I have a feeling he might also say that it's more likely that the robbers will target another inn or house instead of returning here." Looking as confident as he ever did, he said, "Trust me, Beverly. I know about this sort of thing."

"You mentioned that earlier. How would you know so much about robberies? Have you been robbed before?"

Instead of looking irritated by her quip as she'd expected, he shook his head. "No, but I know something about robberies."

He was talking in circles. "How come?"

A muscle in his jaw jumped as he looked away. "You know what? How I know isn't important."

He was going to brush off her request for an explanation again. Refusing to let that happen, she pressed a hand flat on the table. "Oh, no, you're not going to set me up and then not tell me what you meant. Explain."

"Not right now." He held up the pen again. "Now, what cleaning supplies should I pick up?"

"No, Eric, I don't want to wait. Just tell me what you meant."

"You're not going to like what you hear," he hedged.

She'd started out being confrontational because she felt helpless and scared. And she knew she'd been lashing out at him because he had been acting so cocky and sure of himself. But now she was really curious. She was also fairly sure that whatever he was hiding was important to both of them. He needed to share it and she needed to hear it.

"I thought we already knew a lot about each other, Eric," she said. "I thought you trusted me. I promise, I would never betray any of your secrets."

"It's not that."

"Then what is it?"

"Beverly, I know a lot about you. But you don't really know much about me. We haven't talked about my past all that much."

She was embarrassed. Eric was right. Absolutely right. So much of their time together had been focused on her loss and her past. "I'm sorry. I haven't meant to be self-centered."

"You weren't. I intentionally kept our conversations focused on you. I didn't want to talk about my past."

"Eric, I want to know you as well as you know me. I want to be as good a friend to you as you've been to me," she coaxed. "I promise I won't judge."

Tossing the pen down on the table, he pushed it and the pad of paper away. "You don't know what you're promising."

"I'm tougher than you think. I was raised Amish but I'm not completely naïve about life." Softly, she added, "And I'd like to think that I'm pretty compassionate."

"Before on the phone, I lied." He closed his eyes. "I actually do have some experience with break-ins."

She gasped. "Oh, Eric. I am so sorry." She continued, her words practically tripping over each other as she tried to make amends. "Yet again, I've been running around, acting like I'm the only person in the world who has had something bad happen to them." Leaning toward him, she reached out and gently grasped his forearm. "When were you robbed? Was it recently? Was it terrible? What did you lose?"

His expression was completely pained now. "It wasn't quite like that."

"What was it like?"

Pulling his arm out of her grasp, he said, "You know what? Don't worry about it."

Though she knew it might be easier for him if she dropped the subject, she didn't dare. Whatever he was reluctant to tell her had to be pretty important. In all the time she'd known him, he'd never looked so secretive or hesitant.

Therefore, she pushed a little more. "Eric, I can't get to know you better if you refuse to share your past. What happened?"

He gazed at her steadily, as if he was judging just how she would take his news.

Giving in to impulse, she reached out to him again, this time curving a hand around one of his. Immediately, his hand turned and he gripped her fingers. Keeping her with him.

That was all she needed to know that she was doing the right thing by pushing. "Eric," she began gently, "I want to be the kind of friend that you can count on, not someone who takes and takes. Please, just tell me."

"Fine." He swallowed, looked like he was gathering his courage, then blurted, "I used to break in to houses when I was a teen."

His admission was such a surprise, she jerked her hand back but he held her fingers more tightly, as if she were his lifeline.

"You robbed people?" She couldn't wrap her head around the news. Couldn't equate his words with what she knew about him.

"I got mixed up with some bad kids." He paused, shook his head, then said, "No, that's not true. I was one of the bad kids."

She smiled. "Of course you weren't." Surely he was overstating things. He was one of the nicest men she'd ever met. Hadn't he just dropped everything to come to Sarasota?

"I'm telling you the truth, Bev."

"Perhaps you are exaggerating? I mean, my goodness. You went to college and got your accounting license, too. You're smart and a hard worker."

"I did do those things. And I might be that person now. But back then, years ago, I was wild and on a pretty bad path. Beverly, when I was sixteen, I spent nine months in a juvenile detention center."

At last what he was saying sank in. And with that came the sudden, awful realization that he hadn't been exaggerating. He had been *bad*. She hadn't really known him at all. "Why? What did you do?"

"I broke into two houses. And I got caught." He looked uncomfortable and strained and embarrassed and angry. "I can't believe I'm telling you this. I never wanted you to know about my past."

He'd intended to keep his past a secret from her?

Feeling betrayed, she ached to push away from him, to let go of his hand and gain some distance. But his pained expression, combined with her promise to hear him out, made her stay where she was. Though it was difficult, she forced herself to look him in the eye. "Maybe you could explain to me what happened."

"I don't have much family. My dad is a recluse and my mother passed away years ago, back when I was just a child."

"How old were you when she passed?"

He swallowed hard. "Five."

"Oh, Eric."

Visibly steeling himself, he continued. "When I was growing up, we weren't just poor, we had *no* money. My only meals were ones I got at school or when my aunt brought us food from the food pantry."

"So you stole because you were hungry?" She grasped at that excuse, needing him to have had a reason to stray from what was right.

"Yes and no. By the time I was fourteen, my father had become even more withdrawn. He was literally afraid to leave the apartment. We subsisted on his welfare checks and even those weren't regular. So my older brother, Jack, took things into his own hands. He got involved with a gang, started dealing."

Try as she might, she couldn't keep the dismay from her voice. "He was dealing drugs?"

"Yeah." Eric glanced at her, but his eyes darted away before he continued. "What he did wasn't right, Bev. I know that. But because of him, we had money. For the first time in years, we had food in the house. I could even buy some clothes."

"What did your *daed* say?"

He blinked. "Say?"

"About the money? About the food and the clothes. Surely he was curious about how Jack had gotten such things?"

"My father wasn't like your dad. He wasn't involved with our lives, so he didn't really notice. If he noticed anything, it was probably that I wasn't whining." He exhaled again. "Anyway, I liked having money. I liked having clothes that fit. I liked not being hungry."

"That is easy to understand."

"I began to idolize Jack. He protected me from anyone trying to give me a hard time at school and he took care of me at home. He was the only person in my life I could depend on."

It was hard for her to visualize Eric living such a life. She hated to think of him being hungry. So even though she didn't approve of his brother's actions, she couldn't bear to fault Eric for them. "I'm glad you had Jack."

"I am, too." After a brief pause, he continued. "Because I idolized him, because I knew he was responsible for making my life better, I would have done anything for him."

"So you did."

He nodded. "One night Jack came into my room and said he needed my help. I immediately stood up and pulled on my jacket. I didn't need to know why."

"You were simply glad to do something for him," she said softly.

"Yeah."

"Um . . . was that the night you robbed a house?"

There was a glint in his eyes now. That almost-amused look he got when he thought she was terribly naïve. "No, Bev. That was simply the first time I did things I wasn't supposed to." When he blinked, his smirk was replaced by pain. She realized then that he was not only embarrassed by his past, he also was ashamed. But he was willing to let her see his vulnerability, and at the same time, was opening himself up for her anger and derision.

She swallowed, trying to keep her expression as neutral as possible. But it was hard because she felt like she was staring at a man who was changing right in front of her eyes. "I see," she said weakly.

Still looking like it was taking everything inside him to meet her gaze, he shook his head. "No, I don't think you do. I did a lot of terrible things. A lot of things I've spent years making up for. I was eventually arrested for robbery." He shifted, looking just beyond her. "I was still a teenager, thank God, and my brother had run interference for me a lot, keeping me from doing anything that I would regret for the rest of my life. It's because of him that I only did a stint in juvie. He kept me from going completely down the wrong path."

Eric was making it all sound logical, but it didn't make sense to her. Not at all. He might as well have been speaking Greek. "Oh."

"Beverly, the reason I'm telling you all this is because I doubt whoever robbed you will come back, or that they meant to actually harm you. This inn is probably known to do good business. Whoever broke in most likely thought you had more cash lying around than you did."

She clung to that information. "I hope you're right. I rarely have cash. Most folks pay for their visits with credit cards."

"I know."

"I only have that lockbox in case they ask for change for large bills. Or want a cookbook."

"I know," he repeated, his voice soft. After almost a whole minute passed, Eric said, "Beverly, you haven't met my gaze in five minutes. Are you ever going to be able to look at me again?"

"I don't know," she said honestly. She'd wanted to accept anything he told her, like she'd promised she would, but . . . well, that was before she'd learned that he'd been a criminal.

Raising her chin to look directly into his eyes, she said, "Eric, you've just told me that you did a great many bad things. Illegal things. How can I accept that?"

"I'm still the same man you've grown to know. I realize this is probably hard to hear, but once you take a moment to think about it, I'm sure you'll understand what I'm trying to say."

"I don't know how I'm supposed to understand. You just told me that you've stolen and lied but that it was okay."

"No, I told you that I did things I'm not proud of but that I learned from my mistakes. There's a difference."

"All I know is that you've been intentionally keeping parts of your past a secret. You let me think you were a different sort of man than you are." Though it was ruthless, she ignored his look of disbelief and hurt. She needed to think about herself and what was right for her future.

"What are you saying?"

"I'm not saying anything, other than the fact that every time I think I know you, I learn something new."

"That's how relationships usually go, Bev."

"Perhaps it is. But I, for one, can let you know right now that I haven't ever stolen from people, been in a gang, or spent time in prison. Just in case you were wondering."

Hurt flashed in his eyes. "No, you're just judgmental."

"I don't think I'm being judgmental. I'm simply telling you how I feel."

"Well, I hear you loud and clear. Now, do you care which room I stay in?"

It was probably best to act like she wasn't hurt by his reaction. "If you don't mind, I'd like you to take the attic room."

He scowled. "The one with three twin beds?"

"*Jah.* That's a hard room to fill. If and when we open again, most people would rather be in one of the standard guest rooms."

Looking resigned, he reached for his bag. "I'll take my things up there. Then, we can get started cleaning up." He raised an eyebrow. "Unless you're having second thoughts about me staying here?"

She was having second thoughts about everything, especially how she felt about the possibility of dating him.

But instead of recounting even more of her doubts and judgments, she simply stated the obvious. "This is your inn, Eric. Of course you must stay here. And yes, let's get started cleaning up. There is much to do."

"Thank the Lord for that. Otherwise, you'd probably throw me out."

Of course she wouldn't do anything like that. But she didn't dare say so. Therefore, she kept her silence, which Eric seemed to take as yet another sign of her doubt. So she just sat rigidly as he climbed the stairs and disappeared from view. Yet the moment she was sure she was completely alone, she rubbed her eyes and tried not to cry.

But just like learning about Eric's past, it seemed that some things were unavoidable.

Chapter 5

December 3

"I'm going to be sleeping in a Barbie Dream House," Eric muttered to himself as he walked into the attic room.

Looking around at the beds outfitted with coordinating quilts, the bright curtains, and the adjoining bathroom—which was decorated in pinks and purples—he laughed. He'd definitely never slept in a room like this before. It was a far cry from the modern Danish bedroom set at home that had cost him an arm and a leg—and served to remind him that he'd made something of himself. At last.

The blatantly feminine décor was even further from the stark utilitarian surroundings he'd lived with during his nine months in the juvenile detention center.

If the guys he'd shared space with back then could see him

now, he'd likely never live down their ribbing. Actually, he wouldn't be upset about their teasing, either. There were some things in life that one never expected to happen, and sleeping in an ultrafeminine girls' room in the attic of the Orange Blossom Inn—the very inn that he owned—was at the top of Eric's list.

He ultimately chose the bed farthest from the window, hoping perhaps that spot would shield him a bit from the worst of the sun's glare—though it was doubtful he'd be able to sleep much past seven or eight in the morning. But now that he'd taken care of that important decision, he was at a loss as to what to do next. Part of him wanted to formulate a plan for how to patch things up with Beverly, yet he feared there wasn't much for either of them to say. They'd had their share of rocky conversations over the past few months but this one had been the hardest so far.

Maybe because he didn't blame Beverly for feeling the way she did.

From the day he'd first met her in the local library and discovered that she ran the inn he'd just inherited—though she'd thought *she* was the rightful owner—they'd been playing a rather difficult game of chess. Lawyers had been involved and hours of conversations had ensued. But eventually, they'd come to an agreement of sorts: Eric had taken over handling the financial aspects of the inn while she'd continued to run it.

Along the way, however, something had begun to grow between them. Their rocky animosity had first settled into a partnership of sorts before at last becoming a true, warm friendship. More recently, that friendship had begun to change as well. There was a new thread of awareness between them. He'd always thought Beverly was attractive, but lately he'd started to think of her as far more than just that. With her green eyes, thick brown hair, and slim build, he'd begun to think she was one of the prettiest women he'd ever known.

But ultimately, it had been her vulnerability that had drawn him to her in a romantic way—though that trait was encased in a tough shell of prickly self-preservation. Eric found himself wanting to spar with her and hold her in his arms—all at the same time.

If he was being honest with himself, even before the break-in, he'd been missing her so much that he had thought about making plans to see her again. Though he'd told her he hadn't wanted to leave until his house sold, he'd begun to feel like he needed to see her as soon as possible. It had become a physical thing—he'd taken to dreaming about her at night and worrying about her during the day. He was hardly getting any work done. As it was, he'd spent many a night imagining his return and far too many hours visualizing how it would feel to take that next step, to tell Beverly how he felt about her. He'd even thought about their first "real" dates, and how he would take things slow, allowing Beverly to get used to the idea of them being together.

But now it didn't look like that was ever going to happen. He'd broken her trust when he kept his past from her.

And today? Today she'd shown him that he was never going to be good enough.

Here it was, almost Christmas, and instead of feeling like he'd finally come home, he was wondering when he could go back to Pennsylvania.

Or perhaps he should just plan to move somewhere else entirely. Thinking of his brother, Eric wondered what it would be like to reconnect with Jack again. Their lives had veered in such different directions, they probably didn't have anything in common anymore. But they might. Fishing his cell from his back pocket, he thought about giving Jack a call, but he wasn't ready. He felt too vulnerable.

Still, he couldn't seem to concentrate on anything other than the mess he'd made with Beverly. He had a broken heart and he had no idea how to fix it.

As he stewed on that, a sense of peace settled over him when he realized the answer had been there all along. He could go to the place he always went when he was troubled.

Taking a seat on his twin mattress, Eric lowered his head, clasped his hands together, and prayed.

"Well, here we are," Effie said when they were out of Violet's car. Sometimes Violet parked and walked in with her, but today she'd simply dropped them off, saying she had a couple of errands to run.

"Yep."

Josiah smiled, but it was so subdued that she wasn't sure if he was happy they'd at last arrived or if she'd once again said something goofy. She didn't want to think about what it was she might have said, because the truth was there were about a hundred things that she could have said that would have made him laugh. She had been prattling away the whole time they'd been together, from the moment Violet had picked them up at school, until now. And even as they were heading up the front walk, she was tempted to start chattering on yet again.

It was Josiah's fault, anyway. Though he'd never been a chatterbox, that afternoon he'd been unusually quiet. So quiet, Effie kept thinking he was upset about something. And he'd looked so relieved that he didn't have to carry the conversation that Effie had gone a little overboard.

Now that they stood on her front porch, Effie knew the right thing to do would be to open the front door, lead him to her kitchen, and give him a generous helping of cake.

But still . . . she hesitated. She didn't bring kids home very often. Practically never. So she wasn't quite sure what to say. Because of that, she kept overthinking things and was weighing each word before she spoke. Her halting manner was no doubt sounding as ridiculous as she felt. Why, Josiah would no doubt get up and leave as soon as he ate that piece of cake. And from the way he'd been acting, all quiet and awkward, Effie was pretty sure he regretted ever agreeing to come over in the first place.

So she simply stood there, her hands clasped behind her pale blue dress.

Like an idiot.

"Your sister, Violet, is nice," Josiah said at last.

It took her a second to follow his train of thought. Then at last she nodded. "*Jah*, she is. My parents weren't happy when she made the choice to join the Palm Grove Mennonite Church instead of being baptized Amish, so for a while I didn't see her much. But now that they've patched things up, she's around all the time again. I think my parents might even agree that her decision to become Mennonite and take driving lessons is helpful on days like today."

"Did she have a hard time learning to drive?"

Effie shrugged. "I don't think I ever asked. She didn't talk much about her driving. But that was out of respect for our parents. They had a hard enough time coming to terms with her decision without having to deal with worries about driving a car. In the end, I think her boyfriend taught her."

"That was thoughtful." Gripping the porch railing, he said, "You two seem really close."

"We are. Violet has always been there for me," she added. "All three of my siblings have. My eldest brother, Karl, used to sit with me for hours after surgeries, and my other brother, Zack, is so patient. He's given up a lot of time with his friends to take me to physical therapy and doctors' appointments. I'm really blessed."

"Maybe that's what older brothers do, huh?"

"What?"

"Do things for their siblings. Take care of them . . ." He cleared his throat. "My *bruder* Peter looks out for me. He always has."

Glad they had something in common, she smiled. "Siblings are supposed to look out for each other. Ain't so?"

"Maybe, though I don't know if that's always the case."

Thinking some more, she nodded. "I guess I do know a lot of girls who always fight with their older sisters."

"Maybe we just got lucky?"

"I guess so." Funny, she'd always assumed that Zack and Violet had looked after her out of a sense of duty—because of her braces—but it was nice to think about their concern in a new way. "Well, um, we might as well go in," she said as she opened the front door. "Mamm, I'm home! Josiah is here, too." *Please don't make a fuss*, she added silently.

Effie heard a clatter of dishes before her mother walked out of the kitchen. "Hi, you two," she said.

"I was telling Josiah that you've been baking today. I asked him over for a slice of cake. I hope you don't mind?"

"Not at all," Mamm said as she started back toward the kitchen. As usual, she was bustling around. "But I hope you won't only have one piece of cake, Josiah. I made a pot of chili, too. How about a cup of that with some corn bread?"

Effie inwardly groaned. So much for not making a fuss. "Chili, Mamm?"

"It's December. We might be living in Florida, but I've always liked chili in the winter. Would you like some, Josiah?"

Effie was just about to warn him that he didn't have to eat anything he didn't want when he spoke. "*Danke*, Mrs. Kaufmann. Your chili sounds mighty *gut*."

Looking pleased, and a bit smug, her mother turned to her. "Effie, do you want any?"

"No, thanks. I'll wait for supper."

Josiah looked her way. "Sorry, do you mind if I have some?"

"Of course not." She pointed to the table. "Take a seat and I'll bring you a bowl."

"I'll get myself a bowl. You don't have to serve me, Ef."

"It's no trouble."

"You're our guest, Josiah. Please sit down," her mother said. "Effie, why don't you fetch something to drink?"

"*Jah*. Sure." After getting them both tall glasses of iced tea, she sat next to him and slowly noticed two things: First, those shadows around his eyes that she'd seen earlier had worsened. Second, after her mother placed a heaping bowl in front of him, topped with grated cheddar cheese and served with a thick square of fresh corn bread lathered with melting butter, she realized Josiah was hungry. Really hungry.

After closing his eyes in silent prayer for the briefest of seconds, he picked up his spoon and started eating. "This is really *gut*, Mrs. Kaufmann," he said before Effie had even placed her napkin in her lap.

"I'm glad you like it, Josiah," Mamm said with a bright smile. "We've got plenty, so be sure to have seconds. I always make too much."

"Danke."

As she sat there sipping tea, Effie noticed that Josiah was fixated on that chili like he'd never had anything so good in ages. A little worried and a bit embarrassed that something so small could make him so happy, Effie snuck a glance at her mother. She was still at the stove, stirring the pot. However, it was clear that Mamm was mighty aware of Josiah's hunger, too. She kept peeking at Josiah, looking truly concerned. It was the type of expression she wore whenever one of them got a fever. Or when she and Effie were waiting to hear test results at the doctor's office.

As if suddenly realizing he was wolfing down the food, Josiah set down his spoon. "Sorry. I'm actin' like a pig."

"You weren't acting like that at all," her mother said in her kind way.

He took a drink of his tea while Effie struggled to say something to ease his concern.

Luckily, her mother came to the rescue again. Chuckling softly, she said, "Josiah, you've been doing me a great favor. I can't seem to stop cooking for six people, you see. Why, you'd be doing me a favor if you came here every afternoon, just so I wouldn't have so many leftovers to store." She set a fresh piece of corn bread on his plate. "Here you go, dear. This slice is still warm. Eat up."

"Want some corn bread?" he asked Effie, holding up the plate.

"Danke, nee." Realizing that she was going to have to say something to take the focus off his food, she blurted, "I think this is going to be the longest month in the world."

"Because of the upcoming break?" he asked, taking another bite of chili.

"Jah." After debating a minute, she added, "And because Jennifer C. came up to me and was being her usual self."

Immediately, Josiah's posture became straighter, more confident. "Effie, you've got to stop letting her bother you."

"She didn't bother me."

He set his spoon down. "You sure? What did she say today?"

"Nothing important."

"Sure?"

"Jah." Because he was still staring at her, she said, "Sometimes I think she's surprised that you and I are friends."

He grinned. Then, to her amazement, he shrugged. "Maybe when she hears that I came home with you she'll stop being so surprised."

She was completely tongue-tied. "Josiah, I promise I won't tell anyone—"

"You won't need to. Everyone saw us leave together."

"I suppose they did."

"That girl," her mother interrupted as she came back to stand next to them, "is simply mean. She's a terrible gossip, too."

"Mamm, you shouldn't talk like that!" Effie protested. Her cheeks heated when Josiah raised his brows. No doubt he was thinking that she was one to talk. Here Effie was, gossiping about Jennifer.

Mamm picked up Josiah's bowl, took it to the stove, and ladled a second helping into it. "I'm not going to pretend she's nicer than she is, Effie," she said as she placed the bowl in front of him.

Effie bit her bottom lip. This was awful. Beyond awful.

A few minutes later, her mother spoke up again. "Josiah, I am sure you have a lot to do, but would you mind coming home with Effie once or twice a week?"

She. Could. Not. Believe. This. Was. Happening. "Mamm!"

Ignoring her protest, her mother continued. "Now that Effie is moving better, she could probably handle walking from the bus stop."

"Her legs are that strong?" Josiah asked.

"I believe so. Her physical therapist said more walking would be good for her, too. That is, if someone was by her side."

As if it wasn't bad enough to be gossiping, now they were talking about her disability, too. Things had gone beyond awful. They had now settled firmly on something bordering true, stark embarrassment. "*Muddah*, please—"

"Yeah, sure," Josiah said quickly. "I mean, if you want me to I will. And if Effie doesn't mind."

"She doesn't mind. Do you, Effie, dear?" Mamm called over her shoulder as she pulled a cake out of the refrigerator.

"I don't mind," she mumbled. Actually, she didn't know what she thought. Here the boy she'd secretly had a crush on for ages was going to be walking her home several times a week . . . but for all the wrong reasons. She didn't know whether to be nervous and excited or filled with embarrassment.

Josiah smiled. *"Gut."*

And then she was saved by the arrival of two thick slices of yellow cake with her mother's homemade chocolate buttercream frosting. Josiah's was easily double the width of hers. "This is a lot of cake, Mamm."

"I know!" She patted Josiah on the shoulder. "Josiah, you have single-handedly saved me from a lecture from my husband. He always says I bake too much. Now I can tell him that I made it for you and Effie."

He grinned. "Glad I could help."

Her mother's eyes softened before she said, "Effie, I'm going to go outside and see Violet. She's sitting out on the patio."

"She is? I thought she'd gone to run errands. I guess she simply parked the car and then decided to stay outside."

"She probably didn't tell you, but she's been reading some new book in a series she loves. Violet said all she wanted to do today was read." Her mother sighed dramatically. "And that's practically all she's done. I got her to help me bake a chocolate cake and two pies, but that's it."

Josiah looked like he was struggling to keep a straight face. "One cake and two pies sounds like kind of a lot, Mrs. Kaufmann."

"It would be, if I wasn't so behind in my holiday baking. I've got cookies and more cookies to bake so I can give them out as gifts. I had been hoping Violet would be more into the spirit of the season."

"If Violet is that involved in her book, you better be careful, Mamm," Effie warned. "She's probably not going to want you to bother her. Violet gets crabby when people interrupt her." Privately, Effie thought her sister's interest in the book might have more to do with taking a break from kitchen chores. Violet liked washing dishes even less than she did.

"Before she picked you two up, she sat out there for two whole hours." Drumming her fingers on the countertop, her mother looked over at the back door. "I bet she's probably ready for a little break." Before Effie could comment on that, she started Violet's way.

Effie was both thankful that she had a few minutes alone with Josiah and embarrassed by her mother's antics. "Josiah, I'm so sorry that my *mamm* practically forced you to say you'd come over here again," she blurted. "And I'm sorry you had to witness her getting so excited about baking, too."

"I didn't mind. Your mother is a nice lady, Effie. It's really kind of her to ask me to come over again."

Her mother was nice, but she was also not afraid to ask people to help Effie. "Just to let you know, you don't, um, have to feel responsible for me. I can walk by myself."

"I know."

"And Jennifer C. is kind of a brat. She always has been. But she hasn't been picking on me. I'm not worried about her saying mean things." At least, not *too* worried.

"I do like to give those girls something to talk about, but I want to be with you, too."

"You . . . you do?"

"*Jah.* I like being around you, Ef. You're easy. You don't talk nonstop like most girls. And you're nice to everyone. I like that."

Effie felt her pulse race. What was she supposed to say to that? Thank you?

While she was figuring out the right response, he took a breath, then added, "And if you want to know the truth . . . things aren't great at my house right now. I was kind of looking for a reason not to go home."

She was about to ask why when a new awareness settled inside her. Maybe it was because she'd often pretended things were fine even when they weren't. Or maybe it was because she was in junior high and not a kid anymore. Regardless, she knew better than to ask him any more about his reasons.

And for the first time in her life, she realized that her disability was going to come in handy. If it gave her an excuse to be with Josiah, and Josiah an excuse to come over and eat, then she was going to start thinking of it as a blessing.

"I like hanging out with you, too, Josiah," she said at last. "I am glad we're friends." Then she smiled.

When he smiled back, she knew all the awkwardness and second-guessing she'd been feeling was worth it. For the first time, she would be the person helping out instead of the recipient of a good deed.

It was a blessing.

And, well, now that she knew she was going to get to spend even more time with Josiah, she felt a little warm inside, too.

Chapter 6

December 4

After spending most of the night tossing and turning, Beverly knew something had to be done.

As the sun was taking its time starting the day, she slipped on a light cotton sweater and went for a walk. Watching the pink and rose streaks begin to color the sky, she breathed deeply. If she concentrated, she could smell the salt of the ocean from the nearby keys. The fresh air felt rejuvenating and clean. Exactly what she needed—a way to clear her head and put things into perspective.

Yes, her inn had been robbed.

And it had been scary.

But it wasn't the end of the world.

And Eric? Well, he was still the man he'd been when they'd

first met. He was the same Eric she'd been secretly developing feelings for over the last six months. The only difference was that he now trusted her enough to tell her about his past.

She deeply regretted taking that trust and practically throwing it away.

"Why, Lord?" she murmured as the sky began changing again. The pink rays of light dissipated, leaving the heavens a pale blue tinged with golden light. It was beautiful. Perfect in its simplicity.

A verse from Proverbs settled in her heart: *A pretentious, showy life is an empty life; a plain and simple life is a full life.* Wasn't that what she should remember? There was no need to analyze and worry and make things more complicated than they already were.

"Have I been doing that with Eric, Lord?" she murmured.

Of course, the answer was right there before her. Dawn's arrival was neither simple nor uncomplicated. Its appearance was also never the same two days in a row.

Why would she expect her life to be any different?

"All right," she mumbled under her breath. "I get your point."

"Beverly, are you talking to yourself?" Ginny Kaufmann's voice called out from behind her.

"Maybe." She turned and smiled sheepishly. "I didn't see you there, Ginny."

"That may be my fault," she said as she approached, sporty white tennis shoes on her feet. "When I saw you up ahead I raced to catch up to you. It's always more fun to walk with a friend."

"I agree. It's *gut* to see you, too. I was just thinking how nice it was to see this morning's sunrise." Beverly's lips twitched. "And, yes, I was talking to the Lord, too."

Ginny looked embarrassed. "Oh, I'm sorry. Here you were, praying, and I barged in." Looking like she was ready to turn around, she asked, "Would you like me to leave you in peace?"

"Not at all. I've been meaning to thank you again for your hospitality the other night. I truly appreciate you all having me over."

Ginny smiled. "It was our pleasure. I was happy to help you. And I still am. Please let me know if I can do anything at all."

Beverly was thankful to have a friend like her. And because she knew Ginny was being sincere, she said, "Actually, I was just puzzling over something. If you have time to listen, I could use your ear."

"Of course I have time for you. There's a teacher meeting or something this morning, so school doesn't even start until lunchtime."

"Lucky you," Beverly teased. She remembered that Ginny worked part-time as a teachers' assistant and classroom aide at the public elementary school.

Ginny beamed. "I thought so. I decided to use the extra time to get a little exercise. Effie will be sleeping as long as she can, no doubt. What's going on?"

"Everything," Beverly blurted as they turned right.

"Whoa! That's a lot. Are you upset about the break-in?"

"I am, but that's not what kept me up last night. See, I learned something upsetting about Eric and I don't know what to think about it."

"That sounds intriguing. Is it about him and his girlfriend?"

Beverly shook her head. "*Nee.* He broke up with Amy months ago. What I keep thinking about has to do with his past."

"How far in the past?"

"Years." Doing some quick mental calculating, she said, "Probably fifteen years or so."

Ginny slowed. "So it happened long before you knew each other."

"It did." After a pause, Beverly added, "I don't want to betray Eric's confidence, but I feel like I need to talk about what he told me."

"If you'd care to share it, I promise I will keep it to myself."

Beverly had a feeling that the Lord had brought Ginny Kaufmann to her side on purpose. She could either trust Ginny enough to help her get through her worries or continue to fret on her own. Put that way, there seemed to be no other choice.

"Basically, Eric told me that he got into some trouble when he was young. He, um, actually robbed houses."

Ginny stopped and stared. "Goodness!"

Ginny's exclamation was so similar to how she'd been feeling, Beverly almost smiled. "I know! I've been trying to pray my way through my feelings, but I'm embarrassed to say that I haven't come to terms with it yet."

"What are you hoping to come to terms with? Do you want to accept his past or reject it?"

"It's not quite that easy, Ginny."

"I kind of think it is," she countered as they started walking again. "After all, this happened years ago. Long before he knew you or the inn or anything."

"That is true." Then, because she didn't want Ginny seeing

Eric in a poor light, she added, "He said he had a difficult home life. One that forced him to make some bad choices."

"That's probably true, don't you think?"

"Jah."

"So, what did he do?" Ginny asked. "Did he rob lots of people? Did he get caught?" Her blue eyes widened. "Did he get hurt or hurt someone else?"

"Well, he got sent to jail."

Ginny's eyebrows rose. "He went to prison?"

"Not exactly. I mean, he went to a prison for children." Remembering the exact phrase, she said, "It was a juvenile detention center."

"Ah."

"He said when he got out of that place, he made the choice to do things differently." Thinking of how agitated he'd looked, she added, "I think he feels really guilty about his crimes. It weighs on him."

Ginny glanced at her again. "So he's changed since then."

"*Jah*. He is different. Much different."

They turned right and continued their brisk walk. Beverly noticed that the sun was now hovering over the horizon, its golden rays illuminating the area, making everything look bright and clean.

"I made a mistake, didn't I?" she said at last. "I've been penalizing Eric for something he did when he was a child. Something he's already paid the price for." With a sinking feeling, Beverly made herself say the rest. "If he hadn't told me any of this, I would have never known. He trusted me and I betrayed that trust."

"I've never been in your situation," Ginny said, "but I can share that whenever something has happened with my children, I try to remember that we each have our own path to follow. And as time passes, we grow and change; we're never the same people that we were the day before."

"I shouldn't judge Eric on who he was as a teenager, should I?"

"That is your decision, Beverly. I'm just saying that I think judging folks on who they used to be is a slippery slope." Waving a hand at the remainder of the beautiful sunrise, Ginny added, "Just imagine how awful it would be if day broke the same way every morning."

It wouldn't be as glorious. Each morning's sunrise was special and different. Worth celebrating.

Perhaps that was why the Lord gave them so many days on the earth. One needed time to celebrate each day. As they turned right again and headed back toward the inn, Beverly nodded. "You're right about so much, Ginny. I feel better about Eric's past. Even better about the robbery. *Danke* for lending me your ear."

"Anytime, dear. And don't worry. I won't say a word about what you shared."

"Thank you. I would feel awful if Eric heard and thought I was gossiping about him."

"For what it's worth, I don't think you've been gossiping. You're merely sharing a bit of yourself and your worries with a friend. We all need our friends, I think. There's not a thing wrong with that, either."

As they approached the inn, Beverly smiled brightly. "*Danke*, Ginny. Not only have you given me shelter, you've been a great friend this morning. I don't know how to thank you."

"You never need to do that. Friends are there for each other." With a meaningful look at the sky, she added, "Rain or shine."

Beverly smiled and waved good-bye. As she walked into the inn with the rays of sunlight just starting to warm the air and ground, she felt better than she had in days.

After they'd argued yesterday, Beverly and Eric had spent the evening cleaning up the worst of the mess. Things now looked neat enough for her to tackle the guest log. She was still staring at it when she heard Eric coming downstairs just after nine.

She knew it was time to face him, though she still had no idea how she was going to ever attempt to make things better between them. However, she needed to do something. The guilt she felt was practically making her sick to her stomach.

By the time he reached the bottom step, his feet bare as usual, she was up and waiting for him. "*Gut matin*," she said in a rush.

"Good morning." Eric's words were smooth but his glance wary. And it was no less than she deserved.

She stepped closer. "Eric, please let me apologize for everything I said last night."

"You don't need to apologize. I should've told you about my past months ago."

"Of course you didn't need to do that. Your past is your business, not mine."

"That's not quite true. The fact that I was locked up is a pretty big deal, Bev. I can understand why it would have caught you off guard." Looking more vulnerable than she'd ever seen him before, he said, "Do you want to talk about my past some more?"

"*Nee*. There's nothing more to say, is there? Unless you have more dark experiences to share?" She attempted to joke.

Her joke fell flat.

"Not really." Looking at her quietly, he crossed his arms over his chest. Today he wore a snug white T-shirt half tucked into a pair of faded jeans.

She bit her lip so she wouldn't stare at him. Even when they argued, she couldn't deny that she found him attractive. Confused about that, and her mixed-up, crazy emotions wherever he was concerned, she turned toward the kitchen. "I'd like a cup of *kaffi*. Would you like one, too?"

"Coffee would be good," he said as he followed her into the kitchen. "Now, what were you working on?"

"I was trying to figure out who to call to help with the broken window."

"You don't need to worry about that. I'll call around and make sure the window is taken care of today."

"You think you can get it replaced that fast?" She knew she sounded mulish, but she couldn't seem to help herself. She hated that he had a solution for everything. She hated that he seemed to be taking everything in stride while she jumped at every creak and groan in the house.

"I know we can." Looking at her directly, he placed his hands on his hips. "So, how about we open the doors tomorrow?"

"Tomorrow?" She gulped. "But . . . that seems sudden. Don't you think it's a little soon?"

"The rooms are in good order and we got the worst of the gathering room cleaned up last night. What else is there to do?"

"I would need to call and email all the guests whose reservations I just cancelled."

"I can make those phone calls. I bet Sadie or another friend could help, too."

"But I have a certain way I keep track of everything."

"I can figure out your system, Beverly."

"And bake," she said, grabbing hold of the next excuse. "I can't have guests without any of my freshly baked goods. I'm going to have to bake all day to be ready for guests tomorrow."

"You bake, then."

"But there are still the broken lamps and the scuffed walls . . ."

"How about you let me take care of that? I've been meaning to talk to Emma and Jay Hilty and pick up some produce from their farm. They'll know who to see about getting some lamps. Frank Kaufmann will no doubt help, too." Still looking at her carefully, he said, "I'm going to go ask Tricia to lend a hand as well."

"But Tricia doesn't work here any longer." Though Tricia had worked for Beverly for six months, she was a newlywed now. She was setting up her own house. She didn't need to worry about the inn.

"Tricia is your niece, Bev," Eric replied patiently. "If you ask her for some help, I'm sure she can give you a few hours. Besides, you know she would be upset if she discovered that you needed her help but never asked."

She thought he probably had a point there. "All right. But

there's still a chance that we won't be able to get everything done—"

"We can try, right?" He finished his coffee, then poured himself another cup. "Now, go get out your flour and sugar and start baking. I'm going to get those phone calls taken care of and then run over to Tricia's."

Though he seemed hopeful, Beverly noticed that Eric still wasn't exactly facing her. Some of the warm light that usually shone in his eyes was absent, too. He didn't trust her any longer.

"Eric, are we going to be okay?"

"We're going to be just fine, Bev."

"Are you sure?" Because she certainly wasn't.

He lifted up a pair of kitchen towels with fanciful reindeer appliquéd on them, a sweet gift from a frequent guest. "It's almost Christmas. All around us, people are thinking of others, making holiday plans, planning special memories."

She didn't follow. "So?"

"So, holidays come in spite of troubles. Friendships and family still matter even when we are sick or troubled. Life happens."

"I know, but—"

"We can't just sit still and worry, Beverly. The rest of the world doesn't stop when we do."

"I suppose it doesn't, at that."

"Then, let's move forward, too. After all, what other option is there?"

"None, I suppose."

"All right, you get busy in here. I'll be back soon."

Once Eric was gone, Beverly turned back to the pantry. As

always, it was immaculate and neatly organized. Before the robbery, the pantry had been one of the things in her life she was most proud of. Now it seemed like nothing more than a surplus of food. She frowned but then remembered what all those ingredients could eventually be made into.

And how much Eric liked homemade meals.

Maybe it was time to make something special for him. She needed to do something to ease things between them. And to make amends for betraying his trust. Even if he never found out that she'd shared his story with Ginny Kaufmann she knew that it hadn't been the nicest thing to do. If she couldn't let him know how much he meant to her through words, she would have to show him through her actions.

At the very least, it was worth a try.

Chapter 7

December 4

Mark Hilty knew he shouldn't be hanging around the Quick Stop, the small convenience store on Bahia Vista that most of the Englisher tourists favored, but Laura Beachy worked there.

And lately, wherever Laura was, he wanted to be there, too. Luckily, it usually wasn't too busy this time of day. Which meant he'd have her all to himself.

"How much longer until you get off this afternoon?" he asked her, trying not to stare at her long blond hair like he usually did.

"The same as always," she said in mock annoyance. "Six o'clock."

"One more hour." He smiled.

"Yep. One more hour, then you can walk me home."

"Or you can come home with me to the farm." His father

owned an organic farm that was open to the public. They'd moved to Sarasota a couple of months ago from Charm, Ohio, after Mark's *mamm* had passed away. At first the move had been kind of hard, though he would never have told his father that.

When they'd arrived, his *daed* had given him the option of attending high school. At first he'd said no in favor of helping with the family farm, but at the beginning of November, he'd changed his mind. On his first day of school, he'd met Laura. She'd been wearing loose jeans and a faded blue shirt that matched her eyes. He'd thought she was the prettiest girl he'd ever seen.

"I'll think about coming over. I love seeing your stepsisters."

"Yeah, they're cute." That was another big change. His father had fallen in love with a widowed mother of three little girls. Mark, his older brother Ben, and younger brother William, had been taken aback at first, but had come to love both Emma and her daughters. Emma was a great mother and she made their father really happy.

So things were finally going well.

"I could come over for a couple of hours."

"Great. Emma's cooking."

"Then I'm definitely coming over," she teased, then stilled as the shop's door opened.

Mark turned around, wondering about her reaction. When he saw it was Peter Yoder, he understood. Peter was their age, but like most Amish kids, had stopped going to school after the eighth grade.

That was where the similarities ended, though. Most Amish guys Mark knew were working with their fathers or apprenticing with a local business. No one had any idea what Peter did. It was obvious that his family didn't have a lot of money; Peter always looked like he needed to wash his clothes better and get some that actually fit.

Immediately, Mark felt guilty for even thinking that. Laura had told him that Peter's mother had died a couple of years ago, and Mark knew all about making due without a mother.

"Hey, Peter," Laura said.

"Hi," he replied. When he noticed Mark standing there, he nodded. "Hi. Mark, right?"

"*Jah*. Hi." They'd met at Pinecraft Park when he'd first moved there and had even seen each other at church, but they'd never really had much occasion to talk.

Peter looked at them both a little awkwardly and Laura cleared her throat. "Can I help ya with something?"

"*Nee*. I, um, came in for a couple of things."

"Oh, sure." She smiled again, then started fiddling with the stack of plastic cups on the counter.

When Peter picked up a mesh basket and started walking up and down the aisles, popping all kinds of things into it, Mark exchanged glances with Laura. Buying so many things at the Quick Mart was pretty unusual. Prices were higher here than just about anywhere else. Most people simply ran into the store to grab a quart of milk or a can of soda or a couple of candy bars. Hardly anyone ever picked up a basket.

He'd sure never seen anyone picking up so much stuff at one time.

Annoyed with himself for judging the guy yet again, Mark leaned on the counter. "Everyone's talking about the Christmas parade," he said to get their attention off Peter. "Do you ever go?"

"Oh, *jah*. Everyone goes."

"Maybe we could sit together?"

"Maybe," she teased. "But if you want to sit with me, you're going to have to come early. Everyone starts staking out spots around noon."

"I'll ask Emma and my *daed* what time they want to eat on Christmas, then I'll let you know."

She smiled softly, making his insides turn to mush. He really liked her but he didn't know what kind of future they had. She'd told him when her family had first moved to Sarasota, she'd been Amish, too. Now, at age sixteen, she was as English as any girl who'd grown up watching TV or using a computer. He'd never even seen her in a dress. She pretty much wore only jeans and T-shirts.

From what she said, at first her parents had stayed true to their beliefs, but after a time they'd slowly drifted away from their church. Then, when Laura was seven, her father had received the chance to work at the airport for a lot more money, and he'd decided to break away from the church entirely. And though her parents' decision was the result of weeks and months of prayer and debating, Laura had told Mark that it had still felt sudden: one day she was Amish, and the next she wasn't.

Mark was still in the middle of his *rumspringa*, which meant that his *daed* was letting him see Laura without a bit of criticism or a word of caution. But if they got serious, that would change.

His *daed* would likely try to put a stop to things. He'd made no secret that he hoped Mark and his brothers would eventually join the church and marry Amish girls.

He was brought out of his thoughts when Peter walked up to the counter, his basket pretty much overflowing.

Laura pulled the basket close to the cash register. "So, are you trying to empty our shelves or something?" she joked.

Peter started, looked a little embarrassed, and then seemed to catch himself. "Nah. Just, um, doing a little shopping."

Mark gave him an understanding look. "She's just kidding."

Peter shrugged. "I, uh, didn't have time to run over to Yoder's."

"Don't get me wrong. I'm glad you're here. I need something to do," Laura quipped.

"Hey," Mark said. "You said you liked hanging out with me."

"I do, but I'm supposed to be working, too." She smiled at Peter.

When Peter smiled hesitantly back, Mark felt a little jealous—until he noticed that Laura was looking pretty uncomfortable. As she rang up the cans of soup and set them in a paper sack, she said awkwardly, "I love this soup."

Peter looked at her curiously. "Why? It's just vegetable."

"Nothing wrong with that," Mark interjected. It was obvious that Laura was merely trying to ease the tension between them all. "Vegetable soup is great. It tastes great and it's *gut* for you, too." The moment he said the words, he wished he could take them back. He sounded like an advertisement.

"It's low in fat, too," Laura added.

"I'll keep that in mind." For the first time since he'd walked up to the counter, Peter looked relaxed. "Just for the record, Laura, you don't have to worry about eating anything low fat."

"*Danke*. I mean, thanks." Laura's cheeks bloomed.

Peter chuckled. "Listen to you. I guess you haven't forgotten all of your Deutsch?"

"Of course not."

Mark moved a little farther away, letting the two of them talk without him looming. Their easy conversation reminded Mark that Laura and Peter had been friends for years.

Laura had told him that once she'd stopped being Amish, a lot of kids had teased her. For a while she'd had quite a time fitting into a new group. She wasn't worldly enough for most English kids but was too different for most Amish kids to accept her. She'd constantly made mistakes and was teased. However, her friendship with Peter had stayed true, so Mark didn't feel too concerned about Laura's smiles for him.

Well, he *tried* not to be too concerned.

"Peter, you still look Amish. Are you?" she teased as she continued to ring up his items.

"I was last time I checked. I'll let you know if something changes though."

She rang up a box of cereal. And then a quart of milk. Mark was starting to think Peter's purchases were pretty strange. Not only did it seem weird that he was the one buying groceries instead of an adult, it would definitely be cheaper for him to shop someplace else. So why was Peter really there? Did he like Laura after all?

"So, are you two dating?" Peter asked suddenly.

Mark stepped closer. "*Jah.*"

Meeting Mark's gaze, Laura blushed then picked up a can of chili. "What about you, Peter? Are you seeing anybody?"

"*Nee*. I, uh, don't have time for a girlfriend."

"I guess not, seeing as you're spending your afternoons grocery shopping and all," Mark said.

Like a switch had been flipped, Peter's expression shuttered. "Is there something wrong with that?"

"*Nee*," Mark said quickly, wishing that he hadn't let his jealousy get the best of him. If his older brother, Ben, were there, he'd be calling him a jerk. Anxious to make amends, he said, "Sorry. I don't know why I said that."

But instead of responding, Peter kept his focus solely on Laura. "How much do I owe ya?"

Looking contrite, Laura said, "Twenty-eight dollars."

After pulling out a wad of bills, Peter peeled off three tens. "Here."

Trying not to stare at the amount of cash remaining in Peter's grasp, Mark kept silent while Laura hurried to give Peter change. "Here ya go."

He grabbed a sack with one hand. "*Danke*, Laura."

"Sure." After exchanging a glance with Mark, she said, "I'll see you around."

"Maybe. Maybe not." Now ignoring Mark completely, Peter picked up his other two bags and walked out the door.

After watching Peter dart across the parking lot, Mark turned to Laura. "Well, that was weird."

She nodded. "Yes, it was." Resting her elbows on the counter, she said, "I've known him for years, Mark, but I've never seen him act like that. He looked nervous."

"I thought so, too."

She bit her lip. "I thought at first it was because you were here, but now, I don't know."

"I've talked to him a couple of times. I never got the impression that his family had much money."

"I don't think they do." Still staring out the window, she said, "Their home isn't very nice and his clothes and stuff always look kind of worn and used."

"So how come he has all that money?" Mark asked. "Laura, I bet he had a couple of hundred dollars in his hand."

"I sure don't know. Nothing about his visit makes sense, does it?"

Mark shook his head. Laura was right. Peter's visit to the Quick Stop didn't make much sense at all.

Chapter 8

December 4

"Mamm, are you upset with me for bringing Josiah over here yesterday?"

The idea had been bothering Effie since yesterday but she hadn't been quite sure how to ask her mother. But then, as she'd watched her mother continually gaze out the window after Effie had gotten home from school, almost as if she were expecting more people to come barging into their house, she had known it was time to say something.

Her mother popped her head up in surprise. "Not at all. Why do you ask?"

"No reason. Except that you seemed pretty sad when he left." Grasping at straws, she continued. "Did Josiah upset you or something?"

"Of course not. He's a polite young man." Her mother gazed out the window for another long moment before continuing. "But you are not wrong, dear. I guess I have been feeling a little off-kilter ever since he left."

"Why?"

"I know you're in middle school now, but when I was with you in the grade school building, I had the occasion to work with Josiah and his older brother, Peter."

Effie had forgotten that with her position as a teacher's aide, her mother knew just about every child in the school system. "What's wrong with that? Josiah is really smart. Even in math."

"Oh, you're right about that. He is smart. His brother Peter was, too." She glanced over to the kitchen table where Effie and Josiah had sat yesterday. "I guess I'm simply a little worried about those boys." More quietly, she added, "I'm also a little upset with myself for forgetting about them. Amazing how sometimes things really are out of mind when they're out of one's sight."

"Why would you be worried about him at all? I told you, Mamm, he's just about the most popular boy in my class. Everyone likes him."

"There is more to life than popularity, Effie," she chided.

"I know that," Effie retorted, feeling stung. "I'm just trying to say that you don't have anything to worry about. Josiah is not only smart, he makes very good grades."

"Effie, there's more to a person than being smart, too." She sighed. "You may not have known this, but his mother passed away a couple of years ago. From what I remember, she'd been ill for several months before she went on to heaven. Since then, I think their family has really suffered."

"Poor Josiah." Effie hadn't known about Josiah's mother passing. Until last year, she had been so introverted because of her Perthes disease that she hadn't made any friends. Besides, Josiah was fairly closemouthed about his family. But even still, it seemed a little odd that her mother was so concerned. "Are you worried about Peter and Josiah because they're still grieving?"

"*Nee*, dear. I meant financially." She took a deep breath. "I think he's going hungry."

Effie was shocked. "Mamm, he's never said anything about being hungry. If he would have said something, I would've tried to help him."

"Most kids aren't going to talk about bad things going on at home." She turned from the window and walked to Effie's side. "Especially not about something like being hungry or not having food. People like you and me take good meals for granted."

Her mother probably had a point. Effie had certainly never thought about how blessed she was to have plenty to eat.

Then the worst sort of doubts hit her hard—the selfish ones. "Mamm, do you think that's why Josiah came over? For the food?"

"I think he came over because he likes spending time with you. You two are friends." Looking at her sternly, her mother added, "Don't make this about you, Effie. I'm genuinely worried about him."

"What can we do?"

"You can be his friend. Continue to ask him over once a week."

"Mamm, you already asked him to walk home from the bus with me a few times a week."

"That is true, I did. But I can promise that your invitation is going to mean so much more than mine. Please promise me that you'll continue to ask him over."

"I can do that. What else?"

"I think that's all, at least for now. He needs your friendship more than anything." She pursed her lips. "But I can do something more. I'm going to go over to the Borntragers' old farm. Emma married the owner, you know. She's such a dear, and I know she'll really feel for Josiah's *daed* and his boys. Emma might have an idea about how to donate some food without embarrassing the family."

Hearing her mother's plan made it all seem more real. "How could I not have guessed that Josiah needed food?"

"Because rarely do we want the rest of the world to know our faults," her mother said.

"But if he's going hungry—"

"Effie, how many days have your legs really pained you but yet you've said nothing?"

Effie felt her cheeks flush. The truth was she'd probably hidden her pain more times than she could count. "I guess you have a point."

"But before you give yourself too hard a time, please remember that this isn't your fault. You didn't know about this because he didn't want you to know. And you're a child. If anyone is at fault, it is me. I remember several ladies at school worrying about those boys, but all we did was gossip and talk about things that we should do for them. Unfortunately we never *did* anything. Well, this time I'm going to do something. Actions speak louder than words, you know."

"I know, Mamm." Right then and there, Effie vowed to let her actions speak louder than her words, too. And suddenly, she needed to do something for Josiah. To concentrate on someone else's needs, rather than her own.

Why, if she could help Josiah have a better Christmas, that would surely be the best gift she could ever hope to give.

"KNOCK, KNOCK," A FAMILIAR, pretty voice called from the foyer. "Aunt Beverly, where are you?"

"I'm down here, Tricia," Beverly replied from the kitchen floor. She attempted to pop up far enough to catch her niece's eye as she entered.

"Any reason why you're on the floor?"

Oh, but Tricia did have a sense of humor! "I'm looking for another bread pan," she grumbled.

"Oh, Aunt Bev. Do you need me to come over and organize for you?"

Giving up the search, Beverly got to her feet. "I do. Any chance you came over here to do just that?" Her niece couldn't cook very well, and her cleaning skills weren't much better, but she could organize things better than Beverly ever could. Many a time Beverly had entered the kitchen to find whatever recipe Tricia was working on long forgotten but the spices and seasonings neatly organized and in alphabetical order.

Tricia crossed the room, and she looked so at peace that Beverly felt her spirits lift. "You look beautiful, dear," she said as she got to her feet and quickly hugged the young woman. "Positively glowing."

"Danke." Tricia hugged her back. "I've been worried about you, though." When they separated, she asked, "Are you okay?"

Beverly wasn't sure if she was or not. "I'm better," she said honestly.

"Sure?"

"Positive." She shook her head when Tricia looked ready to ask a dozen more questions. "I'd much rather talk about you and Ben."

She shrugged, a faint smile playing on her lips. "We're happy."

"Married life seems to agree with you." Tricia was wearing a bright yellow dress that brought out the gold flecks in her green eyes. As pretty as a picture.

"It does, but I'm here to help you. Thank goodness I saw Eric this morning. He said you could use my help."

"I do—if you are sure you can spare the time?"

"Aunt Beverly, you're being silly. Like I said, I've been worried about you. I tried to call but you didn't pick up the phone."

I ended up spending the night at the Kaufmanns' house the first night, then Eric arrived. I'm sorry, I should have called." Noticing that Tricia still looked worried, she added, "Everything will get better. I'll be okay."

"Especially now that Eric is back."

Beverly didn't know how to agree with that without revealing too much. "I am glad he came right away."

"So, what do you need me to do? Help you cook or help you clean?"

"Cook. I want to make some mini cranberry bread loaves and some sour cream Christmas cutouts. And maybe some spiced cider. And we need to make some fresh cinnamon rolls, too."

Walking to the drawer where Beverly kept all of her long dishtowels, Tricia pulled one out and tied it around her waist. "I'll get to work on the cinnamon roll dough. You look for the bread pans. Then we can tackle the cider." She looked at the phone. "Would you like me to give Penny a call? I'm sure she could stop by, too. She can work in the guest rooms. No one can make a bed as perfectly as she can."

Beverly hid a smile, recalling what a poor housekeeper Tricia had been, especially compared to Penny. Penny had shown up one day, desperate for a job and soon became indispensable. Then, all too soon, she'd fallen in love with Michael Knoxx and gotten married. "I don't think we'll need Penny's expertise, but I'll keep that in mind."

"Okay, but just remember that the only way you'll be overwhelmed is if you don't reach out and ask for help. You are surrounded by people in Pinecraft who would love to return some of your many favors."

"*Danke,* Tricia. You're right. I am mighty blessed to have so many helping hands at my disposal. Now, tell me about Ben and what you two have been doing. I feel like it's been weeks since you've filled me on your married life."

Tricia's smile was near blinding. "Are you sure you really want to hear? Because it might take a while."

"We've got lots of cookies and bread to make. Hours' worth!" she proclaimed. "Tell me everything."

Tricia rested her elbows on the counter. "Well, first off, I've discovered that Ben is a morning person."

Beverly pulled out some more measuring cups and started making a batch of Christmas cutouts. Tricia was right, it was obvious that her stories were going to take a while, but Beverly was glad. She was going to treasure every single minute of it.

Chapter 9

December 5

"Refill, Eric?" the proprietor of the Cozy Café called out as she approached the trio of tables on the café's front porch. "Your cup looks like it could stand to be heated up."

"Hmm? Oh, sorry." He looked down at his half-empty mug from the neighborhood coffeehouse. "Thanks. I guess my mind was drifting."

After she filled the cup, she smiled. "Don't worry about that. Everyone needs to take a break every now and then. Drift away," she joked.

Eric grinned. But as he sipped from his cup, he realized everything he'd been thinking about wasn't all that comforting. He'd been thinking about his past—and how he'd somehow neatly removed much of his crazy "troubled" years from memory. Well, not entirely. He still vividly remembered tagging behind his brother, Jack, and feeling his pulse accelerate as he watched the older boys break into a house.

But ever since he'd made the decision to change his life, to become someone he could be proud of, he'd very carefully, very precisely, pushed the memories of those transgressions away. Now, decades later, it felt as if all the trouble he'd gotten into had been done by another person. A kid who wasn't very smart. A boy who had been missing his parents. A teen who hadn't had a lot of self-respect and had attempted to discover his worth by running around with a group of hoodlums.

Not him.

But ever since he'd broken his cardinal rule and shared his story with Beverly, he hadn't been able to help but wonder about his past and his general reluctance to come to terms with it. Was it because the memories were too painful? Or because with those memories came the reminder that Jack had gone to prison while Eric had gone to college?

Now, as he sipped his hot coffee and watched the tourists walk by on the sidewalk in front of him, Eric replayed his conversation with Beverly. He'd been so full of fire and misplaced indignation. He'd actually chastised her for being close-minded when he'd been a champion of doing just that for the last fifteen years. Furthermore, he had seen how his words had affected her. When he'd arrived in Pinecraft, she'd been scared by the robbery. Now she was scared by the robbery *and* embarrassed by her reaction to his past.

He needed to fix this.

"You seem awfully deep in thought for a newly arrived

Northerner, Eric!" Michael Knoxx called out from the sidewalk. "Don't you know you're only supposed to worry about the state of your tan?"

Eric was thankful for the reprieve from his dark thoughts. "I'll try to keep that in mind," he said as he walked over to greet his friend. "It's good to see you. Happy holidays."

Michael, all good looks and brash humor, grinned. "Happy holidays to you, too. Last time Penny and I saw Beverly, she didn't say a word about you visiting. Seeing you out and about is a nice surprise. Are you staying until Christmas?"

"Yep. I wasn't planning to come back until my place sold. But when Beverly called to tell me about the robbery, I knew I couldn't let her handle everything herself."

"Of course not." Turning somber, Michael shook his head in dismay. "I still can hardly believe such a thing happened here in Pinecraft. Sorry we haven't stopped by already. We were planning on Sunday after church. How is Beverly doing?"

"She's still pretty shaken up. I hope you both will drop by when you can. I know she'll be happy to see you."

"What have the police said? Do they have any idea who broke in?"

"If they know, they haven't told us. I'm going to keep checking in with them, though. Right now we're focusing on getting the inn back open for business."

Michael raised his brows. "So soon?"

"I think it's for the best. The inn was booked solid, and nothing like this has ever happened before. It would be a shame to lose all that business." Folding his arms across his chest, he added, "Besides, if she's focused on baking and running the inn,

Bev won't be dwelling on what happened or second guessing herself. Those things can really run a person ragged."

"Sounds like you intend to make things a bit easier for her."

"I'm trying. Well, trying my best."

"I wouldn't expect anything less. I know you care about her," Michael replied with a grin.

There was something in both Michael's hearty tone and wide smile that gave Eric pause. "Beverly does work for me, you know. I mean, she's the manager, but I own the inn. I'm merely trying to do what I should."

"I haven't forgotten anything about your relationship." After a brief pause, he said, "It doesn't sound like you have, either."

It sounded like Michael was referring to more than he and Beverly's business partnership. "Hey—"

Michael cut him off. "Sorry if I'm sounding a bit presumptuous. But you really don't expect me to believe that you only care about Beverly because she's your employee." When Eric merely stared at him, Michael prodded. "Do you?"

"Well, I'm not sure—"

"After all, anyone can see that there's a lot more between the two of you than just work."

"Yeah, I guess there is." He was about to say what good friends he and Beverly were, but something told him that Michael would simply start laughing.

And he might even be justified in doing so.

Eric decided to switch topics instead. "How is your bride? And how are you doing? Have you adapted to sleeping in the same house every night or are you missing life on the road?"

"Right now I'd be happy if I don't pack a suitcase ever again.

And Penny is doing *wunderbaar*." He lowered his voice. "She's expecting a baby, you know."

"No, I didn't know!" He clasped Michael's hand again. "Congratulations! That's wonderful news."

"*Danke*. We think it's wonderful, too. This *boppli* is a true blessing for both of us. For both of our families, too. Her parents are so excited and my family feels the same. They're coming to Pinecraft on the twentieth and will stay for three weeks."

"That's great. I'm happy everything has worked out." He pointed to Michael's prosthesis. Michael had lost part of his leg after getting caught in a ravine for almost twenty-four hours. For years, he toured with his family to share his story. "You also look like you're getting around just fine now."

"Absolutely. This new prosthesis has a kind of vacuum that seals itself on my stump. It's so comfortable, it feels like a part of me." With a laugh, he added, "Matter of fact, I've been teasing Penny that sometimes I feel like I could play basketball again."

"I know a lot of men run, bike, and do all kinds of things with their fancy bionic legs. But go slowly for our sakes, okay?"

"Don't worry. Right now, I'm simply walking a lot. I'll move on to more activity when the doctors say I can."

"Good. Let me know if I can help you in any way."

"*Nee*, you let me know if I can help *you*. Don't be shy, okay?"

"Thanks. I won't."

"And be sure to tell Beverly that Penny is more than happy to come out and help her, too. She needs only to ask."

"Will do," he said as they shook hands. They parted ways, and Eric continued on to the police station. When he'd called Officer Roberts that morning, the officer had told Eric to stop by in a couple of hours. For Beverly's sake he wanted to hear what the man had to say.

Maybe it was simply a guy thing or maybe it was because he was suddenly thinking about his checkered past, but suddenly Eric felt very protective over Beverly. Whatever the reason, he knew he needed to hear from the officers themselves about the break-in. He also wanted to learn what clues they'd found and which suspects, if any, they were pursuing. Only then would Eric know he could go back and begin mending things with Beverly. He needed to do something to prove himself to her, to prove to her that he was responsible, no longer that troubled teen he'd told her he once was.

But just as important, he needed to remind himself that he was different. He'd turned his life around and made something of himself. He could talk to the police, too, even if it brought back bad memories. Eric was going to push himself to continue to be a man he could be proud of, to be the man his brother, Jack, had always assured him he could be—just so long as he didn't follow his path.

"I'VE GOT ANOTHER ONE," Sadie called out from her make-shift desk—the kitchen table. "I'm so excited, Beverly. By the end of next week, you'll have three guest rooms filled."

It took everything Beverly had to smile right back. "That is wonderful. Thank you for calling so many people today." Though Eric had been going to make the calls, in the end they decided that it would be better if he went out and ran errands and let Sadie make the calls while Beverly bustled around the house.

Sadie's excited expression dimmed slightly. "It weren't no trouble. Actually, once I got used to telling folks about the break-in it wasn't hard at all."

"You told guests that we were robbed?" She hadn't planned on being quite that frank.

"Well, *jah.* That's what happened." The last of Sadie's happy smile disappeared. "Was I not supposed to tell them the truth?"

"I hadn't planned to," she said honestly. "When I called everyone to cancel the reservations, I simply told them that something had come up and we were no longer going to be able to entertain guests until after the first of the year. No good is going to come from telling people about the robbery."

"No one seemed upset. Most folks were concerned about ya. Some were even happy to learn the reason for their reservation being cancelled in the first place."

"I guess that does make sense." Some of the inn's longtime guests had probably been confused.

Sadie rubbed the line that had just appeared between her brows. "Now, there was one lady from Arkansas who wasn't real happy about my phone call or the robbery. But I wouldn't worry about that none. After all, you can't please everybody."

"Arkansas?" Beverly tried to remember which of her regular customers came from that state. But her mind was in such a muddle, she could hardly remember what she'd planned to cook for supper, let alone where all her guests hailed from. "Who was it? Do you remember her name?"

"Nee." She bent over the neat stack of papers on the table. "But if you'll give me a minute, I can find out."

"There's no need to trouble yourself."

"It's no trouble. I'm sorry, Beverly. I hope you won't be upset with me for long."

It was the *for long* phrase that did it. Here her friend had given up hours of her afternoon and Beverly had hardly thanked her.

Crossing the kitchen, Beverly said, "Sadie, please forgive me. I've been so scattered and worried about getting this big house back in order, I fear I've let it get the best of me. Thank you for calling all of those people. I'm not upset about the Arkansas lady, and you're exactly right. You can't please everyone all of the time. Once more, I'm glad you were honest and told them about the break-in. Now I won't have to worry about them discovering it."

Immediately, Sadie's posture relaxed. "I didn't think about that, but I bet that would've happened. The robbery has been the talk of the town, you know."

"Believe me, I know." She could only imagine what people were saying and wondered if anyone had been talking about anything *but* the break-in.

Despite all that, it had been a busy morning and Sadie had been very helpful. She'd come just as Tricia was on her way out. Beverly was more than ready to relax, have a cup of hot tea, and try to convince herself that everything was going to be all right. "I bet you have lots to do, so if you don't mind, I'm going to send you on home."

"Already?" Sadie got to her feet, looking a little lost. "Are you sure you don't want to sit and chat for a while?" Dimples formed in her cheeks. "I can tell you all about the guests who are coming. It's all mighty exciting. Why, one lady is ninety years old."

"She does sound interesting and, um, spry, but I am kind of ready to simply sit in the quiet for a bit. I have a small headache."

"Oh! Well, *jah.* Some rest and relaxation will do you good, I think." Sadie turned back to the table and carefully put her reading glasses in her pocketbook, before she lovingly straightened the stacks of papers again. "I'll come over in the morning to see if you need any more help."

"*Danke.* Sadie, you really are so sweet."

"Not so much sweet as interested. This was great fun, and I had a nice break from doing my usual chore today. Laundry."

"You always look on the bright side of things. It's wonderful."

"I didn't always used to do that, but it's become a habit." With a wink, she added, "One day I'll tell you all about my dark and stormy past."

"I'll look forward to hearing about it," Beverly said with a smile. She couldn't begin to guess what kinds of "dark and stormy" things Sadie had gotten into.

After exchanging yet another round of farewells, Beverly shut the door and leaned against it in relief. Now, if she could let out all the doubts and depression that had been lurking in the corners of her mind, she would be better. As the seemingly ever-present tears pricked her eyes, she gave in to temptation, sat down in the chair that Sadie had vacated, and let herself have a good cry. It wouldn't solve all her problems, but it would surely release some of the tension that she'd been carrying around.

The truth was, she was afraid. She didn't feel safe anymore. She didn't trust the locks on her windows or doors and no longer assumed that all the people who walked by the inn or drove down the street were friendly. For all she knew, they were secretly making plans to break inside and steal from her again.

But now there was a new concern: having guests in the house. They were strangers, after all. What had she been thinking? Was she really ready to let a bunch of people she didn't know sleep in the same house as her? Why, any one of them could be very dangerous! And she wouldn't know until it was too late.

Though she instinctively knew she was overreacting and that everything was going to be fine, a part of Beverly hadn't actually wanted anyone to book a room. She had only let Sadie call her guests because she knew that was the polite thing to do. What had surprised her was the fact that the news about the robbery hadn't deterred anyone. Her guests seemed to be as excited as ever about their upcoming visits. Though, remembering Murphy's Law, she figured there was no doubt that someone would misplace a piece of jewelry and start worrying that the robber had returned.

"Hey, Bev?"

Her heart just about stopped. "Eric? Is that you?"

"Of course it is. Hey, you okay?" Eric asked as he entered the kitchen. "I, ah, just wanted to let you know that I'm back."

"Sorry. You startled me. I didn't hear the door open."

"Really? You can usually hear that door from every room in the inn."

"I must have been lost in a daydream." She was embarrassed that she hadn't heard the door, but perhaps she shouldn't be too surprised. She'd been letting her worries about having strangers underfoot get the best of her, after all.

"Sorry about that." Concern lit his brown eyes. "I just wanted to say hello and see what you were making for supper."

"It's all right. I was going to make you something special, but I'm afraid I haven't gotten too far." Realizing that nothing would get done if she continued sitting at the table like a child, she stood up. "I'll get started now."

"Not so fast. What's wrong?"

"Nothing. I'm just a little tired, that's all. I'll throw together something to eat right away." Thinking of her go-to dish, she said, "How does chicken and dumplings sound?"

Eric touched her shoulder, effectively preventing her from scurrying out of his reach. "Hey. You know I'm teasing, right? I don't expect you to cook for me. We can go to Yoder's or der Dutchman or into Sarasota for steaks or seafood."

"I know."

"Wait, you've been crying." Before she could step away from him, he reached for her hands and clasped them securely in his own. "What happened? Is something wrong? Did you discover something else important is missing? I stopped by the police station and spoke with Officer Reynolds, by the way. He said not to be embarrassed if you suddenly discover something else is gone. He thought there was a good chance that might happen in a big place like this."

"It's not that."

To her dismay, he stepped a little closer. And swung their linked hands a bit, as if they didn't have a care in the world. "What is it, then?"

"Nothing."

"Beverly, don't push me away."

She didn't want to. At least, she didn't think she did. But just as important, she didn't want to lean on him. Beverly doubted that he'd even understand all of her concerns. After all, they were such different people. Not only was he English, used to living in a big city, and a man . . . he'd actually robbed people. He would likely dismiss her worries as feminine fears or be unable to understand them in the first place.

"Beverly," he said again, his voice turning low and silky. "What is it?"

"I'm . . . ah. Sadie got hold of some of the people who had reservations. They rebooked."

His lips curved up. "Hey, that's good."

"*Jah.* It, um, is."

His smile disappeared. "But not to you?"

"Eric, this is so silly, but a part of me doesn't want strangers here."

"Ah."

She closed her eyes, wishing she were anywhere else. "I know this is an inn. I know that I've been taking care of the Orange Blossom for years. But all of the sudden, I'm not thinking about the people coming here as *guests*. I'm thinking of them as scary strangers."

"Uh-oh."

She exhaled. *"Jah."* Warily, she met his gaze. "I know. You think I'm being ridiculous. I'll get over it, I'm sure." Hopefully very soon.

His voice softened. "Hey, did you happen to notice something?"

"What?" She scanned the kitchen but saw nothing amiss. What else could have happened?

"Silly, look at me."

Right away, she brought her eyes to his. Noticed how dark his eyes were. Saw that same faint scar on his cheekbone. But where there was usually humor shining in his eyes, now she saw seriousness. He wasn't laughing. He didn't think she was being absurd.

But she still wasn't sure what he was referring to. "What do you want me to see?" she whispered.

He squeezed her hands. "Me."

"You?"

"Me. That I'm still here, Beverly. I'm not going anywhere."

She gulped. "Of course you are. You've got to go back to Pennsylvania and wait for your house to sell."

He shook his head. "I'm not going back. Not anytime soon, anyway."

She couldn't believe it. "But I thought your Realtor said that you needed to be there?"

"She said that, yes. But I called her today and explained that it's not going to happen."

"You're allowed to do that?"

He nodded. Still looking serious, he said, "I'm not going to leave you here to deal with everything on your own, Beverly."

She was so relieved she felt a lump form in her throat. She hadn't known how she was going to be brave enough to greet her first guests with a smile.

But then another thought occurred to her. "Did you do this because you thought I might be scared?"

"I did it because I own this place," he said. "It's my responsibility." As he looked down at their linked fingers, he added softly, "And because you work for me, so you are my responsibility, too."

"I see." She began to pull her hands away. The last thing she wanted to be to him was another burden.

But instead of relaxing his grip, he held her hands tighter. "No, you don't. More than anything, I decided to stay because you need me. You need someone to have your back. To be your friend. To talk to the cops and to check the doors. You might be very careful and immensely competent . . . but you are definitely not alone."

You are not alone. She knew her lips were parted. She knew she was staring at him in wonder, like a child looking at twinkling lights on a tall Christmas tree.

His voice lowered as he leaned closer. "Do you understand what I'm trying to say, Bev?"

She closed her lips and stared at him. Not trusting herself to speak just yet, she nodded.

"I hope so. I'm not going to let you be worried and scared late at night. I'm not going to make you serve guests breakfast all by yourself in the mornings."

He really did understand. *"Danke."*

"You're welcome, Bev. After all, I'd hate for you to ever think that I wasn't there for you." He ran a finger along her knuckles, then, to her surprise, raised her hand and pressed it to his lips.

She bit her lip to prevent a torrent of words from gushing out. She was so tempted to tell him that she wanted to be there for him, too. And that he mattered to her a lot. A whole lot. But her natural reticence, combined with an ex-fiancé's betrayal that she could never seem to completely forget, kept her mute.

But perhaps that was just as well.

Eric had just taken her breath away by promising the world. And all while holding her hands.

It was quite a spectacular moment.

Chapter 10

December 11

This was the third time Effie had ridden the bus home by Josiah Yoder's side.

The first time, she'd been a nervous wreck. It had felt as if the whole student body had been staring at them, and more than a couple of kids had whispered as they'd walked by. By the time her bus had pulled up and opened its doors, Effie had been half afraid that Josiah was going to walk away.

But he hadn't.

To make matters worse, two of his best friends rode her bus, too. When they first saw him there, they hadn't realized that Josiah was on the bus with Effie. Instead they'd kept asking him to sit with them. It was only when Josiah had said in a very cool, very firm voice, "*Danke*, but I'm going home with Effie," that the boys had quieted. Then, to Effie's amazement, they'd said hi to her and started talking with the two of them, like she was part of their group.

Josiah, for his part, had acted as relaxed and unflappable as ever. He took their conversation in stride and even managed to get her to talk, too. Before she knew it, she was even smiling at some of their jokes.

The second time he rode with her, it hadn't been as big of a shock to the student body, but he'd seemed preoccupied. When she'd tried to talk to him about the assembly they'd had during first bell, he'd stared at her blankly. Then, when she'd noticed that he had a bruise on his cheek and asked if it hurt, he'd told her that it wasn't any big deal.

But she was kind of thinking it was.

Now, they were sitting together for the third time and no one seemed surprised. Josiah was more relaxed, too. As if he was completely used to going home with Effie.

After his buddies left, he turned to her. "You seem like you aren't as nervous about talking to the guys now."

"At first I thought they would just ignore me or ask about my legs or something."

"They wouldn't do that."

"I guess not."

"You're walking pretty good now. Do your legs hurt?"

She debated whether to tell him the truth. Deciding she had nothing to lose, she shrugged. *"Jah."*

He frowned. "Badly?"

"*Nee.* I'm having to do more exercises to help strengthen the muscles. That makes them sore. And, um, well, my leg that was broken still feels a little shaky, so I guess I have to keep working it."

Looking concerned, he said, "I never really thought about how you always have to deal with your disease's effects. You never talk about being in pain. But walking is pretty tough, isn't it?"

"Some days it's hard." She shrugged, hating to focus any more of their conversation on her disease. "I'm all right."

"Sure?"

"Positive. My legs are a little weak, that's all."

"Okay. But if you are hurting, let me know."

"I will, but like I said, I'll be fine. I used to think my Perthes disease was the worst thing in the world. Now I know it isn't."

"That's the way to think."

She smiled, liking that there seemed to be new respect for her in his eyes. It made her proud. She didn't want to be a source of pity for him. She wanted him to think of her as an equal. But as she took a turn studying him, Effie realized that while he might be looking at her differently, there was a shadow of regret in his eyes, too. That was new.

"Josiah, are you okay?"

He looked around, saw a couple of kids from their class, and nodded. "*Jah.* I've got some things going on, but I don't want to talk about them here."

"Oh."

When they got off the bus five minutes later, Josiah did what he always did and took Effie's backpack for her. After the bus drove off and the other kids wandered away, she said, "So, what's going on?"

He smirked. "You don't waste much time, do you?"

"You don't have to answer if you don't want to," she replied as they walked side by side.

"I don't mind. My brother is in some trouble. He did something bad and I don't know what to do." He paused. "I am worried about it but I don't want him to go to jail."

Jail? "Oh my gosh, Josiah! I'm so sorry."

"*Danke.*" He pressed his lips together, almost as if he was afraid to reveal too much.

"Is there anything I can do?" She didn't actually know how she could help, but she was more than willing to try.

He looked a little amused by her offer. "*Nee.* I'll be all right."

They walked on. Effie looked up at him, noticed that his head was down. He looked tired. "Have ya talked to your father? What did he say?" Even if her parents got mad at her, they would try to help.

He kept his eyes averted. "I can't talk to my father about much. Um, when my *mamm* passed away a couple of years ago, my father changed," he said slowly. "And well, my *daed* can't really handle any more bad news." Kicking at something with the toe of his tennis shoe, he mumbled, "He can't really handle much at all . . . when he's around, that is."

More bad news? When he's around? Effie had to physically keep her mouth from dropping open. And though it wasn't any of her business, she wanted to try to help him in some way. But in order to do that, she also had to actually know what was happening. "Josiah, what's wrong with your *daed*? Is he still grieving?"

When he didn't say anything for a full minute, she knew she had gone too far. She shouldn't have pushed. After all, it wasn't like they were great friends. Merely starting-to-be-good ones.

There was a difference.

"I don't know how much to tell you," he said at last.

"You don't have to tell me anything. But if you want to share, I'd like to listen." They were walking slowly side by side, Josiah mainly looking at his worn sneakers, Effie looking mainly at him.

After they had walked almost another half block, he spoke. "My *daed* is pretty tough to live with. He has a temper. And, well, he doesn't have a lot of luck finding a job and keeping it. Now, though, he seems to be happier when he's not at home. He leaves for days at a time."

Effie couldn't think of anything sadder. It was obvious that Josiah's mother's passing had been hard. Not just because he missed her, but because he now had no parents on whom he could depend. "Do you have any other relatives who look after you when he's not around?"

"Nee." That one word was sharp and full of pain.

So much so, she didn't dare ask him any more about it. "Oh."

For the first time since they'd gotten off the bus, he smiled. It wasn't a full smile, just a slight rise in the corners of his lips, but it was enough to let her see that she'd amused him. "Oh? That's all you are gonna say?"

His sudden teasing brought her up short. She didn't know what to say. "Well, I figure if you want to tell me more you will."

"It's not that I don't want to tell you more, Ef, it's just that I probably shouldn't. There's a difference."

"I'm not sure what that difference is."

"If you knew more, it might be too much for you to handle."

"Why don't you let me determine that?" After all, being the only girl in school with braces on her legs hadn't exactly been easy. Effie thought she was pretty strong.

But he continued as if she hadn't spoken. "Even if you did know everything that's been going on, there ain't anything you could do about it. Talking isn't going to solve anything."

"Sometimes talking does help."

"Not my problems. They aren't going away anytime soon."

As much as Effie wanted to help him, she knew she also had to respect his decision. If she pushed too hard, she could lose his friendship and she really didn't want that to happen. "I understand," she said simply.

"I'm glad."

But despite the fact that she'd just promised herself she'd be quiet, she blurted, "If you do happen to change your mind, I hope you'll let me know."

"Ef."

"I could listen. I'm a mighty *gut* listener. Or even get you help."

"I doubt that."

"You might be surprised. My family knows just about everyone in Pinecraft, you know."

"Look at you." His blue eyes flickered over her, looking suspiciously proud of her. "You used to hardly say a word. Now you're all sassy and bossy."

She hoped he would never know how much she liked his compliments. Even though his attention embarrassed her, it also felt wonderful. "Not so much. But I am your friend," she said in a rush.

"Yeah. That is what we are. We are friends. I'm glad about that. I need a friend like you."

She tried to act like his words didn't mean the world to her. But they did. They meant a lot, just like he meant a lot to her. If he knew how fond she was of him, though, he might become uncomfortable.

Actually, she was sure he would be.

As they continued on, Josiah looking pensive by her side, Effie thought about everything he'd shared about his home life. It wasn't much—he'd been studiously closemouthed about his family. Why, she hadn't even known his mother had passed away!

But now everything he'd been saying—and not saying—was suddenly starting to come together: The way he was never in a hurry to go home. The way he ate her mother's cooking like he didn't have a meal waiting for him at home, and maybe wouldn't have one anytime soon. And his comments about his father. About his brother possibly being in very bad trouble.

Something was very wrong at Josiah's house and he was hiding it, too.

She felt closer to him than ever before but, unfortunately, she still couldn't be the person he needed her to be.

If she betrayed his trust, told his story to her parents and they tried to do something, he would never forgive her. Without a doubt, she would lose his friendship.

But if she did nothing, he would continue to suffer.

She didn't want to hurt him, or have him mad at her, either. But she had to do something. Even if it meant that he'd never walk home with her again or, worse, if he started ignoring her at school.

But that was how much she cared for him, she realized. She was willing to do anything she could to help him—even if her actions would haunt her.

December 11

Mark stepped off the SCAT bus on South Beneva Road and ran smack into Peter Yoder.

Reaching out, Mark grasped Peter's arm before steadying himself. "Sorry. I wasn't looking where I was going." Actually, he'd been looking at a text from Laura on his cell phone. They were now texting each other all the time, something Mark was discovering he was addicted to. He was really going to hate giving up his cell phone when his *rumspringa* was over.

Peter glanced at Mark's cell phone with something that looked like jealousy before shrugging. "It's nothing. See you around."

Mark knew he should say good-bye and walk away. But on the other hand, the guy really looked like he could use a friend. Besides, Mark hadn't been able to stop thinking about the things Laura had said about Peter.

Or about the money that had been in his pocket.

Noticing that Peter was heading toward the post office and the parking lot where all the Amish tourists arrived on buses, Mark said, "Do you have relatives coming in?"

"*Nee*. I was just going for a walk."

"Oh. Okay." No one their age simply went for walks. Realizing that Peter was also going in the direction of the Quick Stop, he blurted, "Laura's not working," before he could stop himself.

Instead of looking irritated, Peter smiled. "You must really like her. I promise, there's nothing between us. We're just friends."

Mark felt his cheeks flush. Now he felt like a jealous, insecure idiot. "Sorry. I do, um, really like her."

Peter's smile transformed into a full-fledged grin. "Just so you know, I'm not headed toward the Quick Stop. I wanted to take a break before heading home." He paused. "Actually, I'm putting off going home. I've got a ton of chores to do there and I've been applying for jobs all day."

Reminded again of the money Peter had been carrying in the Quick Stop, he wondered why he even was looking for work in the first place. "Do you mind if I walk with you?"

Peter eyed him suspiciously. "Why? You don't have anything else to do?"

"Not at the moment." Mark didn't dare say that Peter looked even worse than usual. His shirt had a tear in it, and his pants were stained. Even after working in the fields all day, Mark's father would never have let him go out in such dirty clothes.

But more worrisome than the state of Peter's clothes was his strained expression, as if he had the weight of the world on his shoulders. The poor guy looked like he shouldn't be alone.

"I don't care if you walk with me, but I can't promise to be much company."

"That's okay."

They walked a couple of blocks in silence, averting their eyes from most of the people they passed. As they walked, the tension between them started to ease. They smiled at a little girl holding a puppy and shared a look when they saw a kid just a few years younger than them make a fool out of himself in front of a girl.

"So, where all did you apply?" Mark asked after a while.

"At a couple of landscaping companies."

"Any luck?"

"Not yet." He frowned. "Actually, I haven't had much luck anywhere. I tried a couple of stores two days ago. Most everyone said they weren't hiring right now."

With Christmas around the corner, Mark could believe that. "You should try some of the hotels. High season isn't far off. All the tourists will be coming in February and March."

"I don't know if I want to work at a hotel."

"Sure? Some people tip really well. They make good money."

"Maybe. But working a hotel ain't for me."

Remembering all the rumors and talk surrounding the Orange Blossom Inn, Mark said, "Hey, you could always try Beverly Overholt. She might need some help, especially with all that happened at her inn recently."

Peter froze. "What happened?"

"The inn was robbed almost two weeks ago." Thinking how no

one had been able to talk about anything else after it happened, Mark looked at him curiously. "Didn't you hear about it?"

"Why would I know about that?"

"Because it's all anyone has been talking about. The people broke in through a window and took Beverly's money. I heard they got a lot, too."

"You sure know a lot about it. How come you're so concerned about an inn?"

"We stayed there for a couple of weeks before we could move to our farm. Beverly is really nice."

Peter's eyes looked troubled though he shrugged like he didn't care. "I don't know her."

"No reason you should since you have a house here, but I have to tell ya that even my *daed* was shocked. He couldn't believe something like that had happened right here in Pinecraft."

"Crime happens everywhere. Pinecraft ain't no different."

"I know," Mark mused. "But I guess since I stayed at the Orange Blossom Inn, I've paid a lot of attention to the news about it. I really am surprised you hadn't heard."

"I try to keep to myself."

Mark thought that was a pretty strange remark but he let it pass. After all, who was he to say what someone should be interested in?

Sneaking a glance at him as they walked toward Pinecraft Park, Mark thought Peter looked even more perturbed. "You've lived here longer than I have. Who do you think it was? A tourist or someone local?"

Peter stopped and pointed to a street behind him. "You know, I've gotta go. My *bruder*, Josiah, is probably home by now."

"Oh? Oh, well, all right." Great. Even when he was trying to be nice he ended up saying the wrong things. "Next time we meet, I'll try not to run over ya."

But Peter didn't respond. Instead he turned and walked away. Without another word.

Chapter 11

December 12

After consuming a couple bowls of cereal at the inn, sorting through some bills, and calling the insurance company, Eric had ventured out to do some errands. There were still quite a few finishing touches that needed to be done around the inn before the initial guests arrived.

First he went to the hardware store and bought a new bucket of white paint to touch up the baseboards in some of the guest rooms. Then he drove to the other side of Sarasota and bought a pair of lamps for the gathering room. They were Tiffany inspired and were going to look terrific. Even better, he knew Beverly was going to love them.

Now, he was sitting in the back corner of the Cozy Café, sipping a large cappuccino and staring at his smartphone resting on the table. Again.

What he needed to do was pick it up, thumb through his contacts, and call his brother, Jack. After all, they hadn't talked in almost a year. That was far too long to go without checking in. Because of that, he supposed he didn't have to come up with a legitimate reason to give Jack a call. All he needed to do was pick up the phone and say hello.

But he'd tried to come up with several excuses not to anyway. There was too much between them to pretend they had a close relationship.

But maybe it was time to start creating one. Besides, it was almost Christmas. Didn't most people call their siblings around Christmas? Even when Jack was in prison, Eric had made sure to call him on Christmas Day. Jack had been out of prison for years now. One of them needed to push things forward. It might as well be him.

Before he generated another half dozen excuses or procrastinated a second more, Eric found Jack's number, pressed Send, and held the cell phone to his ear. When the fourth ring got cut off by a terse, recorded message, Eric heaved a sigh of relief. Jack wasn't available. Now he could leave a message and know that he had done the right thing and called.

"Hey, Jack. It's me. Don't want anything. I just thought I'd call and—"

The phone clicked, then clicked again. "Hello? Eric?" Jack said quickly, urgently, almost as if he was afraid he would miss Eric's call.

"Hey," he said, hoping he didn't sound quite as awkward as he felt. "I was leaving you a message."

"Why? What's wrong?"

Eric shifted in his chair. "Nothing. I was, um, just thinking about you."

"Yeah?" That one word made Jack sound far more relaxed. Almost like the brother he'd been before they'd grown up and so much had changed between them.

Eric almost smiled. "Yeah. So, how are you?"

He paused. "About the same as I was when we talked last. When was that? Last Christmas?"

Eric was pretty sure that was right but he was too embarrassed to admit that truth. "I'm pretty sure we've talked since then. Like in June. Around your birthday?" At least, he'd *thought* about calling Jack then.

"Oh. Yeah. I bet we did talk then."

Feeling even more awkward, Eric said, "So, what have you been up to?"

"I got a job."

Jack sounded proud. Eric smiled. "Hey, that's great. What are you doing?"

"Construction. Turns out the recession is slowly making its way out of Cleveland. I've been working on some crews downtown."

"Hey, that's great." He winced. Did his voice sound as full of forced joviality as he thought?

"It's not great," Jack corrected. "But it's good."

"Good is good enough," he said, using the familiar quote they'd shared at least once a week when they were small.

Jack chuckled. "I haven't heard that phrase in years."

"Me neither." He smiled, and felt his shoulders relax. At last, they were conversing easily. Maybe, finally, things would change between them and they could recapture the bond they'd shared back before they'd both made choices they shouldn't have. Maybe Eric wouldn't feel so guilty about the way their lives had turned out.

Relief mixed with that same old feeling of dread and churned in his stomach. After they'd been arrested, Jack had threatened to beat Eric if he got into trouble again. There hadn't been anything sweet or kind in his brother's threats; Eric had firmly believed Jack really would hurt him if he stopped going to school and started hanging out with the gangs again. Little by little, Eric had joined clubs, volunteered, and gotten a job at the grocery store in the next town over. Anything to keep away from the guys who wanted him to get into trouble with them.

And Eric had flourished. His grades had gone up. And his clear head had enabled him to achieve high scores on all the college entrance exams, which had given him scholarships, which, in turn, had made his teachers and counselors take a renewed interest in him. His future suddenly held a multitude of bright possibilities. Far more than he'd ever dreamed.

Jack, on the other hand, had stayed on his downward path. Alcohol, drugs, petty theft. Then grand theft. Then jail.

Through it all, Jack had kept his distance from Eric, continuing to threaten bodily harm at times if Eric strayed from his goals while also telling him that he was their only hope.

Realizing that probably a whole minute had passed without a single word, Eric rushed to fill the silence. "So, I'm in Sarasota."

"Where's that?"

"Florida. West coast. Do you remember me ever talking about my old neighbor John?"

"Kind of."

"Well, he died and left me an inn."

"No way. Why would he do a thing like that?"

"I don't know. I guess he thought I needed something." Thinking about it, Eric figured John had known from the moment they'd first met that Eric had needed an anchor in his life. For a few years, John had been that anchor. He'd asked about Eric's life and his goals and even joined him for dinner once a week. John had been his best friend and, in many ways, a father figure. But it was only after his death that Eric realized how much more John had done for him. He'd taught him to trust, but he'd also taught him about church, the Bible, and faith.

"You must have done something good for the guy if he gave you an inn," Eric pointed out. "Or is the place a mess?"

"It's nice. Real nice. I don't know if I ever did anything to deserve this place. I kind of doubt it." Actually, John's gift had felt a lot like God's grace—a gift that was undeserved.

Now, sitting by himself in the corner of a coffee shop in Sarasota, eclectic artwork hanging on brightly painted teal walls, an idea came to mind. He decided to propose it before he dismissed it. If he actually thought about the consequences, he knew he'd get off the phone as quickly as he could. "So, anyway, I was thinking that it's pretty warm down here. It's a pretty good place to spend Christmas . . ."

"I bet." Jack's voice held no trace of envy or bitterness. "If anyone deserves it, you do. Get a tan for me, okay? And thanks for calling."

"No, wait. What I'm trying to say is, why don't you come down and stay with me for a couple of days?"

"Really?" he asked after a pause. "You want me there?"

The lump that had been in Eric's throat turned into a rock. "Yeah, I really do. We haven't spent Christmas together in years."

"In probably twenty, at least."

Eric was now holding the phone with a death grip. "Twenty years is too long, don't you think?"

After another a lengthy pause, Jack cleared his throat. "Hey, I appreciate your invitation. That's, um, real nice of you. But—"

"There's plenty of room," Eric said. "Actually, I'm staying up in the attic, in one of three twin beds. You could share my room."

"Just like old times, huh?"

"Yeah, though these beds are a lot more comfortable than our old bunk beds. They're narrow, but comfortable."

"I'd be all right. I've slept on worse."

Eric swallowed. Yes, he supposed Jack had. Clearing his throat, he said, "Beverly, the gal who runs the inn, is a great cook. Best food you'll ever have in your life."

"Is that right? You got something going with her, E?"

Eric felt his neck flush but told himself it was from being called "E" for the first time in decades. "Of course I don't."

"Sure about that?"

"No."

"No?" Jack's voice now held a touch of humor.

He chuckled. "I don't know. There might be something between us. It's kind of hard to tell." Embarrassed that he could sound so flustered at his age, he redirected things. "So, hey, what do you think? Want to come to Florida for Christmas? It's sure to be warmer than Cleveland." Funny how much easier it was to talk about the warmth being the draw instead of himself.

"Florida would be a lot warmer." Jack inhaled, then Eric heard nothing but imaginary crickets.

Eric pursed his lips and waited. And he found himself hoping for something, just like he'd used to back when they were kids and Eric had wanted his big brother to do something with him.

At last, Jack spoke. "Listen, I, um, really appreciate it. But I don't think I can swing it. Not this year, anyway. I'm working, but guys at my level aren't making a mint."

Eric knew Jack had included that last part as his way of apology. But now that he'd gotten this far, he pushed a little bit more. Something told him that Jack needed him this Christmas.

"Let me buy you the ticket."

"That's not necessary."

"Yeah. Yeah, it is. Because I really want you to come." As he said the words, he realized he was speaking the truth. He needed his brother, too. "Please," he added. "I've got the money. Let me use it."

"You really are serious, aren't you?"

Was that wonder in his brother's voice? "I'm serious as a heart attack," he said. Just like their dad used to say.

"I couldn't come for long. I have a real job, you know."

Eric swallowed hard. The emotion he felt was coming through powerfully. "You don't have to stay long. Stay for a week. Or five days. Or, I don't care, just come for two nights."

"You'd actually buy me a ticket to see you for two nights?"

Eric was realizing he'd spend the money to see his brother for two hours. "I would. Jack, come on the twenty-fourth. Leave on the twenty-sixth."

"Let me think about it."

"There's nothing to think about, is there?"

"I need to check my work schedule. And, well, I do need to think about it for a day or two. Do you mind giving me a little bit of time?"

Eric knew Jack wasn't simply thinking about spending two nights together under the same roof for the first time in almost two decades. He was asking if Eric thought they could start to have a relationship again.

"I can give you that." He swallowed hard again. "I'll call again on the fourteenth or fifteenth."

"Okay. Or I'll call you."

"Can you believe this? We're actually talking about seeing each other. And speaking more than once a year." He was smiling like he'd just won the lottery.

"It's pretty cool. Hey, uh, E?"

"Hmm?"

"Thanks for picking up the phone."

"I should have called you months ago. I'm sorry."

"I should have called you, too. After all, you are my kid brother."

"I'm hardly that."

"You'll always be that. Always."

After they said good-bye, Eric wondered if Jack's voice had really sounded as husky as he'd imagined.

Or was it how he was feeling?

Chapter 12

December 12

When the doorbell chimed at three in the afternoon, Beverly rushed to answer it. This was it! The first guests since the break-in had arrived. A handful of emotions swirled inside her. She felt nervous and awkward, excited and worried.

But, of course, the guests could never know this.

Instead, she forced herself to smile and act gracious as she opened the door to the four Englishers on the doorstep. *"Wilcom!"* she said. "Welcome to the Orange Blossom Inn."

"Thank you," one of the gentlemen said. "I'm Bryan Evans. This is my wife, Betty, and daughter, Amy, and her husband, Colten."

Beverly nodded and smiled at everyone as she introduced herself. "I am Beverly Overholt, the manager of the inn." Stepping back, she waved an arm with a little flourish. "Please, come in and make yourself at home."

She knew everything looked as pretty and clean as it possibly could. Eric had painted trim for hours yesterday while she'd polished the furniture until every piece in the gathering room gleamed. On two of the tables sat new lamps. They were made of stained glass and looked perfectly elegant. Two fresh balsam candles scented the room.

As they entered and hung their jackets on the brass coatrack next to the door, Bryan looked around the entryway with a critical eye and said, "We were really glad one of your employees called and said that you were still open for business."

"We've been planning to spend Christmas here in Sarasota for almost a year," Betty said. "So when you emailed to say that you had decided to not host guests until January, we were devastated."

Beverly thought about the evasive way she'd cancelled their reservation and realized that Sadie had been exactly right. It had been wrong for her to simply cancel without providing a good reason. "I'm glad you were still able to stay here."

"It was a matter of us being pretty desperate. No place else had room in their inn," her husband replied, smiling at his little Christmas-themed quip.

Beverly had a feeling she was going to be hearing comments like that a lot. "Well, you're here now. Please, come in. We have coffee and tea and some cookies that I baked fresh this morning if you'd like some. After you sign in, I'll show you to your rooms so you can get settled."

"I'll take care of the credit card, Betty," Bryan said. "You three go look around."

While they walked around the gathering room and helped themselves to some snickerdoodles, Beverly guided Bryan to her small desk located along the side of the room. Soon she was running his credit card through the machine and having him sign the reservation form.

Less than five minutes later, she handed him their welcome packet. "Your keys are inside, Bryan. Please don't be afraid to let me know how I can help make your stay as pleasant as possible."

"You can tell that rain to move out," he said with a wink, referring to the rare December soaker outside. "We came from snow in Indiana. We're ready for some sun."

"I'll do my best to get the weather to cooperate," she joked.

After waiting for Bryan to get a cup of coffee and a couple of cookies, she walked them upstairs to their rooms. She'd worked hard on the rooms, or actually she and Tricia had. Usually Beverly felt a tremendous sense of pride when she showed her guests their quarters, but this time, she felt her smile grow brittle and a knot of tension settle between her shoulder blades.

This was the first time she'd ever had to act pleased about guests arriving.

A BIT LATER, AFTER Eric had joined her and then eventually escorted another set of people to their rooms, Beverly was feeling so stressed and agitated she was on the verge of tears. Instead of being grateful for the business, she secretly hoped that some of her other reservations never turned up. And knowing the way she was scrutinizing every guest who walked through the door made her feel even worse.

Truly like Scrooge.

How was she going to survive the holiday season with an attitude like this? If she didn't find a way to cope with her negative thoughts, she was going to run off her guests. However, she feared that was easier said than done. It was likely going to be the longest December in history.

And the worst Christmas ever.

December 13

As Eric leaned against one of the pale blue walls in the laundry room, he realized something had to be done.

In front of him, Beverly was carefully ironing pillowcases. Every couple of minutes, she would spray starch on the cotton, glide the iron over the fabric, painstakingly fold it, then press the iron firmly down again. They were surely going to be the stiffest, best-pressed pillowcases in the state of Florida.

"Sure I can't help you with that, Bev?" he asked for the second time in five minutes.

"Positive. I like these pillowcases ironed a specific way."

As he watched her frown and fold with the precision of a robot, Eric shifted. Something was bothering her and it was bothering her a lot. "What's wrong?"

She didn't look at him. Instead, she chewed on her bottom lip as she folded the white cotton pillowcase into thirds and pressed the iron to the fabric. "Nothing. I simply have a lot to do."

Eric couldn't accept that answer any longer. For two days, now, Beverly had been acting out of sorts. Usually, she sipped coffee in the mornings and took time to relax with a cup of tea and shortbread cookies in the evenings. But now she was constantly on the go. It was as if she feared sitting alone or having too much time to reflect.

He could understand her need to stay busy, to a point. What concerned him more was the worry in her eyes. Even now, she was simply going through the motions of looking after guests. Even when he was standing by her side, Beverly didn't look all that pleased to see their customers. Everything that used to make her happy—baking, fussing over her flowers out front, chatting with guests in the morning—now seemed like a burden to her.

And, instead of allowing him to step in further, or accepting additional help from her large group of friends, she seemed intent on shouldering all those burdens by herself.

Yesterday, when Eric had walked down the second-floor hallway and seen her on her hands and knees carefully cleaning the wood trim, he'd gently tried to redirect her energies. That hadn't worked. When he'd mentioned reading about some various holiday events going on in town, she hadn't batted an eye.

"That's nice, Eric," she'd said. "But I have too much to do around here. Plus, we have guests."

"I know we have guests. But you've never let a full house prevent you from taking a break for a few hours."

"I don't want to leave the inn."

"Then let Tricia or Sadie fill in for you for a couple of hours." When she still refused to budge, he'd nudged her playfully. "Come on, Bev. It's Christmastime."

"It is, to be sure. But you forget, I'm an innkeeper. This is a mighty busy time for me."

That had been when he'd realized she was in trouble. Beverly only used Amish expressions when she was feeling particularly stressed or anxious.

To make matters more complicated, he was starting to wonder if she was a hundred percent okay with his new, larger role at the Orange Blossom Inn. Though he'd stayed there before, of course, he now was attempting to be more involved. But instead of his presence easing her mind, it seemed to only fluster Beverly more. She often stumbled over whom to refer to as being in charge, which confused him. They both knew who the heart and soul of the inn was—and it definitely wasn't him.

Then, of course, there was the fact that the police still hadn't figured out who'd robbed the inn. Other than being fairly sure the culprits were teens, they were no closer to making an arrest than they had been on the day of the incident.

It was time to take matters into his own hands. Eric was going to make her take a break from this place, even if he had to pull her out the front door. He was just about to tell her to grab her purse because he was taking her out to lunch when one of the guests approached with a map of Sarasota and a long list of questions. Beverly had jumped up from the ironing, as if anxious to be of use—though, more likely, anxious to put some space between herself and his goals.

"Bev, we need to talk."

She stared at him. She must have been struck by something she saw in his eyes because she sighed. "All right. Give me thirty minutes to finish up these pillowcases. Then I'll meet you in the kitchen."

"Can't we talk now?" he pressed, beginning to feel annoyed. "I'm sure you can iron and talk to me at the same time."

"I can, but I'd rather not. Please, just give me a half an hour. That's not too long to wait."

"All right, but I'm warning you now, I'm not going to let you push me away today."

BEVERLY LOOKED AT ERIC in surprise when he strode into the kitchen a half an hour later. She'd pulled everything out of one of the cabinets and had a bottle of spray cleaner in her hands.

"Beverly, what are you doing? I told you we needed to talk."

"We can talk while I clean the cabinets."

"You suddenly decided you needed to clean them?"

"I'm, uh, taking stock, too."

"Bev."

She kept her eyes focused on something just to his left. "You know I've been going through everything since the robbery."

"Nobody stole anything from the cabinets. We both know that. Besides, you organized it the other day. I stood here and watched you."

Those green eyes of hers that he loved so much filled with distress. "I need to keep busy, Eric."

His heart softened as he heard the distress in her voice, too. He walked to her side and took the bottle of cleaner out of her hand. Then kept his hands on hers and gently squeezed. "I can appreciate that, but you aren't behaving rationally. I'm worried about you."

"Thank you for that, but there is no need to worry. I am fine."

"You are not fine at all. You're working yourself into a dither, and I'm concerned."

She pulled her hands from his and crossed them over her chest. "I don't get into *dithers*, Eric. I have merely been cooking and cleaning and getting the inn organized."

"That's *all* you've been doing."

"We had a robbery. Strangers went through the whole inn. They stole a television, remember?"

"I bought a new one."

"Things are a mess."

"No, things *were* a mess. Now everything is bright and shiny. It looks as pretty as I've ever seen it."

She looked up at him in wonder. Her wide-set eyes appeared even greener than usual, thanks to the forest-green dress she was wearing. And though her brown hair was pinned up, more than a couple of strands had fallen around her face, making her appear younger. And to his surprise, even prettier. Bemused, he found himself leaning against the doorjamb that led to the back patio, content to simply admire her—which wasn't good, seeing as how it was absolutely *not* why he'd wanted to talk to her.

"Eric? You are staring." She fidgeted, pushing a lock of hair back behind her ear and smoothing her dress.

"I know." Unable to keep a straight face, he grinned.

"Why are you staring at me? And smiling? What's wrong?"

"Not a single thing. I'm simply taken with you."

"Surely not. Have you never seen a woman organize a kitchen before?"

He honestly couldn't say that he had. He'd never dated a woman seriously enough to be around her when she was simply doing chores at home. But he couldn't say that. "Not one who wore a pretty green dress while she did it."

Now she was looking flustered. Which was good. Now, at least, they were on even ground.

She brushed back another strand of hair. Honestly, every strand looked in serious danger of escaping from its pins and falling around her shoulders.

"Let's go play hooky for a little while."

"I'm not going to the beach, Eric."

"I wasn't thinking about Siesta Key. I was thinking that we should go shopping."

"I can't go shopping for groceries until I finish this inventory."

"Not for food." Suddenly the perfect idea came to him. "Let's go get a Christmas tree."

"A what?" Her eyes were wide and a look of true dismay filled her expression.

He chuckled. "Beverly, you do know what a Christmas tree is, right? One of those green things you put lights on? Decorate with bright, shiny ornaments?"

"There's no need to use that tone. Of course I know what a Christmas tree is. It's just that the Amish don't have Christmas trees." Standing up a bit primly, she said, "The Amish don't believe in the need for all of those commercial entrapments to celebrate Jesus' birthday."

She looked so earnest, it took everything he had to keep from smiling. "I know that."

"If you know that, then you must also know that I do not want a Christmas tree in the inn."

It was time to pull out the big guns. "Did you forget that this is technically my inn?"

"*Nee.* Of course I didn't forget that."

Taking care to keep his tone light, he added, "And, I don't know if you've noticed, but I'm not Amish."

"I know you aren't."

"And, last time I checked, you weren't, either."

After staring at him a moment longer, Beverly turned to the refrigerator, pulled out a pitcher of cold water, poured herself a tall glass, and drank half of it. "Eric, I may not be Amish anymore, but that don't mean I want to start adopting all kinds of fancy English traditions."

Though Eric had wanted a Christmas tree anyway, he'd suggested it mainly as something they could do to get her mind off the robbery. But now he was starting to think that they needed one really just to shake things up a bit.

Actually, a pretty green tree in the window would look really pretty. Festive.

"I'm not talking about purchasing an inflatable Santa and sticking him on your lawn, Bev," he said gently. "Instead, I think we should head to the empty lot next to the hardware store and buy us a six- or seven-foot Christmas tree. A real one, so the whole room will smell like Christmas."

"Like evergreens," she mused. "Heavenly."

"It would be perfect." If he hadn't seen the fresh wave of longing in her eyes, he would have thought he'd imagined it. He pressed a bit further. "We don't even have to put any ornaments on it if you don't want."

Ironically, she looked a bit peeved. "Eric, we can't have a plain, bare tree simply sitting around. What would people say?"

It was becoming difficult to keep a straight face. "How about we put lights on it? Just a bunch of white lights?"

"White lights would look pretty."

"Christmasy, yet plain."

"The Amish don't use electricity. So not too Plain."

He started laughing. "You are so literal sometimes, Beverly Overholt. Honestly, you crack me up. I meant that we won't have a tree with all kinds of ornaments and stuffed birds hanging from the branches."

"Absolutely not. We have birds outside."

She sounded so prim and proper, he was tempted to remind her that there were trees outside, too, but he was pretty sure that would work against his plan. "So what do you say? Will you go get a Christmas tree with me?"

She bit her lip, glanced around the neatly organized room, and then seemed to have made her decision. *"Jah."*

"Thank you. I think it's going to look great. And I promise I won't make you get the biggest tree in the lot."

"*Gut*. It would take up the whole gathering room."

"We can't have that. It's going to be hard enough to get it set up." He clapped his hands together. "How long is it going to take you to finish your inventory?"

Looking sheepish, she said, "I don't actually need to sort through all of this right now. I did a big shopping run right after Thanksgiving. Want to leave around ten?"

"Ten sounds perfect." He noticed that her eyes were glowing. For the first time since his arrival, she didn't look as if she was scared to face the day. "You know if we go look at trees, we might as well pick up a wreath, too."

She nodded. "I thought of that. And I would like to get some pretty red ribbon, too."

"You going to make a bow for the wreath?"

"*Nee.* But I do want to hang Christmas cards up on the walls." She smiled then, gifting him with a bit of her happiness. "*Danke*, Eric. I am looking forward to this."

"Me, too. I can hardly wait."

Chapter 13

December 13

If anyone had asked, Beverly would have denied that picking out a tree was an exciting task. To admit such a thing would be childish and vaguely embarrassing.

The miracle of Jesus' birth should've always been first and foremost in her mind. But she couldn't help considering how a lit Christmas tree, ribbons, and a wreath would make the inn look more welcoming and cozy. They would also erase any stain that remained on the inn's reputation from the robbery.

But inside, Beverly was practically jumping up and down. She was also taking in every sight and sound around them and depositing them in her memory to revisit on future days when she was sitting alone and feeling a little blue. The pine smelled fresh and reminded her of her childhood home in Ohio and the woods nearby, of growing up and seeing snow covering every surface in December.

That was when she realized Eric really had known what she needed. Sometimes a person had to take a step outside what was comfortable and allow themselves to enjoy something different.

She was glad to not be worrying about police reports and guests' needs and what to cook. She was glad to be out of the inn, and for once not remembering the damage that had been done to the cozy bed-and-breakfast that had given her so much comfort over the last few years.

As she embraced that thought, she started noticing all sorts of things: children scampering among the trees, pointing out their favorites and tugging on their parents' sleeves. Some were even playing hide-and-seek among the displays. It was a little bit naughty, but Beverly couldn't help but smile as she watched them. Their antics reminded her further of growing up and the many enjoyable hours she'd spent in the wide open fields near her family's farm.

But the sight that struck her most was of a little girl who couldn't have been more than four or five examining each tree with wide eyes. Compared to her size, the Christmas trees looked stalwart and tall. But her expression mirrored exactly how Beverly was feeling: wondrous. Knowing that she had something in common with that little girl made her heart warm.

Even the arguments taking place near the various parked vehicles made her grin. It seemed that buying the tree wasn't necessarily the hardest part. Strapping it onto the length of a car in a secure way looked like it was a job and a half.

"You okay, Bev?" Eric asked.

Beverly started, realizing that she'd been staring blankly into the distance. "Oh, I'm fine. My mind went wandering for a minute, but I'm better now."

His lips tilted up for a moment, but he was still gazing at her with a hint of worry. "Sure?"

"Very sure. This was exactly what I needed, Eric. *Danke*."

His smile grew, and she knew she'd pleased him.

"All right, let's do this."

Shaking her head at his expression, she led the way, walking up and down the lot. The trees were bunched rather close together, and before long, they were surrounded by the smell of pine. Sometimes they even had to gently raise or lower branches in order to examine each tree.

And examine them they did!

After twenty minutes passed, Eric sighed. "Bev, what was wrong with that blue spruce? I thought it looked fine."

"It didn't look very fresh."

"They aren't going to be *that* fresh. They were carted down here to Florida."

"It looked a little lopsided, too."

"None are going to be perfect."

"One will be," she said with a smile. "And don't complain. This was your idea, remember."

"I haven't forgotten," he grumbled.

But Beverly did notice that his eyes had lit up. She led the way down the rows again, stopping to feel the branches and needles, inspecting each tree from every angle.

After another thirty minutes, Eric reached for her hand.

"Beverly, I can't take it much longer. Pick a tree. Pick *any* tree. Please."

"Oh, all right." Turning around, she marched back to the front of the lot. "This one," she said at last, pointing to a slim, seven-foot-tall pine.

He tilted his head to one side. "That one? Are you sure?"

"Positive."

Later, as they stood by the cash register and Eric paid too much for a tree that they didn't actually need, Beverly said, "Eric, how are we going to get this tree home? You've got a small car just like that couple over there. And, um, I fear I'm not quite tall enough to help you tie it on the roof."

"You don't need to worry about that. We're going to get it delivered."

"They do that?"

He pointed to the sign. "Looks like it."

Somewhat embarrassed, she noticed that there was, indeed, a sign that said that delivery was available. "That is a *gut* idea."

"I thought so, too." After he paid the men and set up a time for delivery, he turned to her. "Now, it's time to go get lights and ribbon."

"I suppose it is," she said with a laugh.

He opened her car door to let her in. Then, after he got settled in the driver's side, he turned right onto the street. Minutes later, they had left the quaint buildings of Pinecraft and were in the traffic of Sarasota. She, of course, was familiar with the area though she didn't drive.

"The traffic has already started to get worse," she commented as she eyed the cars slowly easing through the intersection and the bicyclists maneuvering in and out of traffic. "By January first or second, no one will want to drive if they don't have to. The streets get so congested with automobiles and bicycling tourists, it takes twice as long to get anywhere."

"That's the consequence of living someplace so beautiful, I guess."

She nodded and leaned back in her seat, realizing as she did so that she now felt completely comfortable around Eric. She didn't worry about what to say to him, or how he might react to different situations. Actually, more than anything, she trusted him. She was so grateful to have him as her friend.

"Have I told you how glad I am that you came here?"

"You have, and I've also told you that I was happy to come."

"You took the first flight here. I don't even want to think about how much that cost."

"I don't want you to worry about that. Every penny I spent was well worth it." Lowering his voice, he said, "Beverly, don't you realize that I didn't want to be anywhere else? I hated the thought of you being in the inn alone and scared."

His words meant so much to her. Although they sometimes had their rocky moments, it was nice to know that her instincts had been right. Eric was a man she could completely depend on. Even when she was grumpy or scared or, well, being silly. No matter what she did or what her mood, he was there for her.

She sincerely hoped that he felt the same way about her.

"Do you have any family or friends back in Philadelphia who are upset that you left so abruptly?" she asked. The question was blunt—and maybe none of her business—but she was eager to move the conversation on. "Will they be disappointed that you won't be there for Christmas?" Of course, the moment she asked such things, she wished she could take them back. She sounded vaguely callous. Almost insinuating that she would be surprised if he had family and friends who cared about him. "Sorry if that came out wrong," she said quickly. "I didn't mean to sound like—"

"I know what you meant." As he stopped at a traffic light, he looked her way. "Mind if I ask why you want to know?"

She realized that she'd struck a nerve. His question had struck one, too, and it made her come to terms with her feelings for him. Eric meant more to her every day. "I guess I want to know more about you," she said hesitantly. "If that's okay."

"You can ask me anything you want," he said as the light turned green and he accelerated the car forward.

"Ah, here we go," he murmured as they came upon a big retailer that sold pretty much anything one might need. He clicked on his turning signal and moved to the right lane. "To answer your question, no, there's not really anyone in Philly who is going to be that upset that I won't be spending Christmas with them."

"What about Jack? What is he doing for Christmas?"

"I'm not sure . . ."

"Would he like to come here?" Feeling happy that she could push him a little, she said, "You should ask him, Eric. I would enjoy getting to know your brother."

He winced. "Believe it or not, I did ask him yesterday when I was at the Cozy Café." After a pause, he added, "I should have talked to you first. I'm sorry."

"No need to apologize. I'm glad you asked him." She smiled,

wanting Eric to see that she really was happy he'd reached out to his brother. "No one should be alone for Christmas."

To her surprise, Eric still looked a little hesitant. "Beverly, don't forget that Jack has some regrets about this past, too."

She swallowed, remembering. However, although she recalled every bit of Eric's past, she couldn't remember the particulars of his brother's story. "What does he regret?"

"A lot of things, but most of all, for going to prison for robbery."

"He went to prison . . . for robbery." She clenched her hands together in an attempt to maintain her composure. "I see."

"He's not dangerous or anything, Bev," Eric said quickly. "I promise, I would never put you in danger. Gosh, I wouldn't want him anywhere around you if I was worried about that. But you do need to know that, well . . . he made some mistakes and he paid the price."

She realized then that Eric was giving her a way out. Though it was clear that he wanted Jack to visit, Beverly knew if she told him that she couldn't handle having an ex-convict at the inn he would abide her wishes. However, the expression on his face told her everything she needed to know. He loved his brother and he wanted to see him.

And because of that, she needed to overcome her prejudices and welcome Jack into her home. "We all have a past, Eric," she said, realizing with some surprise that it was just as true for her. "Everything will be fine."

"You can think about it . . ."

"*Nee*, if you want him here, then I do, too."

"I just want you to be happy, Bev."

Giving into impulse, she reached out and squeezed his arm. "I will be. So, is he for sure coming? Do you know what day he's going to arrive?"

"I don't know if he's actually coming or not. He said he wanted a couple of days to think about it."

She was having a hard time reading Eric. "I'm sorry. Are you worried that he might say yes or he might say no?"

"You know what? I'm not actually sure." Lowering his voice, he said, "There's so much bad between us, you know? Whenever I see him, it seems like everything I've spent my adulthood pretending never happened comes back in a flash. I think it's that way for him, too."

"When was the last time you saw him?"

"Five years ago."

"It sounds like it's time, then. I hope he says he'll come. But if he does, he's going to have to share the attic room with ya."

He grinned. "It's going to be awkward, but he can share my Barbie Dream House with me, no problem."

"I have no idea what a Barbie Dream House is."

"I can remedy that, Bev," he said as they pulled into the supercenter's crowded parking lot. "Come on. We'll go get lights and ribbon for our beautiful tree. And while we're wandering around, I'll take you by the toy section and show you what is usually at the top of every little girl's list to Santa."

"It's that special?"

"It is when you're five or six years old. I don't know a lot, but I can promise you that."

She giggled. "Lead on, Eric."

December 14

At nine thirty the next morning, after helping Beverly serve breakfast and clear the table, Eric got yet another cup of coffee, his iPad, and phone, and walked out to the back patio, his favorite spot to relax.

Beverly popped her head out after him. "Are you going to call Jack?"

"Yep. I want to call before we get busy with the tree."

After Beverly's tree had arrived yesterday, they'd moved around furniture and placed it in the inn's left front window. Eric had been eager to string lights on it and see how it looked, but when he'd noticed how Beverly kept moving it around, fingering the boughs, and generally looking like she was coming to terms with the fact that she had a Christmas tree now sitting in her living room, he'd suggested that they wait a day before decorating it.

As he'd hoped, at the mention of the tree, her eyes lit up. "Take your time, Eric. And don't worry. Jack will say yes."

Eric didn't want to say anything to Beverly, but he was actually kind of afraid of that.

It wasn't that he didn't want to see his brother—he did—he just didn't want to revisit their past all over again. Every time they did that, Jack ended up talking about his years in prison and Eric inevitably felt guilty. Soon after, they usually started talking about their parents and how they'd lost both of them far too early. Which, of course, brought forth yet another set of studiously repressed emotions.

Staring at his cell phone, Eric wondered if it was truly possible to forge a new relationship with a long-lost brother.

There was only one way to find out.

He thumbed through his contacts and pressed Send.

Jack answered on the first ring. "You didn't waste any time, huh?"

"I guess not. Actually, I was telling Beverly yesterday that I asked you to come out here."

"What did she say?"

"I think she's even more hopeful that you'll accept my invitation than I am."

"Really?"

"Yes, really. So, have you looked at your work schedule?"

"Yeah. And I thought about it, too."

"What did you decide?"

"I want to come, Eric. If you're sure you want to be together again."

"I'm sure."

"Well, in that case, Florida sounds great."

"It *is* great. What date do you want to arrive? Any day or time works for me."

"Let's make it from the twenty-fourth to the twenty-sixth, just like we talked about."

"You can stay longer if you want," Eric offered. He was pretty sure Jack would have to make at least one connection in order to get to Sarasota. That meant he'd be spending a good amount of time flying on both Christmas Eve and the twenty sixth.

"No, I think this will be good." His voice turned hesitant. "E, are you sure you don't mind paying for the ticket?"

"I'm positive. I want to pay for it." Eric opened his iPad, ready to start looking up flights, when Jack spoke again.

"Hey, Eric? One more thing."

"Yeah?"

"Does, ah, your Beverly know I'm not like you?"

Even though their lives had veered in different directions, Eric knew they were essentially the same as they ever were. "What are you talking about? We might have different types of jobs but we're still a lot alike where it counts."

"Don't play stupid. You know what I'm talking about. I mean, does Beverly know about my past?"

Eric wasn't going to let Jack take that burden solely on his shoulders anymore. "You mean *our* pasts? Yes, she knows."

"You can pretend we're the same, but we're not. You went to college, Eric. I went to prison. That's kind of a big difference."

"You kept me from going down that path."

"You made choices, too, Eric." Before Eric could argue, Jack blurted, "Are you sure she's okay with having an ex-con in her home?"

"She's more than okay with it." That lump that he'd been pretending hadn't been about to choke him was threatening to block his whole throat. "Okay, before we get all sappy, give me your email address. Do you have one?"

"Of course I have one."

After writing it down, Eric smiled. "Great. I'll make a reservation right now and then email it to you. I'm really glad you're coming here, Jack. It's going to be a great Christmas."

When Eric finally disconnected, he breathed in deeply and exhaled. He felt like he was finally moving forward. At long last.

After he made the flight reservation and sent the confirmation to Jack, he looked for Beverly and found her sitting on the front stoop, sipping coffee and watching a trio of hummingbirds flit around a feeder.

He sat down next to her with a sigh.

"How did it go?" she asked.

Glad that his earlier misgivings had disappeared, he grinned. "He's coming. I booked his flights after we talked."

"I'm so glad." She smiled. "I hope you two have a nice visit together."

"Me, too." After debating whether or not to bring it up, he ventured, "I've kind of noticed that you don't seem so bothered by my past anymore. Is that the case?"

"I suppose." She kicked her feet out straight in front of her. Today she was wearing a red dress. It had short sleeves and shiny black buttons running down the length of it. Matching red flip-flops were on her feet. After setting her coffee cup down, she rested her hands behind her. "Eric, I finally realized that I couldn't fault you or Jack for your pasts. Not when I've had something in my own past to overcome."

"Our pasts are a little different, Beverly. Jack and I broke the law. You suffered a broken engagement."

"That is true, but I let one very bad experience become the focal point of my life. The first couple of years here, I kept being jilted a secret. But then, when I finally started talking about it, I realized that I've been giving it too much power over my life. Yes, it was painful, but it doesn't define me. And it was wrong of me to let some poor decisions you made as a teen define you for me."

He was speechless. He'd never expected her to accept his past so easily.

"Sorry. I guess I sound a little preachy."

"No, you don't."

Looking back his way, she reached out and touched his sleeve. "Please know I'm not suggesting that what happened to me can compare to what you went through."

"Yeah, you haven't gotten arrested." Even though he tried to make light of it, he knew his voice was bitter.

She shook her head. "Eric, I've always had people in my life looking out for me. That's what I meant. I wish you and Jack had had the same thing."

"I did have that. Jack looked out for me. He made sacrifices for me. The older I get, the more I realize that, too."

"Then it's good you called him. Ain't so?"

Hope and relief and well, *love*, flowed through him as he stared at her. "You really mean that, don't you?"

"*Jah*, Eric. I really mean it." Then, as if she couldn't resist teasing him a bit, she added, "Besides, it's your inn, you know."

Though he was tempted to take the bait and roll his eyes, he resisted. What they were talking about was too important to him. And maybe to her, too. "Bev, what if it wasn't? What if it was still your inn and we were just friends? Would you want Jack to stay here then?"

"*Jah*. Because he is *your brother*, Eric. I would want him here because *he matters to you*. And, well, because everyone needs a chance to begin again." With a sigh, she leaned against him, so her shoulder was resting against his arm. "I'm happy Jack is going to join us for Christmas, Eric. Mighty happy."

He curved an arm around her shoulders and held her close.

Right there, out in the open. Smack in the middle of the front porch of the inn.

For a split second, there was so much pain and hope in his heart he felt like it was on the verge of bursting.

Or maybe he would simply break down and cry.

After a few minutes, Beverly rested her head against his chest. He thought about how right she felt. How right they felt together.

How much it was going to hurt when she realized that she could do much better than him.

Chapter 14

December 18

When Mark walked into the Quick Stop at ten minutes to five, he expected to see Laura looking as eager to see him as he was to see her. After all, they had something pretty big planned for later: Her mother was allowing Laura to spend the evening with him.

First he was going to take her home to the farm to have supper with the family, then the two of them were going to go hang out at Pinecraft Park. More and more Amish had arrived from up north and Mark was pretty sure two of his buddies from Charm had arrived earlier in the day. He was as anxious to see them as he was to spend time with Laura.

But before they did any of that, he needed to figure out what was wrong. Instead of greeting him with a smile, she looked as if she was on the verge of tears.

"Mark, I'm so glad you're here!" she called as she walked out from behind the counter. After giving a small wave in her manager's direction, he put an arm around Laura's shoulders.

"What's wrong?" he asked. His imagination started going crazy, and every bit of it settled on something bad. "Laura, are ya hurt?" He scanned her face, her simple white blouse and jean skirt, looking for any sign that could give him a hint of what had made her so upset. "Did someone bad come in here and scare you?" He always worried about her safety, working in a convenience store like she did.

"*Nee*, it's nothing like that. I'll tell you when we leave." Looking over her shoulder, she said, "Scott, its five to five. Can I go ahead and punch out?"

Her boss walked over to a machine on the back wall. "That's fine, Laura. You go ahead and punch out."

"Thanks."

"Sure. But don't forget what we talked about."

"I won't forget. Thanks." After grabbing her backpack from a closet near the back, she followed Mark outside.

Though Laura no longer looked as shaken up as she had when he'd entered the store, Mark was still concerned about her. "Where do you want to go?" he asked easily, just as if he were still thinking about nothing but taking her out on a date. "We'd talked about me taking you to our farm. Do you still want to do that?"

"I'd love to do that. But I . . . I think I need to go to the police station first. Will . . . will you go with me?"

The police station? "Of course I will," Mark replied as they walked out of the parking lot and onto the sidewalk. "But how about you tell me what's going on first? You've got me pretty worried, Laura."

"I know. I'm worried, too." She tucked her chin to her chest and sighed, the movement causing a piece of her long, honey-golden hair to cover her cheek.

Mark thought she was so pretty. Before he thought about how she might react, he slipped his hand around hers. When she lifted her chin and met his gaze with a grateful smile, he knew he'd done the right thing.

"Can we go sit over there first?" she asked, pointing to a bench in front of a casual seafood restaurant.

Keeping her hand in his, he led the way.

The moment they were sitting down, she continued. "Mark, Peter Yoder came back today."

Mark was really surprised that Peter was the source of her anxiety. "What's wrong about that?"

"He bought a bunch more stuff."

"Isn't that why people come in?"

"Yeah, but like I've told you before, no one buys that much. It's usually just a couple of things. Items people don't want to go to the big markets for. Anyway, Mark bought a bunch of groceries again and then he paid for it all with a fifty-dollar bill. And he looked real nervous the whole time."

"What did you do?" he finally asked.

Laura grimaced. "Honestly, I shouldn't have said anything. But, well, I teased him about buying so many groceries here again. And then I said something like, it must be nice to have so much cash. And that I'd have to tell my girlfriends that he's the boy to like because he could take them out for pizza."

Mark moaned. "Laura."

"It was stupid, I know. But I was just teasing."

"What happened next?"

"He got all nervous and scared. And then he told me that I had better not tell anyone that he'd been spending so much money. He pretty much acted like he'd been shopping at the Quick Stop when I was working because he knew I wouldn't question him." She frowned. "I couldn't believe it. I mean, I know I'm only sixteen, but I'm not stupid."

Though nothing was funny about their conversation, Mark struggled to keep from smiling. He really liked her spirit, even admired it. Even though she was sweet, she wasn't afraid to speak her mind. "You're right, you're not stupid, Laura. Peter, uh, sounds like he was really worried about something."

She nodded. "After he said all that, I just rang up his things and handed him the bags. He took them and left."

"Did he say anything else?"

"No. He just looked sad." She took a breath. "About an hour after Peter left, Scott came in. Even though Peter probably wouldn't have wanted me to, I told him about Peter's visits."

"I'm glad you did."

"Me, too. Well, I kind of am."

"Because?"

"Because Scott listened. At first he looked kind of shocked. But then he asked if Peter might be the type of boy who would commit a crime for money."

"What did you say?" he asked slowly.

"I said maybe." Her brown eyes searched his face, obviously looking for reassurance that she'd done the right thing. "I mean, think about what happened at the Orange Blossom Inn. Everyone says that whoever broke in really only wanted the lockbox. I'm not saying that Peter did it. But couldn't you see that he might have?"

Mark wasn't sure. Yeah, everyone knew about the robbery, and because his father was friends with Officer Roberts, Mark even knew that the police suspected the robbers were teens. But that said, Mark felt it was kind of mean for Laura to assume so much about Peter. "I'm surprised you told Scott that. I thought you liked Peter."

"I do. But he doesn't have much money, Mark. I'd heard his father doesn't work, and even takes off for weeks at a time. Like, he leaves him and his brother alone. Plus, you know how his clothes never look like they fit right."

Even though he'd thought the same thing, he didn't know if it was right to jump to conclusions like that. "I didn't know all that," he said.

"I'm really afraid he stole that money from the inn and is spending a lot of it at my store. It kind of makes sense."

Though it was painful to admit, Mark had to agree with her. "Does Scott really think you have to talk to the police? I mean, it's not any of your business." Of course, the minute he said that, he knew he was wrong. He knew Beverly pretty well. She'd been really nice to him and his brothers when they'd stayed at the inn. She'd even let William help her garden one afternoon. He couldn't simply pretend that her robbery wasn't his problem.

"Scott said he could call Officer Roberts and ask him to come to the store but that it might be better if I stopped by on my own. That way I would have more privacy."

"I'm surprised he doesn't think it would be scary for you to go to the police station by yourself."

"He knew I wouldn't be alone," she said quickly. "I mean, he knew I'd be with you." She stared at him with so much trust in her eyes, Mark felt she believed he could do anything. "Please don't be upset with me. I didn't know what to do."

He reached for her hand again. "I'm not upset."

"I don't want to accuse Peter of something bad, but I also don't want my boss to think that I know something but kept it to myself."

She was still staring at him, still expecting him to reassure her and make everything all right—or at least give her the support she needed.

With some surprise, Mark realized that he was perfectly happy to do that, too. Funny, a part of him had never understood how his brother Ben had fallen in love with Tricia so fast, but now he was starting to realize that things could definitely happen out of a person's control.

"I think you did the right thing, Laura."

"Are you sure?"

He nodded. "Positive. A hundred percent positive."

"So, you think I should walk over to the police station?"

He looked in the direction of the station. It was only a couple of blocks away, an easy walk. His first impulse was to take her home and ask his *daed* and older brother for advice. But if they did that, it would be too late to go to the police station, and

Laura would worry about it all night. Plus, he was old enough to help Laura himself.

And that was what she was asking for, wasn't it? For him to help her take care of it. She wasn't running home to her parents; she had run to him.

"*Jah*," he said at last. "I think we need to go talk to Officer Roberts. He's a nice man and friends with my *daed*. I, well, *my family* knows Miss Beverly pretty well, too. My brothers and Daed and I stayed at her inn for almost two weeks. If we even *think* we know who robbed her, I could never keep that a secret."

Laura exhaled. "That's what I think, too. But I hope it's not a terrible thing to do."

"Officer Roberts seems like the kind of man who will listen to you, Laura." He shrugged. "And who knows? He might say that we're wrong and that they've already arrested somebody else."

"I hope so. For the first time in my life, I really hope someone tells me that I'm completely wrong."

Standing, he tried to give her an encouraging smile. "No offense, but I hope that happens, too. Let's go get this over with."

"And then, if it's not too late, can we still go by your farm?"

"We can do whatever you want," he said with a smile. As they walked toward the police station, he realized that was the complete truth.

Chapter 15

December 19

"I'm not going to open a single book next week," Christy Emerson said to Effie as they and the rest of their American History class waited for the bell to ring.

"Me, neither," Effie replied. "Well, at least not any history books."

Christy grinned. "Or math." Looking around at the rest of the kids who were watching the clock, she said, "I'm going to Tampa for Christmas. What's everyone else doing?"

As Justin, the freckle-faced boy two seats behind them answered, Effie started gathering her books together. She wasn't missing anything important—for the last couple of days, all anyone talked about was their upcoming Christmas break. During lunch, in between classes, and on the way to the buses after school, Effie's girlfriends chatted about vacation plans, gifts they hoped to receive, the annual Pinecraft Christmas parade, and how excited they were for Christmas dinner. Some of the Amish girls complained about all the stuff they were going to have to do once break started: cooking and baking, extra cleaning and sorting, all in preparation for visiting guests, huge holiday meals, parties, and gift exchanges.

Though Effie never said anything to the contrary when her friends started complaining, she didn't dread having to do those chores at all. The truth was that she was grateful to have the chance to get to do normal things. Finally. For far too long, she'd been either in a wheelchair or on crutches. Though she hadn't exactly been helpless, she'd felt a bit like a burden to her parents and siblings and she'd hated that.

Because of the nature of Perthes disease, just when she'd gotten to the age where she could be of use to her *mamm*, Effie's legs and hips had started paining her too much to do anything. Violet, Karl, and Zack had never complained when they'd had to pick up the slack, though. And her mother had told her over and over that she shouldn't worry about how much she was contributing to the family. She'd assured Effie that her day would come.

Still, Effie had felt the bitter sting of being different from most everyone she knew.

But now, after the surgeries on her hips, months spent in a wheelchair, and continuing physical therapy sessions, Effie was finally getting around well. Every month the pain lessened and her ability to do just a little more increased. Because of that, she was glad she was going to be helping her mother bake and make fleece blankets for the needy. She was also secretly hoping that this Christmas she'd get to be the one who delivered them, just like her sister, Violet, had at her age.

In any case, everyone was counting the days until they were out of school for two full weeks . . . except for Josiah.

Effie knew him well enough now to see through his quiet manner when everyone sitting around him started talking about their holiday plans. Most everyone thought he remained quiet because of his cool nature, but his lack of sharing wasn't because he thought the conversations were childish or beneath him.

It was because, Effie knew, he was dreading two weeks at home. What, exactly, he was dreading, she didn't know for sure. She wished he trusted her enough to share more about his home life, but it seemed like that kind of trust—like most everything else—took time.

Because of that, they still had a complicated school relationship. He was Amish and so was she, so it wasn't uncommon for them to talk. Most kids knew, too, that he had started to walk her out to the bus and was even coming over to her house once or twice a week.

But Effie's girlfriends had confided that most everybody was sure that the only reason Josiah was going over to Effie's after school a couple of days a week was because he felt sorry for her. Pitied her. Like she was a sort of charitable project. Josiah himself had never said such a thing. He even told people that they were friends. However, nobody really believed him. The most popular boy in school did not choose to hang out with the awkward, shy girl with braces on her legs.

Effie didn't refute everyone's assumptions, though secretly she wanted to. But she didn't want to mistakenly misrepresent their relationship and somehow end up embarrassing him. The truth was that she did feel especially close to Josiah and she was pretty sure he felt the same way. They were friends. They'd become good friends.

All of this was going through her mind as she walked out of her American history class by Josiah's side. Not only did he seem a little quieter than usual, he also had a note from the office in his hand. Josiah held that pink slip of paper in a death grip, looking like he would give just about anything to simply throw it on the ground and keep walking.

"Did you get some bad news or something?" she asked as they stopped at his locker. He was a good student and well liked by all the teachers and staff. She couldn't imagine what the note was all about.

He glanced at her in surprise, almost as if he'd forgotten she'd been standing there. "Hey, Ef, I'm sorry, but I canna walk you home today."

"That's all right." She was disappointed that she wouldn't get to spend the afternoon with him but she understood. Trying again to bring him out of his daze, she said, "Are you all right?"

Again he sidestepped her question. "Since I can't help you get home, who would you like me to ask to give you a hand?"

That was Josiah. All she had to do was give him a name and he would pressure anyone in the school to take care of her without a second thought. It made her feel both really special and kind of embarrassed. No matter what he might think, she was definitely not his responsibility. "I can get home on my own just fine." Giving him an out, she turned to walk to her locker.

But instead of looking relieved that he was off the hook, her statement only made him more stressed. "Come on, Effie. You know I'm not going to let you do that."

"I'm not injured or helpless, Josiah," she said as she put her history book inside her locker and placed her math textbook and some spiral notebooks in her backpack. "And even if you haven't noticed, I've been able to get off the bus and walk home pretty well. I may walk a little slower than you but I can do it."

He shook his head as she slammed her locker shut. "I have noticed that you're walking better, but you still can't go by yourself."

After slipping her backpack on, she sighed. "Why not?"

"Because I promised myself that I'd help you."

She loved that. She loved that he didn't say that he'd promised her mother or make up any other excuses about why he was helping her so much. But she couldn't let him start asking kids to walk her around as a favor to him. She couldn't think of anything more embarrassing. "Josiah, what do you have to do? Do you have to go right home?"

"Jah."

"Did something happen? Can I help you for a change?"

He didn't meet her eyes. "Effie, it's getting late. We've got to get you on that bus." His eyes scanned the rapidly thinning crowd in the halls. "Who do you want me to ask?" He was impatient now and looking increasingly tense and worried.

So much so, that Effie decided to take matters into her own hands. "How about I go home with you today?"

Every muscle in his body froze. *"Nee."*

She started to reach for his hand but remembered they were in the hallway at school and dropped it. "Josiah, please, let me go with you. After you take care of things, you can walk me home and have supper with me," she added quickly.

He shook his head. "I don't want you to have to do all that."

"Why not? It's no trouble."

"Never mind why," he said impatiently. "Listen, just tell me who to talk to. But be fast, 'cause you're about to miss the bus." He looked around. It was obvious that he intended to snag someone, *anyone*, to take care of her.

There was no way that was going to happen. It was time to push a little bit. "Josiah, please let me go with you. I promise, just because I don't walk real well doesn't mean I'm helpless."

He still wasn't looking at her. Instead, he was scanning the halls. "How about Samuel?" he asked. "You seem to get along with him fine. He rides your bus, too."

"I don't want to walk with Samuel."

He sighed. "Samuel won't tease you. I'll make sure of it. It'll be fine."

"I'm not thinking about myself. I'm thinking about you." She leaned close enough to whisper in his ear. It was close enough to be a bit too forward, close enough to cause anyone who saw her to gossip. "Josiah, I know you don't want me to see your house, but I want to go with you. Friends help friends."

"You're gonna regret that. My *haus*, it ain't like yours."

Thanks to her mother's hints, she knew that. She also didn't care. "That's okay."

He started to look a little panicked. "It's gonna be dirty. My *bruder* and I haven't had time to clean up much . . ."

"That's okay," she repeated. "I'm real *gut* at cleaning." Okay, that might have been an exaggeration, but she had to do something.

"But—" He looked like a caged animal. Lowering his voice, it turned plaintive. "I don't want you to see how things are."

The voice on the intercom suddenly blared. "Two minutes until buses depart."

"Effie, you've gotta go. If I don't get you on a bus, your *mamm* is gonna worry."

She knew he was right, but she also was pretty sure her *mamm* would realize that Effie was with Josiah.

Besides, suddenly she knew there was no way she was going to let him face whatever he had to face at home all alone.

With a shrug, she said, "I'm real sorry, but there's no way I could make it to the buses in two minutes. I can walk better but not that good. Looks like you're stuck with me now." She smiled at him, pleased that she'd gotten her way.

"Yeah." He didn't smile back. "I guess you're coming home with me."

She felt bad for manipulating him, but not bad enough to actually regret what she'd done. For weeks now he'd been a great friend to her. More than anything she wanted the opportunity to return the favor. "I'm glad about that," she said quietly.

With a sigh, Josiah slid her backpack from her shoulders. "Come on, then. But don't say I didn't warn you."

Then, just like that, he turned and started walking. For the first time, he didn't even look back to make sure he wasn't going too fast. As she trailed behind him, Effie gave praise that she'd become so much stronger. It looked as if she was going to need two strong legs and a great resolve to get through the next few hours.

Twenty minutes later, as they approached his house, Effie was starting to wonder if she'd been just a bit too full of herself. Josiah lived in an area she hadn't been aware existed.

Though it was only a little to the south of Pinecraft Park, it felt miles away from her neat and tidy street. Most houses looked to belong to Englishers, based on the number of cars and other vehicles resting in driveways. Josiah's home was at the end of a narrow cul-de-sac, about a block away from some small hotels, a convenience store, and a rather dilapidated apartment building.

He led the way to a tiny run-down one-story home. It looked kind of sad and neglected: Weeds littered the front yard, the paint on the white siding was peeling, and old cardboard boxes rested on the slanting front porch.

Josiah wore a resigned look as he climbed the front steps. Effie wondered if he was preparing to introduce her to his family or merely bracing himself for whatever had called him home in the first place. She made sure to keep her expression blank and calm. As if she walked into homes like this all the time.

Just before he opened the door, he turned to her, his lips set in a grim line. "Things will go better if you don't say much, okay?"

She nodded. Right now she felt like she couldn't say a word if her life depended on it, so he needn't have worried.

"All right. Let's get this over with then so I can take you home."

As Effie followed him inside, she couldn't help but shiver. His words sounded like a warning.

Chapter 16

"Where have you been?" a voice barked from a chair in the living room.

Effie felt Josiah's body tense next to hers. "School, Daed," he said.

"Your *bruder* was supposed to make sure the school got my note."

"I did get it. I got here as soon as I could." After motioning for her to stay put by the door, Josiah stood in front of her. "When did you get back?"

"Couple of hours ago."

As she watched Josiah become even more agitated, Effie stepped backward up against the wall. Inside the house, the air was warm and thick and smelled stagnant. Two empty bottles rested on a table nearby. Papers and dirty clothes were piled up against one of the doors in the hallway to her right. Effie was torn between wishing she could grab Josiah's hand and pull him out of this place and hanging her head in shame. It seemed she had taken much in her life for granted.

"Are you staying for a while?" Josiah asked, continuing the stilted, painful conversation.

Instead of answering Josiah, his father barked a request. "Someone from that school of yours called. Again. A social worker is coming by. You need to clean this place up."

Glad that Josiah couldn't see her, Effie inhaled sharply. His father sounded so gruff and angry. Effie could feel the tension between them. And his words were confusing, too. Had he really been gone? Had Josiah been living here with just his brother?

"I'll start with the kitchen," Josiah said at last.

"Gut." After what sounded like a yawn, his father added, "Get busy, boy."

When Josiah immediately turned toward the kitchen, Effie followed on his heels. Inside, the mess was about what she had expected: Dishes were stacked on counters and piled high in the sink. Everything looked neglected and dirty. Not dirty like someone had forgotten to clean up the evening's dishes; dirty like no one had cleaned anything in weeks.

At the sink, she located a bottle of dish soap, turned on the faucet, and began hunting for a cloth or sponge of some kind with which to scrub.

"You canna do this, Ef," Josiah said with a pained look.

"Sure I can." Pleased to have found a reasonably clean-looking dishcloth, she wet the corner of it and set to work on a plate.

Looking even more upset, he added, "What I mean is that I don't want you to do our dishes. I don't even want you here." Pulling the cloth from her hands, he stared at it like he wanted to rip it into pieces. "I never wanted you to—"

"Josiah, stop," she blurted. Pulling the dishcloth from his hands, she added gently, "Believe it or not, I've washed my share of dishes. I'm from a big family and my mother entertains a lot. This is nothing. Please, let me do this."

His lips pursed together. *"Nee."*

"You need my help and I want to help you."

His expression turned hard. "I never wanted you to see where I live, Effie."

"I don't care where you live." She turned to face him. "Don't you understand, Josiah? For months now, you've been walking me to class and helping me with my books and my locker. Now you're even coming home with me so I can ride the bus. I want to do something for you."

She didn't dare mention how his presence in her life had made everyone see her in a new light as well. Now she wasn't just the girl with the braces—she was Effie, Josiah's friend.

Her climb in social status had been enormous. And though her mother would claim that such things didn't matter, her mother had also not been in seventh grade in a very long time. Until a person had been stared at or ignored or teased for days at a time they had no idea what it was like for Effie to be able to walk down the hall and have people say hi to her.

"None of that matters."

"It does to me. It's meant a lot to me. Please let me help you. I'm glad that I can do something for you at last. It makes me feel like I'm not such a burden."

"You're not a burden."

"Josiah, what are you doing?" his father called out.

"Nothing, Daed."

"You're lying. I hear it in your voice. Who's here?"

"Just a friend."

"You need to clean, boy."

When Josiah tensed, looking like he was either about to yell or cry, Effie made a shooing motion. "Go work on something else," she mouthed. "I promise, I can wash dishes just fine."

She kept her smile firmly in place until he was out of sight. Then and only then did she dare let her true emotions show on her face.

Josiah lived in a terrible situation.

And something was very wrong with his father.

An hour later, when she left his house, Effie knew she had to do something to help him. She'd stayed long enough to hear Josiah's dad yell at him about almost everything under the sun and long enough to meet Peter, Josiah's brother, who'd looked surprised to see that Josiah had brought a friend home.

She'd stayed just until a car pulled up in front of the house. That's when Josiah had practically pushed her out the back door. "Go on home. Sorry about . . . about everything."

"Don't apologize. I'm glad I stayed." She'd tucked her head then and started home. It was a longer walk than she was used to, easily six or seven blocks. But she'd be able to do it. Actually, she'd never been so glad that her brother Zack had encouraged her to do her leg exercises as she was at that moment.

When she walked up her driveway, her mother ran out. "Effie, where in the world have you been?"

Effie's spirits sank. She'd been so wrapped up in Josiah and his kitchen and everything else that she'd completely forgotten that her mother was going to be wondering what had happened to her. "I went over to Josiah's *haus*."

"You did?" Her voice hardened. "Well, you should have told me that you were planning to do that."

"There wasn't time. It was only decided after school."

"Effie, I was worried," she said as she ushered Effie inside. "I had no idea what had happened to you."

She saw the look of concern on her mother's face, heard the love and worry in her voice, smelled the scents of supper and furniture polish and her mother's favorite lemon candles, and burst into tears. Her life was so different from Josiah's! It was so different that it hurt her heart. She felt so bad for him.

"Oh, Mamm," she said through a wash of tears. "I'm so blessed."

Immediately, her mother's fierce expression faded into one of sheer concern. "What's brought this on? What is wrong?"

But Effie simply cried harder.

Mamm wrapped an arm around her shoulders. "You aren't crying about me being mad, are you?"

Effie shook her head as she hiccupped. She tried to settle herself, finding comfort in her mother's gentle demeanor.

"What happened?"

She debated only a few seconds before making the decision to share. "Oh, Mamm, it was terrible. Josiah got a note at school that said he had to come right home. And he looked so agitated that I went with him because I didn't want him to face whatever was wrong alone. And then . . . and then when we got there . . ." How could she put into words just how his house had looked? How mean his *daed* had sounded?

"What happened?"

"His father said Josiah had to clean up because a social worker was coming over."

Her mother's eyes widened. "A social worker?"

"*Jah*. I'm not even sure why. All I know was that nothing had been cared for and it was obvious that his father hadn't even been living there. Mamm, Josiah was surprised to see him."

"Oh, dear."

"And when his *bruder* Peter showed up, Josiah looked scared to death. Peter glared at me and whispered to Josiah that I should never have been there in the first place. And I felt so guilty because Josiah had kept telling me that he didn't want me to go home with him but I wouldn't listen. So I only made things worse."

"Maybe not."

"I'm fairly sure I did. It was bad. Really, really bad."

Her mother sat down on their large, comfortable couch. "Oh, my."

"Josiah looked so alone, so, well, sad, I couldn't just leave him, Mamm," she added, taking a seat next to her. "Not after everything he's done for me at school."

Her mother brushed a stray tendril of hair away from her face. "Of course not."

Around another hiccup of tears, Effie added, "I went right to the kitchen and started doing dishes. There were dishes every where. And Mamm, they hardly have any food. When I put a bottle of juice in the refrigerator, I saw what was inside."

"What did you see, dear?"

"*Niks!* Practically nothing. There wasn't anything other than a couple of condiments. And all I found in one of the kitchen cabinets were a couple cans of soup."

"That poor boy." She swallowed. "Those poor boys."

"After I cleaned up the kitchen as best I could, I tried to offer to clean the bathroom but Josiah wouldn't let me. Then, when a car pulled up, Josiah made me leave. I'm so worried about him."

"I know you are. I'm worried, too."

"And I feel awful, Mamm. He must have felt so obligated to help me. And here he has so much else to worry about."

"I know, but perhaps he needed to concentrate on your problems. Sometimes it's so much easier to concentrate on other people instead of one's self."

Effie blinked, thinking that her mother was probably right. The whole time she'd been at Josiah's house, she hadn't been thinking about anything beyond washing all those dishes.

"Effie, you were a good friend to him today."

"Was I? I hardly did anything."

Her mother looked at her directly, then spoke. "I debated about whether to tell you anything, but I guess you deserve to know the truth. Josiah is having quite a tough time at home.

Not only has he been going hungry, I've heard stories that his father is in a . . . well, in a bad way."

Effie felt her lip tremble. "He is."

"I wanted him to have some decent food, but also to be around our house, too. I wanted him to feel comfortable here."

"I think he has been." And she was glad for that, but now that she'd seen what his home was like, she wondered if she'd completely misread his reasons for coming over. Maybe he hadn't been trying to be her friend. Maybe he'd really just been hungry.

Mamm clicked her tongue, as if reading her mind. "Now don't look at me that way, Effie. And you mustn't convince yourself that he only came over here for something to eat. He has become your friend. And a good one, at that."

"You think so?" She hated that she was even thinking about herself at a time like this.

"I know so. I've seen the way he looks at you. He genuinely likes being with you, Effie. I'm sure of it."

"What can I do to help him?"

"Just what you're doing now. I talked to Emma Hilty and she and Jay are going to deliver several baskets to some needy families in the area. One of them is going to be Josiah's house."

"*Nee*, Mamm. That ain't enough. We need to help him now."

Her mother studied her, seemed to come to a decision, then walked to the door. "Let's go, then."

Effie rushed to her side. "Where are we going?"

"I think it's time we paid a visit to some people who know a whole lot more about helping those in need than we do."

"Who is that?"

"We're going to go visit with Bishop Metz. Then I think we're going to talk to Beverly and Eric over at the Orange Blossom Inn, too."

"Why Beverly and Eric?"

"Beverly knows a lot of people in the community and I do believe that Eric has some experience being in a similar situation to Josiah and Peter. It's time that all of us worked together to make a difference for those boys. Now."

Effie liked that. She liked the idea of actually doing something. Of making a plan. But most of all, she wanted to be Josiah's friend. And that meant doing everything she could to make sure he was going to be okay.

Chapter 17

December 19

When the doorbell rang at seven o'clock at night, the last people Beverly expected to see was Ginny Kaufmann and her daughter standing on her front stoop. "Hello," she said with a tentative smile. "This is a nice surprise."

"Hi, Beverly. I hope this isn't a bad time?"

Though Beverly was friends with the whole Kaufmann family, they didn't usually call on each other out of the blue. But since they had so graciously let her sleep at their house the evening of the robbery, maybe things had changed? "Did you two come over for tea?" she asked hesitantly.

"*Nee*. We actually came over to seek advice from Eric." Looking rather agitated, Ginny craned her neck. "Is he around, by any chance?"

Beverly was now really surprised. She couldn't imagine what Ginny and Effie could need from Eric. "He is. He's sitting out on the back patio." After ushering them inside, she gestured toward the back door. "Let me take you back."

With a sigh, Effie nodded. Ginny slipped an arm around her, then turned to Beverly. "Would you be able to join us, too? I, um, think maybe you both could give us a lot of *gut* advice."

More curious than ever, Beverly nodded. "I'd be happy to join you. May I get you girls something to drink first?"

"I'm fine. Effie?" Ginny asked.

Effie shook her head. *"Nee. Danke."*

Beverly was fairly curious by the time she'd led the women outside and they'd all said hello to Eric. After they were all sitting down, she said, "So, um, how may Eric and I help you?"

"It's not about me—it's about my friend Josiah," Effie said.

Looking a little embarrassed, Ginny stared at Beverly and Eric. "Beverly, I know I promised that I wouldn't say anything, but I've been thinking a lot about what you said about Eric's past."

Though she felt like the bottom of her world had just fallen out, Beverly simply stared.

Eric's eyes narrowed. "Pardon me?"

"Eric, I hope you don't mind, but the other day Beverly shared with me that you once had some trouble at home." Ginny looked even more pained. "I'm really sorry, Beverly. I know you are probably mighty upset with me."

"Upset" was putting it mildly. She was equally embarrassed and horrified. But she had no one to blame but herself.

She should have known better than to share her worries with anyone. As the silence between them all stretched taut, Beverly could practically feel Eric's heated glare.

"I'm the one who should be apologizing, Eric," she said around a swallow. "The morning after you told me about your past, I was so confused and upset that I went for a walk. When I ran into Ginny, I shared some of what you told me."

Eric braced his hands on his knees. "I never told you to keep my past a secret, Bev. You don't need to apologize."

But of course, everything in his posture told a different story. He looked pensive. Almost like he was afraid Ginny was going to ask him twenty questions about his past. Beverly felt terrible.

"Are you worried about me or something?" Eric asked.

After glancing at her daughter, Ginny cleared her throat. "Of course not. We came here for advice. I thought it was the right thing to do."

"What do you want to know?" Eric asked slowly.

Ginny took a breath. "This afternoon, Effie shared with me that her friend Josiah and his brother have been very likely living on their own."

"Josiah's *daed* was there today, but I don't think he's around much," Effie blurted. "He also doesn't sound very nice. At all." After a pause, she mumbled, "I saw a bruise on Josiah last week, too."

Eric glanced over at Beverly, confusion in his eyes. Beverly shrugged. She was just as at sea as he was.

"Effie also overheard enough to be afraid that Josiah's *bruder* Peter has gotten into some trouble of some sort." Ginny continued in a rush. "Josiah said he feared he might have even broken the law."

"Josiah was really worried about a social worker coming to their home."

Eric's expression hardened. "I'm sorry about your friend, Effie. If a social worker was called, that means his living situation is pretty bad." After taking a moment, he added, "I imagine you are right. His brother might be in a heap of trouble, too."

"And they didn't have any food."

Eric winced. "Again, I'm real sorry. But I don't know how any of what's happening in that house pertains to me."

"What happened to Eric was a long time ago," Beverly interjected, feeling protective of him. "Almost twenty years. I don't think he could offer any advice to Peter or his brother."

Ginny didn't seem to be cowed by Eric's cool tone. "I was hoping you might have suggestions about how we could help those boys without interfering too much."

Beside her, Eric looked equally confused. "Just because I had some problems a long time ago doesn't mean I'm an expert on helping kids who are making bad decisions."

"Of course not," she said quickly, folding her hands tightly in her lap. "Eric, I didn't mean any disrespect. I was only hoping that you might be able to be those boys' friend or something."

Eric blinked. "You came over to see if I could be their friend?"

"*Jah.* Someone needs to check up on them."

"You could do that."

"Yes, of course. But see, Josiah has finally started to trust Effie. I'm afraid if Frank and I get involved, he's going to think Effie told on him."

"Which she did," Eric said. Looking at Effie, he added, "I don't want to hurt your feelings, but he's going to find out that you told your mother about his living situation sooner or later. When he finds out, he's going to be upset. You might as well get it over with."

"These boys need some adults who care about them." Ginny sighed. "I'm afraid if my husband and I simply offered them some food it wouldn't be accepted."

"I doubt me showing up out of the blue is going to be any different."

"Of course not." Ginny hung her head and took a deep breath, then raised her chin and looked Eric in the eye again. "Obviously, I care about Josiah and Peter enough to risk upsetting you and overstepping myself and even betraying a private conversation that Beverly and I shared."

After a moment, Eric nodded. "Effie, if things are as bad at Josiah's home as you think, you need to tell someone who can make a difference. If that social worker doesn't move those boys to a better living situation, you need to go to the police."

Her eyes turned to saucers. "But Josiah would be so mad at me."

"If things are that bad, it doesn't matter." Glancing Beverly's way, a new resolve entered his eyes. "Listen, sometimes a person has to be a good enough friend to risk having someone they care about be upset with them. If Josiah is being neglected or is in danger, then you have to tell the authorities."

"You could even tell one of your teachers," Beverly ventured. "Maybe that is the best way to help your friend and his brother."

Effie bit her lip. "Mamm, I shouldn't have said anything."

"*Nee.* I shouldn't have come over here and bothered Mr. Eric and Miss Beverly," she said softly. "I am sorry. We were simply hoping to do something to help them, you see. Especially since it's almost Christmas and all."

"Don't apologize," Beverly said. "I know your intentions were good. There's simply nothing Eric or I can do."

"Maybe there is," Eric blurted suddenly.

"Eric?" As she watched, Beverly saw pain enter his eyes, but also something real and true. It was so honest, so completely without artifice, it took her breath away.

"Let me do some thinking about our different options," he said at last. "I'll stop by tomorrow and let you know what I think we should do."

"We?" Effie asked.

"Yep, we." Taking a breath, he continued. "Effie, your concern for Josiah makes me realize that I can do something, too. I want to help those boys. It's, ah, *important* that I help them."

Eric's words made Beverly realize that she, too, had changed. She needed to reach out to Effie and her friend and his brother in the same way that so many people had come to her aid after the robbery.

After exchanging a glance with Ginny, she looked Effie in the eye. "I promise, Eric and I will do everything we can."

"Josiah is a really nice boy," Effie said. "He's really popular, too. I, um, had no idea he was having such a bad time at home."

"Not many kids want to share things like that," Eric said quietly. "They're ashamed. But don't worry. We'll do something. Somehow, some way, things will be better by Christmas."

Looking extremely relieved, Ginny stood up. "*Danke.* I didn't want to share secrets, but I didn't feel I had a choice. I truly hate the idea of a child going hungry here in Pinecraft."

"I feel the same way," Beverly said. Then when she noticed how dejected Effie looked, she moved to her side. "Effie, dear?"

The girl stopped and looked at her warily. *"Jah?"*

"I'm glad you came over. I'm glad you told your mother about what you saw, too. It was the right thing to do."

Her lip trembled. "You . . . You don't think Josiah is gonna be mad if he finds out I told you and my *mamm* about what I saw at his house?"

"I don't know. He might. But I do know that sometimes a person doesn't know how much he needs help until he receives it."

Eric walked to her side. "I was in a situation a whole lot like Josiah's. I don't know if anyone ever guessed how bad things were but I can tell you that my brother and I, well, we had to face a lot of consequences because we were all on our own. I wish now that someone would have cared enough to help."

Effie nodded. Then, after a pause, she took her mother's hand. Though she was thirteen, and a teenager, at that moment Beverly knew she was simply a girl who needed her mother.

Beverly stood next to Eric on the porch as they watched Ginny and her daughter walk down the street. It was clear that he was still pretty tense, though she couldn't tell whether he was upset with the situation or with her.

Either way, she knew she needed to apologize again. "Eric, I really am sorry that I betrayed your confidence."

He turned to her, eyebrows lifted. "Why did you? What happened?"

"Well, like I said, the morning after we talked, I was still thinking about what you'd told me. And though a big part of me knew you were right, that your crimes were in your past, I was having trouble with coming to terms with it. I couldn't wrap my mind around the fact that someone I cared so much about had done the same thing to other people that had been done to me."

Something new lit his eyes. "Someone you cared so much about?"

She flushed. It was hard to hear her words on his lips, but she wasn't going to hide behind her embarrassment any longer. He deserved more from her. "Yes."

Then, hoping to shift the conversation away from her latest confession, she added, "Like I said, I was having trouble with it, so I woke up early and went for a walk. That's when I ran into Ginny."

"Just like that?"

"She was walking, too. Next thing I knew, I was telling her your story and sharing how I was feeling."

"What did you think she would say?"

"I didn't know. But, Eric, I wasn't trying to gossip, I simply needed someone to listen. And maybe put everything into perspective. Which she did."

"How so?"

"She has a son who recently married after a very short courtship and a daughter who not only chose not to be baptized Amish but is seriously dating a man who is teaching her how to drive, among other things. And before all that, she and her husband had to deal with Effie's diagnosis, surgeries, and rehabilitation. All of those things were challenges."

His lips twitched. "I'd say so." He looked her way then. "I'm not mad, Beverly."

She sighed in relief. "I'm so glad. Did you happen to notice how worried Effie looked?"

"Of course I noticed." Eric nodded. "I'm glad Ginny brought her over. I don't know if I helped her at all, but if I did, then talking about my past was worth it. And, well, I'll do some thinking about how to reach out to those boys without hurting their pride."

"Do you think that's possible?"

"I think I can try."

His gaze was warm on her, almost tender. She sighed in relief. "I'm glad you aren't upset with me."

"It took me off guard, and if I'm being completely honest, it kind of embarrassed me to be thought of as the go-to guy for troubled teens, but I'm glad she did."

"I'm glad you're not mad."

Throwing his arm around her shoulders, he said, "Beverly, you just told me that you cared a lot about me." He smiled broadly. "That's huge!"

"Not that huge," she grumbled.

Kissing her cheek, he whispered, "It was to me, Bev. Because I care about you just as much." He stepped away and stuffed his hands in the back pockets of his jeans. "Now, let's go string up those lights on the tree."

"All right, Eric." Her pulse was racing and she knew she was probably blushing again.

She just hoped he thought it was from the excitement of decorating her first Christmas tree and not from, well . . . him.

Chapter 18

December 20

"Mark, come join us outside on the front porch, would you?"

After glancing at William and getting only a shrug of shoulders in response, Mark followed his *daed* out the front door. There, he found Emma already sitting on one of the porch's black rocking chairs. His *daed* went right to her side.

"Is anything wrong?" he asked. He couldn't think of anything he'd done that might get him in trouble.

"Nothing's wrong, Mark," Emma said. "We wanted to talk to you about what you and Laura told us the other night about Peter."

It had now been about forty-eight hours since Mark had gone with Laura to talk to Officer Roberts and then taken her to the farm for supper. He'd only seen Laura for a couple of minutes in between classes yesterday and a few minutes after school today.

Just long enough to make sure she was okay and to tell her he'd come see her over the weekend. But first he had to get through the last two days of school before Christmas break. It seemed every teacher had something due that he'd forgotten about.

Today after school, he'd taken the SCAT home, helped Ben with the fruit and vegetable stand, then had supper. By the end of the meal, he could feel his patience starting to slip. He loved his new stepsisters, but they were chatty, busy little girls who loved his attention. While he was usually more than happy to be around them, by eight o'clock, all he'd wanted to do was pass out.

But it seemed his father and Emma now had other plans.

"None of what happened was my idea. I'm just trying to be Laura's friend," he pointed out.

Emma smiled. "You're being a *gut* friend to her, for sure."

"I went up to the station and talked to Officer Roberts this morning," Jay said.

"Why? What did he say?"

"He said that he went to see Peter yesterday at his house." Looking troubled, his father continued. "What he found concerned him."

Mark sat down on the stoop, facing his *daed* and Emma. "Did he find the money?"

"After a time, *jah*."

"So Peter did rob the inn."

"It seems so," Emma said. After clearing her throat, she leaned forward a bit. "Mark, Peter's actions were not good. That is true. But that's not the reason we wanted to talk to you. See, um, Officer Roberts said when he got to Peter's house, the boys' father had left again. It seems he leaves for days or weeks at a time. And when he goes, he puts Peter in charge of Josiah."

"That's too bad."

"It's worse than that, Mark," his father said. "When their father disappears, he doesn't leave them with anything."

"What do you mean by that?"

"He doesn't buy them food or give Peter money to pay for expenses or bills."

Mark was still trying to understand how Peter's father could abandon two teenaged boys without anything. "They didn't have any food? At all?"

His father shook his head. "That was why Peter robbed the inn. He was desperate to get something to feed his brother."

Afraid his *daed* might see the tears that had suddenly sprung up in his eyes, Mark looked away. Now he felt even more guilty about going with Laura to the police station. Peter had only been trying to feed his little brother. "So we shouldn't have said anything."

"That's not what I'm saying at all. You did the right thing, son," his *daed* said. "See, Peter needs help. He and his brother need someone to count on. Actually, they need a lot of people to help them. They've been alone for far too long."

Starting to understand, Mark nodded eagerly. "I can do that. I can ask him if he wants to come over here for supper. Or maybe, Daed, we can bring him some of the produce that no one wants? We've got lots of that."

"Those are good ideas, but the boys need more." After taking a deep breath, he added, "Officer Roberts is going to make sure

Peter pays Beverly back for the damage he did and the money he stole. But what he really has to do is find those boys someone to look after them until everything gets sorted out with their father."

"What does that mean?"

"Officer Roberts has already talked to the social worker that stopped by their *haus*. They were just about to make some calls when I came by." After looking at Emma, his *daed* said, "Mark, I want you to know that Emma and I volunteered to be those boys' foster parents."

Mark had heard of foster kids, but he didn't really know what that meant. "Are you saying they're going to live with us?"

Emma nodded. "After your father talked to Officer Roberts, he came and talked to me. Then we went and met both Josiah and Peter. A social worker is watching them tonight, but they're going to come here tomorrow."

"Forever?" He swallowed hard, trying to take it all in.

His father shrugged. "I don't know what's going to happen in the future. A lot depends on what happens with the boys' father when they locate him. But I did tell Officer Roberts I want the boys to stay with us at least until the New Year."

Emma nodded. "Those poor boys. I think it's been years since they had a good Christmas. I want to give them that at the very least."

"Have you told Ben and William and the girls already?"

"I told Ben but I asked him not to say anything to William or even Tricia," his father said. "I wanted to talk to you first." Leaning forward, his father looked at him closely. "Mark, it's probably too late to ask you this, but are you okay with our decision?"

His father was right. Even if he wasn't okay with Peter coming to live at his house, it was too late for anything to be changed.

But that didn't matter.

What did matter was that Peter and his little brother wouldn't be living in some stranger's house. Or worse, living in their own house with nothing to eat.

"It's okay with me," he said quietly. "We have a big house and a lot of blessings." He turned to Emma, who he privately thought was just about the nicest woman he'd ever met. "Peter and Josiah are going to be really glad to get to know you, Emma."

Emma smiled sweetly. "I'm looking forward to getting to know them."

"If you and Laura hadn't felt compelled to do something about what she suspected, things wouldn't be changing for Peter and Josiah," his father said. "Starting today, their lives have gotten better. I want you to know that I'm really proud of you."

Mark shook his head. "I didn't do anything. Laura just asked me to go with her to the police station."

"I think you might have done more than you know. Laura was able to go to the police because she had you beside her. And Peter told me that you've always been nice to him. Because of your kindness, he is willing to bring Josiah here."

Mark felt humbled. "Things are going to change again, aren't they?"

Emma stood up and gave him a hug. "I imagine so. But in the best ways possible." When she stepped away, she smiled. "Now we just have to hope that they like beagles."

Mark grinned. "As long as Frankie doesn't steal their pizza, they should like him fine."

After supper, Eric and Beverly had just taken a couple of cookies to the front stoop to watch the world go by when a police cruiser pulled up. As they watched the car park on the side of the street and Officer Roberts exit the driver's side door, Eric felt his shoulders and neck begin to tense, just like they used to when he was in the juvenile detention center and felt a guard's eyes settle on him.

Maybe Ginny Kaufmann had come to the right person after all.

It seemed that no matter how much time passed, he was always going to be the guy who was a little afraid of the police.

But Beverly, on the other hand, had no such qualms. Her eyes lit up. "Oh, Eric. It looks like Officer Roberts has some news." She scampered down the porch steps.

"Hi, Beverly," the policeman said with a smile that didn't quite meet his eyes. "I see you are enjoying the evening."

"Oh, *jah*. When one is blessed with warm weather in December, it's hard not to appreciate it."

Officer Roberts nodded, but his tense expression didn't ease. Looking past her, he nodded. "Hello, Eric."

Getting to his feet, Eric asked, "Do you have some news?"

"I do. Do you two have a few minutes to talk?"

"Of course we do," Beverly answered quickly. She pointed to the set of rocking chairs on the porch. "Would you like to sit out here or inside?"

The policeman looked at the chairs, then shrugged. "If you

don't mind sitting outside, I suppose this would work just fine. It is beautiful out."

Once they were settled on the porch, Eric got right to the point. "What's going on?"

Roberts pulled out his smartphone and skimmed through a couple of screens. Eric noticed he was looking at some notes he'd typed on it. "First off, we're fairly sure we found your burglar, Beverly."

Beverly scooted to the end of her chair. "You did? Who was it?"

Eric wrapped an arm around the back of her chair. He wanted to be able to support her in case the news was worse than they thought. "Easy, Bev."

Glancing his way, her green eyes full of warmth, she exhaled and murmured, "I'm fine."

Officer Roberts was still scrolling through his phone. Then he spoke at last. "It looks like our suspicions were right," he said. "Your burglar was a teen."

"Just one?" Beverly asked with a frown. "But there was so much damage."

"It seems that he wanted to make it look like there was a bunch of kids breaking in. This kid, he's kind of a loner."

"Well, he did a good job," Eric murmured. "He trashed several rooms." He stood up. "I'm glad you discovered who did it. Thanks for coming to tell us the news in person. I know Beverly will sleep better now."

"Hold on. We need to talk about this some more," the policeman said.

"How about I stop by in the morning?" Eric asked, feeling protective. Beverly didn't need to hear any of the details, at least not from the cops. Instead, he was sure it would be better if he heard everything, then sat down with Bev and gently told her everything she needed to know. "As long as he's not out trashing more homes, it's all good." When Roberts didn't say anything, Eric said, "I'm assuming you've arrested this kid?"

"No. Not yet."

"And why is that?"

Officer Roberts rolled his shoulders. "This boy is seventeen. It turns out the young man's mother died a few years ago. Since then, he and his younger brother have been essentially making do on their own."

"On their own? What about their father?" Beverly asked. "Is he dead, as well?"

"I can't tell you everything, but he isn't, ah, very involved in their lives." He frowned. "I can share that their father doesn't care for them as he should. He shows up at the house for a while, long enough to give the boys hope that he'll be back, then he takes off again without any notice. This has been going on for a while. Of late, it seems he's been leaving for weeks at a time."

"For weeks? Oh, but that's terrible," Beverly said. "Those poor boys."

Roberts nodded. "Yes, it really is terrible. They have been going through a pretty difficult time."

"How are they able to live?"

"The house was paid for, but the father owes money to just about everyone. It's amazing no one has turned off their water."

Eric winced. The whole situation sounded rough. And far too familiar. Though it had been almost twenty years, he still remembered how it felt to have no one really looking out for him except Jack.

"Beverly," Officer Roberts continued, "when we were talking to the oldest boy and attempting to figure out how he was making ends meet, his younger brother joined us and pretty much gave him away. And then this young man confessed everything. He even took us to a back shed and showed us your television. He also pulled out your lockbox and handed it over."

"Oh, my."

"He'd only used about eighty dollars of the five hundred. He said he's been saving the rest."

"For what, do you think?"

"Food."

Eric felt as if someone had hit him in the stomach. "They've been going hungry."

"But why wouldn't one of the boys simply tell someone that their father kept leaving them?" Beverly asked innocently, her eyes wide. "They could have told a teacher, at the very least."

"If they'd told anyone in a position of authority that person would have been legally bound to do something," Eric said. "The boys might not have liked what would happen next."

Roberts nodded, his expression grim. "That's right. They would have been placed in foster care—if someone was willing to take in two older boys. If not, they would have been split up and put into two different homes or perhaps in a group home."

"What are their ages?" Eric asked.

"Thirteen and seventeen."

Beside him, Beverly gasped. "Officer, by any chance, was this younger boy's name Josiah Yoder?"

Roberts stilled. "Do you know Josiah?"

"*Nee.* But, um, we just had a visit from a friend whose daughter is friends with Josiah. The girl was worried about him."

"She has every right to worry about him. I'm going to need the girl's name."

Beverly bit her lip.

Eric leaned close. "It's just like what Ginny said the other day, Bev. Breaking a confidence is sometimes the right thing to do."

"My friend's name is Ginny Kaufmann. Her daughter Effie is Josiah's friend."

"Thanks," Officer Roberts said. "I know the Kaufmanns. I'll stop by and talk with them tomorrow."

Beverly looked so upset, Eric reached for her hand and gave it a gentle squeeze. "So, what's going to happen now, Officer?"

"They're staying in a temporary home tonight. But a family here in Sarasota knows the boys. They've asked to look after them both until everything gets sorted out."

"Who is taking them in?" Eric asked. "Can you tell us?"

"I probably shouldn't, but Pinecraft is such a tight-knit community everyone will know within an hour. Jay and Emma Hilty are taking them in."

"My goodness. They are newlyweds. I must say I'm surprised," Beverly murmured.

Officer Roberts smiled. "I was caught off guard, too. But then Jay told me that he thought they might be a good fit. He's currently raising six kids and they have a big house. It seems that one of his boys knows Peter and has been worried about him. Their youngest son, William, knows Josiah, too."

"I know Jay and his boys. They stayed here before they moved to their farm," Eric said. "I can see Jay being concerned and wanting to help."

"Beverly, there's a lot of information to sort through in order to make the right decision for both you and the boys. The law says we can arrest Peter and charge him for vandalism and theft. He's admitted it, so he could get fined."

"But because he doesn't have any way to pay those fines, he'll get put in juvie," Eric said. His stomach tightened as he remembered his first night there. He'd been so scared.

"Maybe," Roberts allowed.

Just imagining how being incarcerated would affect an Amish boy for the rest of his life made Eric feel sick. "We can't let that boy go to jail, Bev."

"You're right." Beverly was already shaking her head. "We canna do that. What is the other option?"

Officer Roberts stared at her. "I was thinking that Peter could come over here and apologize for what he put you through. Then, maybe we could come up with a contract together, one that would ensure he'd pay you back the money that he owes you—both the money from the lockbox and the money to replace the broken window and lamps." He hesitated, then added, "But he wouldn't be arrested."

Beverly's eyes were swimming with tears. "I can't believe he was so desperate that he broke into the inn because he needed money to feed his brother."

"It seems to me that he's already been suffering a lot," Eric said.

Officer Roberts nodded slowly. "I was thinking the same

thing. I don't usually get emotionally involved. But this one got to me, you know? Poor kids."

"Did you get hold of their father yet?" Eric asked.

"No. But I have to tell you that part of me hopes we don't find him for another week or two. Those boys deserve a couple of nights in a warm house with some good meals. Jay and Emma Hilty are going to give them that."

"What do you want to do, Beverly?" Eric asked. "I do feel sorry for those boys, but I won't ever forget how shaken up you were. You are the victim here."

"Eric's right," Officer Roberts said. "There is nothing wrong with seeking retribution."

She shook her head. "*Nee.* I don't want retribution. If I've learned anything since the robbery, it's that I have a lot of blessings in my life. I have friends to lean on, I have savings in the bank to pay for crises, and I am stronger than I thought I was. I'd much rather hope and pray that something good will come from this whole situation. I have to think that God planned it this way so I would remember my blessings, but also so that something good would happen for those two boys. I promise, an apology from Peter will be enough."

"I'll stay in touch then," Officer Roberts said, and left a few minutes later.

After he was gone, Eric grabbed her hands. "Are you sure you're all right with this?"

She nodded. "I'm going to be just fine."

"I have to say that you're handling everything well. I'm impressed with how strong you've become."

"You know what? I didn't think I had become stronger, but I know I actually have," she said with a smile. "I've been able to handle things that I wouldn't have even a year ago."

"I'm glad. I wonder what changed."

"That's easy. I now have you. Because I have you to lean on, nothing is insurmountable."

Her honesty blew him away. "I feel the same way, Beverly. You have become incredibly important to me."

Actually, he knew exactly how important she'd become.

He'd fallen in love with her.

said. "By now Peter probably knows that I went with Laura to the police station. I bet he's going to hate me."

Ben sat down on the stoop next to him. Inside, Tricia was reading a book to Lena, Mandy, and Annie. "Peter ain't going to hate you."

"You can't be sure about that."

After nudging Mark's arm, Ben said, "You did what you had to do, Mark. There's nothing wrong with that."

"That's easy for you to say. How would you feel if this happened to you?"

"I have no idea. Stealing money in order to take care of my little brother hasn't happened to me. But then again, I've never had to handle things on my own like Peter had to."

"I guess that's true."

"I can say that if things are really as bad as Emma and Daed made it sound, then I would have probably stolen money, too."

Mark stared at him in surprise. "You really think so?"

"I know so." After a pause, he said, "That's what love is, don't you think?"

Ben had lost him. "Stealing?"

"*Nee*. What I'm trying to say is that love is everything. It's warm and sweet and good, to be sure. But, well, it's also a powerful motivator. It makes men and women and even kids do things they never thought they would."

Put that way, Mark thought, maybe Ben had a point. Love—true love—was so powerful that it could override most any other thing, even the desire to follow rules and obey laws.

"You know, I'd do just about anything to take care of Tricia," Ben said quietly. "I'd do just about anything because I promised

Chapter 19

December 21

A lot had happened over the last couple of days. The whole sequence of events felt amazing to Mark and more than a little too close for comfort.

He'd certainly never anticipated that his *daed* and Emma would have offered to become foster parents to Peter and Josiah!

But now Mark was going to have to face Peter, knowing that he was at least partly responsible for him having to leave his house and being removed from his father's custody. He'd only been trying to help Laura, not trying to get Peter into big trouble.

Mark felt sick inside. Actually, he felt like he was about to throw up.

"Daed and Emma are going to be here any minute, Ben," he

her and God that I would take care of her. And well, I think I would actually do anything to take care of you and William, too. Especially if I thought you were going hungry. You two are my younger brothers."

Mark knew he would, too. Their little brother, William, was a handful. But he was *their* handful. Without a doubt, Mark knew he would do whatever it took to make sure William felt protected and safe, too. He'd even do things he wasn't proud of—if he had to.

"I'd do anything for you and William, too," he said at last.

"That's all you have to tell Peter," Ben said. "Maybe not the minute he gets here. Maybe not even tonight. But if you tell him that you understand why he did something so bad, that you understand what it means to love someone so much that you were willing to sacrifice yourself in order to make sure they eat? Well, I bet there's a good chance that someday, he'll understand why you had to be by Laura's side and help her."

"I hope he does."

"I hope so, too. But Mark, if he doesn't, you can't let that bother you. You did the right thing. You couldn't have looked the other way."

"Are you surprised about Daed and Emma offering to take them in for a while?"

"No. They've both lost people important to them. They know what it's like to grieve. And, well, we do, too."

Mark never thought he'd ever be even a little glad to have lost his mother, but if it meant that he could help Peter and Josiah, he supposed his *mamm* up in heaven would be happy about that. "It's funny how life works, huh?"

"*Nee.* It's good how life works. No matter how hard it is, the Lord always helps. That makes me feel like we're not alone." Suddenly Ben grinned. "They're here. Come on, let's go greet them."

Mark walked slowly down the front steps to where a black SUV had stopped. He watched everyone pile out: Daed, Officer Roberts, Emma, Peter, and Peter's brother, Josiah. He watched Ben shake Officer Roberts's hand and say hi to Peter and Josiah.

"Hey," Mark said. "Josiah, I'm Mark. Glad to know ya." And then it was time.

Peter turned his way, his face an expressionless mask. It felt almost as if he were staring right through Mark.

Mark reminded himself that he might have acted the same way. Looking directly at Peter, he said the only thing he could think of that made sense. *"Wilcom."*

Peter blinked. Then, to Mark's surprise, his eyes lit with a new warmth. *"Danke."*

Two hours had passed since Officer Roberts had come over and relayed everything to Beverly and Eric. Practically the moment he'd left, one of their guests had needed directions to the mall, then another had had some questions about restaurants they'd read about in a magazine. Almost glad for a reason to push aside her worries, Beverly had efficiently answered questions, drawn maps, and given out her opinion. By the time she'd finished, Eric was on the phone.

She took advantage of the break and the quiet. Walking back to the kitchen, she put on the kettle, unfolded one of her favorite chamomile tea bags into a cup, and allowed herself to reflect on both the officer's visit and the news she'd learned.

The mystery surrounding the break-in had been solved. But with this news came the reminder that there were so many things far more important than some cash in a lockbox and a sense of security.

Never had she imagined that the robbery would have set off this whole series of events. From the time she'd walked up her street and seen the three police cars, she'd held so many emotions deep inside her. She'd been holding fear and indignation close to her heart. Then she'd felt anger and resignation. Now? She merely felt sad for those boys.

"Are you as stunned as I am?" Eric asked as he entered the room.

Looking at him, she noticed some new lines of tension around his lips. He seemed dazed by the turn of events, too.

"*Jah*," she replied at last. "I have to admit that almost every evening since the break-in I've gone to bed praying for an answer. I focused so much on this robbery that, to me, it sort of became the most important thing happening in Pinecraft. I'm kind of embarrassed now."

"You don't have a thing to be embarrassed about. Anyone would feel upset and scared after discovering that their home was robbed." He opened up her cookie jar, pulled out a plate, and started piling shortbread cookies on it. "That said, I've gotta tell you that I didn't see this coming."

His words, combined with his tall stack of cookies, made Beverly decide to pour Eric a cup of tea, too. It seemed he could use a little bit of chamomile calm. While he brought the cookies to the table, she poured water into mugs, added a spoonful of sugar into each, then followed him to what had become their spot, the kitchen table.

It occurred to her as they did this that it had become routine. They didn't knock into each other or waste conversation asking each other's preferences.

Now, they already knew.

Two minutes later she was holding her favorite mug, letting the warmth heat her hands. Eric had already had two cookies.

They were now able to discuss things.

"So," she said at last. "Our mystery has been solved."

"It has." He shifted, kicked out his bare feet, then crossed them at the ankles. "I'm glad about that."

"Me, too," she said around a sigh. "It was awful, not knowing."

He nodded. "I know you said you forgave that boy, but are you truly okay with how everything was resolved?"

She thought about it. "I am." Shifting into a more comfortable position, she said, "Eric, when Officer Roberts was telling us about Peter and his brother, all I could think of was how upset I'd been when I first walked inside and saw the mess. I acted like it was the end of the world."

"Don't be so hard on yourself. And don't forget, you called me as soon as everyone left. Besides, anyone would have felt what you did."

"Maybe. Or maybe not. Now that I think about how I carried on so much that you took the first flight out, how I had to sleep over at the Kaufmanns' because I was afraid, how I didn't even want to see new guests because I felt like I'd lost my trust in everyone . . ." She shook her head. "It was a pretty poor response."

"But this inn has meant the world to you. It's been your refuge since your breakup with your fiancé. Then you clung to it for security after your aunt died." He smiled softly. "Most recently, you discovered that the inn you thought was yours was actually mine. All of those things are reasons why this place means so much to you."

It would be easy to let Eric's statement absolve her of her mistakes. But she wasn't going to hide behind excuses. "Eric, while it is true that this inn is mighty special to me, I am still guilty of forgetting about forgiveness and compassion. I was so selfish."

Shifting again, he shook his head. He reached out and took her hand. "You were not, Bev. What Peter did was not good. Stealing from you was not okay. Breaking a window was not okay. Searching through the rooms, looking for things to pawn was wrong, too." His voice was firm. Sure. After taking a breath, he added, "That boy did a lot of damage around here. And after? Instead of confessing, he kept his secrets. Who knows, maybe he would have stolen again. I would have." He grimaced as he let go of her fingers. "I did."

"He was hungry. He was trying to provide for his brother."

"I know. But robbing the inn wasn't the right course of action."

She pressed a hand to her brow. "Those poor boys, afraid to let anyone know that their father had been taking off for weeks at a time." With a sigh, she looked at him. "Why would a father do that?"

His brown eyes darkened with what she guessed was the same pain and confusion she felt. "I have no idea."

"And the worst part is that you tried to warn me. You tried to remind me that there are dozens of reasons why someone might rob the inn. But I didn't listen."

"Bev, I did not warn you about this. I had no idea a hungry teenager was your thief."

"Eric, you told me about yourself and your brother. You explained that there might be more to the story than I had realized. And there was!"

"Yes, there was, but you didn't know that." He shifted in his chair. "Kids sometimes make bad choices. I know I did. I know my brother did, and he paid the consequences. Though Peter's intentions were good, what he did was wrong. I hope he realizes that. I hope we're not letting him off too easy."

"His father left for weeks at a time, leaving him with a little brother to take care of. I think he's already learned that life isn't fair. He's certainly learned the consequences of only thinking about himself."

"I agree." He smiled softly then, and she was reminded how he was always on her side. No matter what happened, he had always been her support. And he'd been more than that to her, as well. Eric had become her friend and her confidant. Together over the last year, they'd navigated a rocky relationship, helped several couples with their romances . . . and become very close.

Now, when Beverly looked at him, she didn't just see a handsome man with a devil-may-care attitude. She saw a man who had been through a lot but still found a way to move forward.

Just as important, she saw a man whom she could move forward with.

"I hope they'll spend time with Emma and Jay," Beverly said. "If anyone can give those boys both love and structure, it's those two. They're such a nice couple."

"They are. I have a feeling that they'll both bend over backward to give those boys a Christmas they'll always remember, too. Bev, I really think that those boys are going to eventually be all right. They now have a lot of people in town looking out for them."

"I hope so. I'd love for them to feel less alone now." She sighed. "Maybe they'll be okay after all."

"And maybe we will, too."

She looked at him in surprise. "We will. We have so much to be grateful for this Christmas."

He tilted his head to one side and studied her carefully. "What are you grateful for?"

Beverly was done hiding her heart. "You."

"You really are okay, aren't you? You don't want to press charges."

"*Nee.*" She shrugged. "I never would have believed this, but I think I needed that break-in, Eric. It jarred me. It made me realize that life happens. God doesn't promise us easy lives. Instead, he promises that we'll have obstacles and bumps and pain . . . and glory and beauty and love and mercy. Yes, being robbed was painful. But learning why it happened means more to me than my false sense of security ever did. Something needed to happen for those boys. And if it took this robbery to spur that change, then I choose to be grateful for it."

"Choose to be grateful. I like that."

"Me, too. I like the idea of the Lord giving us options." Looking him in the eye, she finally felt as if she'd laid herself bare in front of him. "For too long I held tight to my pain and let it influence how I lived my life. And though I was tempted to dwell on how upset I was when my fiancé and best friend fell in love behind my back, I made the choice to do something different. I'm really glad about that. It's a blessing."

"Me, too. And now instead of dwelling on how frightened you were after the break-in, you are choosing to think about two boys' needs instead of your own. That's pretty awesome."

Beverly grinned. "You know, that's true."

"I'm proud of you. Who knows? Maybe Santa will bring you something special, since you've been such a good girl and it's so close to Christmas."

"I guess you could say I did something good in the nick of time."

He winced. "Beverly, are you making Saint Nicholas puns?"

"Maybe." Grabbing a cookie, she said, "That was a good one. Ain't so?"

Lines formed around the corners of his eyes as he smiled at her. "No, it was not a good one. At all." Then he winked. "But it was clever."

"I'll take clever," she said with a smile.

Chapter 20

December 24

Eric had been pacing in front of the Orange Blossom Inn for almost an hour.

Beverly knew because she'd been watching him from the window. Over and over, he walked back and forth like a soldier on parade, sunglasses covering his eyes, his cell phone in hand.

Twice she'd considered walking out to keep him company, but he looked so lost in thought she decided to give him his space. She knew what had him in knots, anyway. His brother was due to arrive at the Sarasota-Bradenton International Airport in just a couple of hours. And though Eric had invited him and was excited to see him, she knew there was also a lingering bit of worry and doubt surrounding the upcoming visit.

She'd experienced those emotions herself.

As she continued to watch him pace, Beverly noticed that he had dressed up for the occasion. Well, as much as Eric liked to dress up. He was still wearing his usual faded jeans, but instead of his favorite flip-flops, he had tan loafers on his feet. He'd also replaced his usual T-shirt with a loose-fitting linen shirt in pale gray. With the haircut he'd gotten yesterday and the close shave that morning, Eric looked very handsome. Very clean-cut, too, she thought. So different from his usual relaxed appearance.

Remembering the faint scent of aftershave that had lingered in the kitchen after he'd gotten his coffee, she knew he smelled good, too.

He was so very appealing.

"How's Eric doing?" Sadie asked from behind her. "Is he still fretting?"

Beverly turned around in surprise. "Sadie, goodness! You startled me! Where in the world did you come from?"

She smiled. "I decided to come in through your kitchen door when I saw how deep in thought Eric was out front."

"That was probably a smart decision. He is in a bit of a daze."

"That's to be expected, I suppose," Sadie mused. "Visits can be stressful experiences. Especially when they are from long-lost brothers."

Beverly blinked in surprise. "How did you know Eric's brother was coming in today?"

"Word gets around, dear," she said in her airy way. "You two have been quite the topic of conversation, you see. Everyone is wondering what's going to happen next."

Beverly could only imagine what gossip had been stirred up around the two of them. She supposed she couldn't blame the speculation. Their relationship was complicated and at times a bit volatile. It had certainly never been boring!

And over the past couple of days, their relationship had shifted again. Their friendship had become far closer. Though she wouldn't exactly say they were dating, they certainly had moved beyond carefully circling each other—which had seemed to be the hallmark of their association so far.

Even though Beverly remained by the window watching Eric walk back and forth, Sadie made herself at home. Sitting down in the center of the couch, Sadie crossed her legs, taking care to smooth the dark green fabric of her dress as she did so. "Everything looks pretty in here, Beverly. Even the Christmas tree."

Beverly glanced over at the next set of windows to where the tree stood decorated with hundreds of white lights. "I must admit that while I would never have bought a tree, I have enjoyed staring at its beauty in the evenings. I'll miss it when it's gone."

"I expect so." Sadie inhaled deeply. "It makes the room smell fresh and lovely. As do the cinnamon-scented candles."

Beverly glanced at the display of red candles she'd set out just yesterday. "At last, it feels like Christmas is about to come. And just in time, too. I can hardly believe that it's Christmas Eve!"

Sadie grinned. "I'm surprised you're not in the kitchen preparing everything for tomorrow's meal."

"I've already made the egg strata and cinnamon rolls for tomorrow's breakfast. The guests staying here will have that, then head to the parade. Eric and I have decided to simply bake a ham and offer a few side dishes later for Jack. It's just going to be the three of us since I never make suppers for the guests."

"I'm going to Winnie's *haus*. She's hosting supper for fourteen."

Beverly whistled low. "I do enjoy having a lot of people over, but this month has been so hectic, I am thankful we're keeping things simple."

"I'm sure you are glad of that." Looking beyond Beverly, Sadie smiled. Then she stood up. "Well, I think it's time I was going."

"So soon?" Beverly had enjoyed simply visiting with her friend.

"Eric is coming up the sidewalk. I do believe he's come lookin' for you," she said cryptically as she opened the front door and stepped outside. "Merry Christmas, Eric!" she said before walking down to her house.

"Same to you, Sadie," he called out as he walked up the front steps.

Beverly met him at the door. "Hi," she said. "So, are you ready to come in for a while?"

He shook his head. Looking a bit like a child getting ready to go to the circus, he said, "It's time for me to go to the airport."

She smiled. "*Wunderbaar*. Let me get my purse and a light sweater and I'll be ready to go."

"There's no need for that."

She tilted her head to one side. "You don't think I'll need my sweater?"

"No. I mean, you don't have to come."

What did that mean? Was he trying to tell her that he didn't want her with him? She wondered if this was another one of those statements where the meaning and the intended message were at cross purposes. "I would like to come with you, if you don't mind."

"I don't mind, but, well, I have to warn you that Jack is a little rough around the edges."

She smiled. "I've realized lately that we all are a little rough around the edges, Eric. I wouldn't want him any other way. I promise, I just want to be there for you. It would mean a lot to me if you'd let me come."

His whole bearing relaxed. "I'd love for you to be there. Rough edges and all."

Feeling pleased with herself, she rushed to her room to get her purse and light white cotton cardigan to wear over her bright blue dress, then carefully made sure the cabinet holding the lockbox was secure. Finally, she locked the front door. Her guests each had their own keys to let themselves in if they returned before she and Eric did.

Eric was standing on the porch, his car keys in hand. "Ready?"

"Very ready."

"I don't know if you noticed, but I'm kind of nervous."

"I noticed."

"Do you think that's strange? I mean, he is my brother."

"Eric, you've witnessed me being nervous about most everything over the last couple of months. I'm actually a little glad that you are nervous about this upcoming reunion. It makes me feel like I'm not the only one that gets tense about meeting relatives."

He laughed. "I'm glad my stressing out has made you feel better, Bev. Anything for you."

They continued their easy conversation the whole way to the airport. She teased him about his fancy loafers and he made her tell him stories about growing up on an Amish farm in Sugarcreek. Later, they lapsed into a comfortable silence as they stood in the greeting area of the airport terminal.

As the minutes ticked by, Eric kept looking at the monitors, glancing at the screen on his smartphone, and jangling his keys. Beverly had never seen him so agitated. Truly, if she hadn't witnessed it herself, she would have never guessed that he could ever be anything but his confident, unflappable self.

Not knowing how to ease his mind—or maybe because she could truly relate to what he was feeling—she didn't try to offer any words of wisdom. Sometimes what she needed the most was simply a friend to stand beside her. That meant more than meaningless assurances.

"Hey, Bev?" Eric blurted, interrupting their silence.

"Jah?" She glanced his way and noticed that the muscles in his jaw were tight.

"What . . . What if we don't have anything in common anymore? What if this long-awaited reunion of ours is a bust?"

The fact was she didn't know his brother, and his fears could very well come to fruition. He and Jack might not have anything in common anymore. They might very well be in store for three days of strained conversation and disappointment that they no longer had much to say to each other.

If that happened, Beverly promised herself that she would do her best to make both men as comfortable as possible. And if all else failed, why, she would cook for them nonstop! An array of home-cooked meals might make even the most difficult visit easier to bear.

Reaching out, she clasped his hand and enfolded it in both of hers. "It will still be all right, Eric."

His eyes searched her face. "How do you know?"

"It will be all right because you both tried," she said simply. "That is all one can do. Ain't so?"

His tense expression relaxed into the grin she was so fond of. "*Jah*. Ain't so."

"Eric, do me a favor and don't even attempt to speak Pennsylvania Dutch to your brother."

"My accent is still that bad?"

"It's worse."

Looking at her smile, Eric felt the warmth of affection that he was coming to realize was a consequence of those smiles. "I'll try to remember to only speak English to Jack. *Danke*."

She rolled her eyes. "Eric, it's '*danke*,' " she said, emphasizing some sound he wasn't sure he was capable of producing.

He was just about to try anyway when he spied a man walking down the hall who looked very familiar. He blinked, wondering if a person's loping walk could stay with him the way it looked like Jack's had. "That's him."

Seeing Jack's stride, along with his faded jeans and boots and the intricate line of tattoos on his forearms, Eric felt a lump rise in his throat. "Excuse me," he uttered to Beverly, not even sure why he was excusing himself.

All he seemed able to do was go to his brother.

When Jack recognized him, he paused, then lifted a hesitant hand. "Hey."

Eric picked up his pace. "Jack. It's good you came," he said, his voice thick with emotion.

Jack's lips twitched. Stuffing one of his hands into a back pocket, he said, "I figured if you took the trouble to ask me to come down here and buy me a ticket, the least I could do is actually show up."

Eric grinned at him, then realized he'd been standing there staring at his brother as if they were strangers. Awkwardly, he stepped closer and hugged him, slapping his shoulder blades as Jack did the same.

When they parted, Eric looked him over. His brother was bigger than him, probably at least two or three inches taller and a good forty pounds heavier, but it was easy to see that all that extra weight was muscle. His construction job obviously kept him in shape. Honestly, between his girth and the tattoos, Jack was imposing enough that a lot of men would probably think twice about messing with him. Amazingly, Eric felt proud about that. It seemed Jack was always going to be the big brother who could take care of anything, anywhere, and at any time.

"You look great. Pale," he teased.

Jack shrugged. "It's been pretty cold and snowy up in Cleveland. Not a lot of chances right now to get a suntan."

"It was cold up in Philly, too. I was never so glad to get on a plane and head south."

Belatedly realizing that they were standing in everyone's way, he pulled Jack closer to the wall. "Seriously, I'm really glad you're here."

"Yeah. Me, too. It's been too long."

Eric reached for his brother's duffel. "Come on, I want you to meet Beverly."

"She's the woman who runs the inn?"

"Yes. But, um, she's more than that," he replied, realizing that he now thought of Beverly in a far more meaningful way.

Jack glanced at him out of the corner of his eye. "What does that mean?"

How could he put it into words for his brother when he was only now coming to terms with it himself? "I'll tell you later."

When he saw that Beverly was watching them approach with a glow in her eyes, he knew she and Jack were going to get along just fine. Beverly was going to enjoy Jack's humor, and Jack was going to think Beverly was both beautiful and a great cook. Because both were true: She was beautiful and she was an outstanding cook.

"Hi, Bev, I'm Jack," he said as he moved to Beverly. "It's great to meet you."

When she held out her hand without a trace of hesitation and smiled at Jack, her green eyes sparkling, Eric noticed that his brother was speaking to her softly. Kindly. Not just because

Beverly was obviously a lady, but, he realized, because Jack knew he was talking to Eric's girl. And that, he realized, was why Jack was going to like her most of all.

Both of them were important to Eric. And Eric was also important to them.

And at the end of the day, that was truly all that mattered.

Chapter 21

December 24

Because of the nature of her job, Beverly cooked for others all the time. She felt a great deal of satisfaction when her guests reacted to her homemade cookies, pies, and cakes with obvious enjoyment. She loved creating her signature French toast and maple-glazed bacon and knowing that she'd made someone's visit to the Orange Blossom Inn a memorable experience.

These achievements were the product of years of careful practice and experimenting. She was proud of them. Despite all this, she could count only a handful of times when she'd felt like one of her meals had been really special.

But as she relaxed after supper that evening, she knew this had just been one of those occasions. She'd served crab cakes, beef filets, a salad dotted with fresh fruit, steamed broccoli, and twice-baked potatoes. For dessert she'd pulled out all the stops and baked a chocolate cake with a chocolate mousse filling and a shiny white seven-minute frosting.

The men had been so attentive to the food, so appreciative, that their conversation had been limited and sparse. Beverly hadn't minded one bit. She had enjoyed watching them together, even if it was doing something as simple as sharing a meal.

Now that she knew some of their past, she felt as if she'd given them a small gift: a hearty dinner served with love on the eve of a holiday. Eric and Jack had joked with each other, gently teased her, and generally acted like it was one of their favorite meals ever. They were so much fun to be around, Beverly knew she would always hold this meal close to her heart. Their reunion was a blessing, for sure. She was so glad Eric had invited Jack to spend the holiday with them.

After Jack consumed the remaining bite of cake on his plate, he leaned back in his chair with a contented sigh. "Beverly, Eric told me you were an outstanding cook, but his praise didn't do you justice. I can honestly say that this was the nicest meal I've ever eaten."

"I'm *verra* glad you enjoyed it," she replied with a smile. And she *was* happy he'd enjoyed it, but when she peeked at Eric and saw how happy he looked, the warm feelings increased tenfold.

"I don't know why you ever leave here, E," Jack continued. "Sarasota is beautiful, these accommodations are like something out of a fancy magazine, and Beverly's food is amazing."

Eric laughed. "Put that way, you're absolutely right. I don't know why I ever went back to Pennsylvania. Now that my house is pretty much packed up, I hope my next visit back to Philly will be short and sweet," he added, his gaze darting her way yet again.

Beverly looked down at her lap before she started blushing like a young girl.

Jack chuckled. "I know I should get up, but I'm almost too full to do that."

"I hope you're not too full, Jack. Tomorrow we're going to have cinnamon rolls for breakfast and then ham for lunch."

"I'm just kidding," he said with a wink. "When I go back to Cleveland, I'll be living on frozen food and takeout again. I fully intend to eat everything you put in front of me."

"I knew you were smart," Eric teased.

"We're going to need plenty of energy for tomorrow's events, anyway. We're going to the parade, right?"

"Oh, *jah*," Beverly said. "No one misses the parade. It's quite the sight, especially if you are a child. Everyone throws lots of Christmas candy."

"Eric and I saw some folks decorating vehicles today. I'm looking forward to seeing everything." With a sigh, Jack stood up. "Now, though, I think it's time we helped you do all the dishes."

Eric picked up two serving dishes. "Yep. These are going to take a while, I think."

While she would usually gladly accept their help, Beverly didn't want Eric to spend what precious time he had with Jack washing pots and pans in her kitchen. "How about you gentlemen help me clear the table, then go outside and enjoy the evening?"

Eric shook his head. "No way, Beverly. It won't take too long if the three of us do them together."

"But there's no reason—"

"There's every reason," Eric interjected. "I know you like to argue with me, but lét me win this time."

She was mildly affronted. "I do not love to argue with you."

"You do, too."

"Eric, for your information, I simply like pointing out when I'm right and when you are wrong." She attempted to keep a straight face but failed. "Which is often."

Jack laughed as he followed her through the swinging door into the kitchen, two water glasses in his hands. "I hate to side against a woman, but I think Eric might be right on this one. You both seem to enjoy bickering."

She was just about to give in gracefully when they heard a knock at the front door. "I wonder who that is? Maybe one of the guests forgot a key?"

Eric frowned. "I'll get it, Bev."

When he left the kitchen, Jack pulled out a dishtowel and picked up one of the saucepans she'd washed earlier. "You two might enjoy bickering, but I happen to think you make a good team."

"Thank you. Eric and I work together well."

"I'm sure you do, but I wasn't thinking about work," Jack said as he placed the saucepan down on the stovetop and grabbed another pot.

"Oh?" There came that maddening blush again. "Well, um, Eric is a nice man." She closed her eyes. That sounded terribly inadequate. "I mean, he's been a *gut* friend. To me," she sputtered. "I mean, he has been a mighty *gut freind*. Helpful and a, um, hard worker, too."

"I'm sure he has been those things. But what I am trying to say is that the two of you would make a good couple. I can see you two together."

"Do you think so?" she blurted before realizing that she should be keeping her feelings to herself. The last thing she needed was for Jack to tell Eric what she was thinking.

"Bev?" Eric called, interrupting her floundering.

"Jah?"

"Hey, you need to come out here."

Beyond happy to have a reason to dart away, she rushed out the door. "Excuse me, Jack." She felt like throwing her arms around Eric and thanking him for getting her out of that conversation.

She knew she was beaming as she walked into the foyer, but she couldn't help it. "Eric, I have to thank you—"

"Beverly, you have some guests," he said, his expression grim. "Peter, Officer Roberts, and Jay Hilty have come calling."

She froze as her gaze skittered from Eric to Peter Yoder and the other men.

Looking apologetic, Officer Roberts stepped forward. "Hi, Beverly. I'm sorry about the timing, but we were hoping to have a few minutes of your time. Can you spare us some?"

"Of course." She smiled wanly at the four men. Jay smiled back but Peter looked scared to death.

Eric came to her side and, lowering his voice, said, "I hope you don't mind me asking them in, but I thought you might as well get this over with."

His expression was so concerned, his presence so steady and true, she was able to regain her composure. "Yes, Eric." Feeling more like herself, good manners and years of hosting led her to say, "We were just finishing supper, but we have lots of cake left." Remembering her former guest's penchant for chocolate, she smiled. "It's chocolate, Jay, and I must admit that it really is rather tasty. May I bring you some?"

Jay Hilty's eyes crinkled. "I will never pass up anything you cook, Beverly."

"Officer Roberts?" Beverly smiled. "Peter?"

"Please," the officer said.

"*Danke*," Peter whispered.

"You sit down, Bev. I'll bring out the cake," Eric said.

"You don't mind?" She gazed into his dark eyes.

Patience and pride shone back at her. "I don't mind at all." Looking at their visitors, Eric gestured to the couches and chairs. "Please, everybody, have a seat."

Though an awkward tension filled the air, everyone sat. In the background, Beverly could hear Eric and Jack clinking around in the kitchen, gathering forks and plates.

Peter was sitting motionless, his hands clasped tightly around his knees. Officer Richards looked far more relaxed but still a bit stiff. Jay seemed to be the only one who was completely at ease. He was leaning back in his chair with one black boot resting casually on his opposite knee. "Beverly, you've got quite the tree there in your window."

She rolled her eyes. "I do. Eric said since he is most definitely not Amish, he wanted to have a lit Christmas tree. I have to admit to liking the white lights."

"It's very pretty. But kind of plain," Officer Roberts said.

Jay raised his eyebrows in an expression of mock annoyance. "Plain? It's covered with hundreds of lights."

"True. But there's not an ornament to be found," the policeman teased.

"I decided to push only my English decorating habits on Beverly a little bit at a time. It's easier that way," Eric said as he entered the gathering room with a tray holding three giant portions of cake. "Beverly, don't say a word about the portions," he warned. "Men like good-sized slices."

She chuckled. "I've been serving cake longer than you have, Eric. I think those are perfectly sized."

"I think it's perfectly terrific cake," Jay said after he'd consumed a generous forkful.

"*Danke*, Jay."

After all three of her visitors had taken a couple of bites, Officer Roberts put his fork down. "Beverly, I brought Peter here to talk to you."

Looking pale, Peter swallowed and put his plate on the coffee table.

"You can talk to us about anything," Eric said. He'd sat down by her side, obviously ready to shield her from any further pain or discomfort.

Beverly was grateful for his efforts. However, she was realizing that she didn't want to rely on him. Placing a hand on his sleeve, she said, "Thank you, Eric, but I think I need to do this on my own."

The muscle under his sleeve contracted. "Are you sure?"

"I am." Not only did she think this would be best for her, but for Peter, too. It was obvious from the way he was sitting that he was scared to death. The last thing he needed was Eric glaring beside her. "Officer Roberts, Jay, would it be permissible if Peter and I talked together first, just the two of us?"

"Peter?" Officer Roberts asked.

Peter looked paler, but he nodded. "*Jah*. That is fine."

Eric stood up. "Jay, Officer Roberts, how about you finish your cake in the kitchen? You can meet my brother."

Jay picked up his dish and headed that way. "I didn't even know you had a brother," Beverly heard him say as the three men slipped through the kitchen door.

When they were alone, Beverly smiled softly. "I hope you'll finish your cake, too."

But instead of picking up his fork, Peter clenched his hands. "Miss Beverly, I'm really sorry."

She knew he needed to apologize in order to clear his conscience. So she simply nodded.

He took a deep breath and continued. "I kept trying to do the right thing but it wasn't going well. I had to look out for Josiah and I was afraid." He closed his eyes. "I was afraid if I told the truth about things at home, the social worker would take him. Someone had told me about your lockbox, how they'd seen a lot of cash in it and I started thinking if I just had some money, I wouldn't have to worry so much. But it was wrong. Instead of the money making my life easier, the guilt I felt for stealing only made things worse."

As much as she simply wanted to accept his apology and move on, Beverly knew she needed to be honest with him. Honest about her feelings, honest about how devastated and afraid his actions had made her.

"You scared me, Peter," she said at last. "When I came home and saw the window broken, I was petrified." Because her hands had started trembling from her memory, she clenched them into tight fists. "I truly wish you hadn't decided to solve your problems by robbing my inn."

"I'm going to pay you back," he said in a rush. "Jay said I could work for him for months until I pay you back everything I owe you."

She nodded. "I'm sure you will. That will be fine."

He looked away. Obviously too ashamed to meet her gaze.

And that's when she realized that she needed the Lord's help to say the right words.

After a quick prayer, she said quietly, "Peter, I have to tell you that something happened to me this month. I . . . I learned something about myself."

He stared at her, motionless.

Though Beverly feared she was going to sound as awkward as the boy obviously felt, she leaned forward and let the words flow. "Through all this, I . . . well, I learned that for much of my life I've been thinking only about myself. Oh, I cook and clean for guests and I do try to help others, but I was looking at everyone and everything through my own experiences and memories." Thinking just how misguided that had been, she averted her eyes. "I realized that over time I have become somewhat narrow-minded. Maybe cynical."

"Cynical?"

She turned to him again. "I wasn't as understanding about others' situations as I should have been." She sighed. "Peter, learning about your situation; learning about the sacrifices that you were willing to make for your brother . . . well, it humbled me."

"I don't understand."

"What I'm trying to say is that you have inspired me, Peter. You have inspired me to want to be more giving. To remember to think of others. Not only at Christmas, but all year round."

He blinked. "Me?"

"Absolutely you," she said with a slight smile. "You were willing to do whatever you could to help your brother, even break the law. Now you are being strong enough to take responsibility for your actions. Why, I know adults who would not handle such things so well. Perhaps this sounds strange, but I have to imagine that years from now, when this time in your life is just a memory, we'll both be glad this happened."

"Do you really think that?"

She nodded, then moved to sit next to him on the couch. She didn't touch him but sat close enough to smell the fresh soap on his skin and see the longing mixed with doubt in his eyes.

After a moment, she said, "Peter, I accept your apology. What's more, I forgive you. Now, I have a favor to ask of you."

"What is it?"

With a small smile, she held out her hand. "I'd like to be your friend."

He simply stared at her hand. "You want to be friends with me?"

"I've learned this year that one can't have too many friends, you see." Still staring at him intently, she said softly, "I know

I'm older. But I'm still nice. And I do make great cakes and pies. That has to count for something, don't you think?"

He nodded slowly. Then slipped his hand in hers. *"Danke."*

Squeezing his hand, which, she realized, was already bigger than hers, she said, "Thank you, Peter. Now finish your cake. And when you're ready to leave, I'll send the rest of it home with you."

His eyes widened. "Are you sure you want me to have the rest of it?"

"Well, Josiah's going to need some." She winked. "And then there are all those little girls to think about."

For the first time since he arrived, Peter's expression lightened. "Lena, Mandy, and Annie would be mighty sad if Josiah got cake and they did not. Not to mention William."

"We certainly can't have that. It is Christmas, you know."

He grinned then.

And that smile was so beautiful, so meaningful, Beverly had to swallow hard so she wouldn't burst into tears.

She had been right. Long after she stopped baking cakes and looking after guests, long after she stopped being an innkeeper and started to look after her own *kinner*, she would always remember this moment.

This wonderful, beautiful moment when she realized that nothing mattered in the world but kindness.

Nothing at all.

Chapter 22

Christmas Day

Effie Kaufmann might have been only thirteen years old, but she was fairly sure that she would remember this Christmas as the best in her life. It was a beautiful, sunny day. As she stood with her family on the corner of Beneva, almost patiently waiting for the annual Christmas parade to start, she decided that she'd rarely been happier. So far, it had been a really special day.

After spending the morning listening to Daed read the nativity story from the Book of Luke, they'd exchanged gifts. Everyone had seemed to like the baskets she'd made. Effie had painted each basket white and filled it with things that each family member liked. For her mother, Effie had put in scented soaps. Daed received a basket of pink grapefruits and oranges.

Karl had received some peanut butter fudge she'd made, and Violet—who had recently taken up quilting—had received all kinds of prettily tied fabric remnants from the Quilt Haus. Zack and Leona's basket had made everyone laugh. In it, Effie had put six cans of cat food, in honor of the kitten she knew Zack had given Leona for Christmas.

She loved the gifts she'd received just as much. Her siblings had given her a little booklet of coupons for her to redeem. They offered everything from rides home from school with Violet to trips to Yoder's for pie and offers of helping with her always dreaded math homework. Mamm and Daed had given her some new dresses and a backpack she'd been pining over for months.

After opening gifts and eating her *mamm*'s fresh banana pancakes, she, Violet, and Mamm had delivered blankets and food to the shelter in town and then spent the next couple of hours preparing lunch. Violet and her mother prepared a lasagna, roasted a chicken, and made a large dish of stuffing. And for the first time, Effie had been allowed to make most of the black forest cake they would serve for dessert.

Her parents were expecting twenty people for the meal. Karl was bringing his girlfriend; Violet was bringing her steady boyfriend, John; Zack and Leona were bringing Leona's parents; and several other neighbors and friends were coming over, too. All the guests were bringing side dishes. It was going to be wonderful.

But Effie thought the day was truly special because of the new sense of contentment that pervaded the family. Not only did everyone get along with one another, they seemed happy. Zack was no longer restless. Now, he was obviously in love with Leona and had made peace with his many jobs throughout the community.

And Violet seemed relieved that their parents were no longer upset with her decision not to become baptized in the Amish faith.

Yes, it was as if they'd all agreed to put aside their differences and give thanks for their blessings.

Effie knew she had much to be grateful for this year as well. The leg she'd broken was healed and strong, and—thanks to all the walking she'd been doing to and from the bus—she could now go several hours without wearing braces on her legs.

But the most wonderful celebration was that Josiah and his brother were going to be all right. He and Peter seemed to be really happy living with the Hiltys. Neither of them had to worry about bills or clothes or when and if they were going to be able to eat.

Now that Jay Hilty and Officer Roberts were working with Peter on reimbursing Beverly Overholt for all the damage he'd done, he no longer had to worry about being discovered or separated from his brother.

Every time Effie thought about that worried look she'd spied in Josiah's eyes, she gave thanks to God for helping to ease his fears.

Now, as everyone in town was getting settled for the annual parade, Effie suddenly caught sight of Josiah sitting next to Emma Hilty and one of her girls on the sidewalk. His elbows were resting on his knees and his expression was quietly shuttered. Just like usual.

But Effie also noticed that he looked far more relaxed than he had recently. He wasn't averting his eyes from the kids who walked by or looking especially worried. Instead, he looked much like the other people milling about; he was simply enjoying the warm weather, the beauty of a Christmas day in Sarasota, and the opportunity to relax.

She couldn't wait any longer to see him.

"Zack, I'm going to go over and say hi to Josiah, okay?"

"Sure, Ef," he said. "I think we're going to sit in that open space on the next block. If you decide to stay here, don't forget to tell me where you're gonna be."

"I won't." She loved that she was old enough and strong enough to do things like a normal teenager. Walking haltingly through the crowds because her mother had asked that she wear her braces on account of the long day and the amount of walking involved, Effie slowly made her way over to Josiah.

When he saw her, he stood up. "Hey, Effie. Merry Christmas."

"Merry Christmas to you," she replied. Looking around him, she smiled at Emma Hilty and little Annie. "Merry Christmas!"

"Merry Christmas to you, dear," Emma said.

"Emma, do you mind if I talk to Effie for a second?"

Emma's eyes softened as she pointed to a grassy area behind them. "Why don't you two go over there for a bit? That way you can have a bit of privacy."

"*Danke*," Josiah said before looking at Effie a bit more directly. "Is that okay with you?"

"It's fine." Of course, Effie would have eagerly agreed to whatever he wanted.

Josiah led the way through the crowds of people, pausing every couple of seconds to make sure Effie didn't need his help. When they got to the grassy area at last, Josiah grinned at her. "You did real *gut*, walking through the crowd, Ef."

"*Danke*. I told ya, I'm getting stronger."

"I'm proud of you."

"*Danke*," she said again, suddenly feeling shy. When she'd first seen him, she'd wanted to give him a hug and ask all about his stay at the Hiltys'. She wanted to ask how his brother was doing. How he was doing. But now she was afraid to bring any of it up. She would hate it if he started thinking that she was simply getting into his business. But she had to say something. He needed to know how much she cared about him. "Josiah, are you okay now?"

He shrugged. "I think so. I know things are better. That's a start, ain't so?"

"I hope so," she said earnestly. "Is your *bruder* doing better, too?"

"Peter is doing much better," he said with a smile. "He and Jay went over to Miss Beverly's last night and talked. He was really nervous about it, but she gave him a bunch of cake to bring home, so I guess it went all right."

Perhaps the right thing to do would be to drop the subject and talk about the upcoming parade, but Effie couldn't pretend that she didn't genuinely care about everything he'd been going through. Even if it made them both uncomfortable, she was pretty sure that it was better to talk about things instead of pretending that nothing had happened.

"I'm really sorry about your *daed*," she blurted.

"Me, too," he said quietly. "Ever since my *mamm* went to

heaven, it's felt like I lost my *daed*, too. He, um, he never used to act the way he did when you came over." He swallowed hard. "He left right after the social worker came and hasn't been back since. Officer Roberts said people are going to look for him but I kinda hope they don't find him anytime soon, you know?"

Effie nodded, not trusting her voice. It was a struggle to think of the right thing to say. But since no words were coming, she simply sighed instead.

Josiah stepped closer. "Don't worry about me, Effie. Everything will be all right."

"I hope so."

"I know so," he said, circling back to her first question. "Emma and Jay Hilty are nice people. So far, they've acted like Peter and I are part of their family and we haven't been part of a family in a mighty long time."

"At least you're with them today." Feeling like she wasn't making herself very clear, she said, "I mean on Christmas. I mean, I'm *verra* glad you and Peter aren't home alone today," she said at last.

He looked at her intently. "I'm thinking being surrounded by nice people and good friends on Christmas Day is the best thing of all."

Her insides warmed as she realized he was speaking about her. That he was thankful for their relationship. "Me, too, Josiah. Being with good friends is important."

He smiled. "Want to sit with me and Emma and her family?"

She couldn't think of anything she'd rather do. "*Jah*. Sure."

"*Gut*. Let's go tell your *bruder*, then we'll get our spots. The parade is about to start and I, for one, intend to get lots of candy."

As Effie walked by his side to do just that, she noticed more than one girl from their class watch her with a bit of envy in their eyes. She lifted her chin, feeling more than a little bit of pride to be seen walking next to the most popular boy in their class. But her smile came from her heart. Yes, Josiah was cute and popular, but what mattered the most was that he was now her friend.

It was such a *wonderful-gut* day. Such a *wonderful-gut* Christmas Day.

Chapter 23

Christmas Day

When she heard footsteps on the stairs, Beverly quickly pulled her white cotton nightgown and thick terry cloth robe more closely around her legs. Ack! She should have known better than to be lounging about in her nightclothes when there were guests around.

But just as she was wondering how to sneak across the sitting room to the kitchen, she realized the interloper was Eric. He was wearing baggy gray sweatpants and a faded T-shirt that fit him snugly. As usual, his feet were bare. His hair was damp, too. It was obvious he'd just gotten out of the shower.

"Hi," she said, attempting to ignore the warm feeling flowing through her at the sight of him. She really needed to stop noticing how attractive he was.

"Hi yourself," he teased as he crossed the room. "I didn't expect to see you here. It's late. What are you still doing awake?"

"I don't usually go to sleep this early, actually," she countered with a smile. "Did you need something?"

"I came down for a sandwich. It's been a couple of hours since we've eaten."

"Indeed. Probably at least four." After they'd come home from the parade, she, Eric, and Jack had pulled out the leftovers from their early lunch. Well, she'd had a small salad. The brothers had constructed hearty ham sandwiches and cut slices from the key lime pie she'd made earlier that morning.

Eric didn't look the least bit sheepish about late-night munching. "Four hours is a lot when your stomach is growling."

"To be sure," she teased. "Is Jack coming down, too?" If so, she was thinking she should go put on a dress. Eric and she were good enough friends to be around each other in nightclothes, but she would never feel as comfortable in front of another man.

"Nope. I think this quick trip has finally caught up with him. He's out like a light." But instead of making his way directly to the kitchen, Eric eyed her carefully. "You sure you're okay?"

"Jah." She pointed at their Christmas tree. "I would never tell my mother, but I've been enjoying this tree. I like the fresh pine smell and I love looking at the lights at night."

He leaned back against the wall and smiled. "Most people do." After another moment, he said slowly, "Bev, you sure you're only thinking about Christmas lights?"

"I was just thinking about a lot of things, if you want to know the truth."

"Let me guess. You were thinking about a certain pair of boys?"

"Maybe."

"I'm not surprised," he said as he settled down next to her, wrapping an arm around her shoulders. "I've been thinking about them, too."

Enjoying his comforting presence, Beverly allowed herself to lean into him. He responded by cupping her shoulder with his palm and bringing her closer. "I looked for them at the parade but I didn't see them. I had hoped to say hello."

"There were a lot of people there. I'm surprised you found anyone you recognized."

She shrugged. "But, still . . ." She let her voice drift off. It was probably for the best that they hadn't intruded on the boys' day, but she had wanted to see for herself that they were doing all right.

"Bev, you and I know Emma and Jay real well. If anyone can help those two boys start healing, it's them." He gave her a little squeeze.

"And Frankie! We canna forget him!"

He laughed. "Who could ever forget that crazy, hungry beagle?"

"No one who's attempted to enjoy a slice of pizza in peace," she joked. The Hiltys' dog had a terrible habit of losing all his manners whenever food was involved. Most everyone in Pinecraft had a story about Frankie and his never-ending quest for food that he shouldn't have.

"If you want, maybe we can stop over to see them in a couple of days," Eric offered. "You can bring a casserole or something."

Liking that they were making plans, Beverly nodded. "I would like that."

"Then that's what we'll have to do."

She practically melted against him, his words were so sweet. "*Danke*, Eric. Thank you for understanding."

"You're welcome," he said lightly. "I want to see them, too. And, well, I figure I'd better keep you smiling so you'll have some happy memories of our first Christmas together."

"You don't have to worry about that."

"Why not?"

How could she tell him how much this day had meant to her? For the first time in years she wasn't a guest in one of her friends' homes for Christmas. She hadn't been that proverbial third wheel. She'd had Eric by her side. And Jack, too!

Turning her head, she realized that Eric, too, was needing reassurance about how things were going between them. "You don't have to worry because it's been a wonderful day. The best."

He shifted so they were almost facing each other. His arm dropped from around her shoulders but then he caught her hand in his. Looking at their linked fingers, he nodded. "It has been a great day. I'll never forget it."

She loved the gentle way he touched her. Never would she take for granted Eric's easy affection. "So, did you enjoy the parade?"

"I did. I don't know what I expected, but what we saw wasn't it."

Beverly knew what he meant. It was a hodgepodge of Amish, Mennonite, English, and kitschy floats. People rode bicycles, cars, flatbed trucks, and everything in between. Local businesses decorated their entries. Why, even the Pioneer Trails bus had a sign. Through it all, everyone chatted to one another, tossed and ate candy, and wished each other Merry Christmas. Everyone said that they couldn't imagine such a parade ever existing anywhere but in Pinecraft.

Beverly sincerely hoped that was true.

Still playing with her fingers, Eric chuckled. "I really enjoyed watching Jack take everything in."

"He seemed to enjoy himself."

"I think he definitely did. He told me a number of times that he liked the area and that he could understand why I was deciding to move here."

"Pinecraft is mighty special."

"It is, but I think he realized that for me its appeal has less to do with quaint restaurants and shops and more to do with one pretty green-eyed lady."

She smiled softly. Eric had a way of making her feel pretty and wanted without feeling overwhelmed or unsure. In fact, she had become accustomed to looking forward to more than just his conversation. She liked the way he looked at her, as if there were no other person in the room. She enjoyed the way he frequently touched her, pressing a palm to her back when they walked, brushing a strand of hair away from her face when they sat together in the kitchen. Just that morning, he'd pressed one of her hands between his when he was making a point. She'd never thought she was the type of woman who would crave contact like that . . . but she certainly craved his.

When he leaned back, propping one bare foot on the opposite knee, and seemed content to simply gaze at the tree, Beverly let her mind drift. It seemed daydreaming about Eric had become one of her favorite activities. She couldn't help it, though. From the moment she'd run into him in the public library last spring he'd been steadily infiltrating her thoughts.

It was no surprise, though; he treated her differently from anyone else in her life. From flying out to Sarasota the day after the robbery to calling the Kaufmanns' to ask them to look after her, to now—when he was making sure she was taking a few hours for herself—Eric always seemed ready to put her needs ahead of his own.

Though she'd always had her family's love, she couldn't remember another person who had gone to such great lengths to see to her happiness. She wished she knew how to convey what he meant to her without making him uncomfortable. The last thing she ever wanted to do was scare him away.

So she made do with generalities. "Eric, today was really special. A beautiful day. Wonderful." Goodness. She'd now told him it was special, beautiful, and wonderful.

Oh, brother!

"I hope next year is just as nice."

"Me, too." She glanced at his face before turning back to the tree, though it no longer held the same appeal as the man beside her. Thinking about next year and wondering if they were simply destined to be friends, if she could ever be attractive enough to capture his interest, she added with false brightness, "I hope the weather will cooperate next year, too."

He smiled. "Yes. Let's hope so."

He was teasing her. She knew it. And why wouldn't he be teasing her? She was going on and on about the weather. And then going on about it some more!

"Sorry," she blurted. "I seem to be rambling. I, ah, must be more tired than I thought."

When he glanced at her again, this time with true concern in his eyes, she inwardly winced. Her voice had trembled and he'd heard it.

"Hey, Bev?"

"Jah?"

"When you think about next year, when you are making plans and such . . . are you only thinking about the weather?"

What could she say? *"Jah."*

"Really?" He looked disappointed.

"Well, um, *nee.* I mean, yes." Now he was staring at her as if she needed medication or something. She pursed her lips together, deciding it would be better for the both of them if she simply stopped talking.

He tilted his head to one side. "You're starting to speak Pennsylvania Dutch again. What has you so flustered?"

It was time to simply be honest. "Eric, I, um, I'm not sure what you expect me to say."

"Wait here a sec, Bev. Okay?"

Confused, she nodded, then bit her bottom lip as she watched him go up the stairs. What could he possibly need to do up there? Two minutes later he returned, now wearing a loose sweatshirt.

"Did you get cold, Eric?" she asked.

"Not really. I, uh, well, I have something for you. I've had it for quite some time," he said as he sat back down beside her.

"Another Christmas present?"

"Not exactly." He pulled out a small box from the pocket of his sweatshirt and held it tightly in his hand. "Beverly, I want you to know how I feel about you. I want you to know that my intentions toward you are pure."

Unable to do anything besides stare at the small box in his hand, her mind spun. What was he talking about? What kind of pure intentions did he have? "Is that some kind of Philadelphia saying?"

He shook his head. Then, to her surprise, flushed. "This is probably why we've had more than our fair share of ups and downs. I'm not all that good at sharing my feelings." He frowned. "And I pretty much stink at surprises."

She yearned to shake him. He was flustering her! "You stink at speeches, too. Eric, you need to be far clearer. What in the world are you talking about?"

He held up the box in a death grip. "I, um, bought you a ring." After looking at the box again, he kind of thrust it at her.

She took it. Held it in her hands carefully, like it might explode. "A ring?"

"Yeah." Staring at her intently, he added, "Beverly, I bought you a ring. It's, um, like an engagement ring."

She was so stunned, she kept staring at the box. "*Like* an engagement ring?"

And as each second passed, he looked more nervous. "Um, I know you grew up Amish. And the Amish don't wear jewelry. But, well, I've always imagined buying you a ring, so I did."

Her heart felt like it was beating a thousand times a minute. "Eric," she whispered. "Are you . . . are you proposing marriage to me?"

"Well, yeah. Aren't you going to open the box?" He paused,

looking even more unsure. "Or are you offended? Do you really not want to wear my ring?"

Oh, she wanted to. She wanted to wear that ring and launch herself into his arms! She wanted to smile and cry and maybe even shout. But first she wanted to hear the words from him that she'd secretly been dreaming about.

Carefully, she set the box on her lap. Then looked directly at him. "Aren't you going to ask me a question?"

His gaze flickered to hers before he nodded. "Yeah." A second later, he shook his head. "I mean, yes, Beverly, I am going to ask you a question."

Before she could ask what he intended to do now, Eric stood up, took a deep breath, and knelt at her feet.

Looking into his handsome face, seeing how earnest he was, Beverly had to remind herself to breathe. This was it! Suddenly, everything around her became brighter, more vivid, more pronounced. She smelled the pine in the room, noticed the glow from the red candles she'd lit over an hour before. Noticed a faint chill in the air.

Realized that everything she'd ever imagined happening was a pale substitute for the bright reality of this moment.

Eric reached for her hand. "Beverly, I don't even know when I fell in love with you. Maybe it was when you knocked into me at the library. Maybe it was when we had our first argument and I realized that you were just as stubborn as I am." Glancing down at their intertwined fingers, he smiled softly. "Who knows? Maybe it was when I realized that you have the prettiest green eyes I've ever seen. As well as the most generous heart I've ever known." Meeting her gaze again, he said, "All I do know is that I want to be your husband. Forever. So, will you marry me?"

"Forever," she repeated.

His eyes lit. "Yeah. I'm not going to want to ever let you go." The faint smile playing at the corners of his lips broadened. "Come on, Bev. Please say you'll marry me. Say you'll be my Christmas bride."

A Christmas bride.

Eric's Christmas bride. Could she have ever imagined anything more romantic? More perfect?

The tension between them tightened. Eric's broad smile dimmed as he waited.

"Yes," she finally replied after struggling to think of something just as perfect and beautiful to say back to him.

"Yes?"

"Yes!" She laughed. "Here," she said as she handed him the ring box.

Instantly, he looked crestfallen. "Bev, you don't even want to see it?"

"Of course I do. But I want you to put it on my finger, silly. I mean, isn't that how you Englishers do things?" she teased.

"Oh. Oh, well, okay, then." Carefully, he opened the box and pulled out a lovely white gold band inlaid with small diamonds all the way around it.

It was so sparkly and stunning, she gasped.

He looked almost apologetic. "I was going to get you a big diamond, but when I looked at the choices, I couldn't do it. Those big, showy diamonds didn't really seem like you. But then the jeweler showed me this. It's called an eternity band. He tried to tell me that it's usually only given for anniversaries . . . but I told him that we do things a little bit different in Philly." He rolled his eyes.

Finally, he held it up, turning it left and right, so it twinkled against the lights glistening on the tree. "Do you like it?"

She held out her left hand. "Let's see."

He held her hand and carefully slid it on her finger. The band felt warm from his touch. Though feeling it around her finger was a little strange, it was so very beautiful. She loved the idea of Eric wanting the world to know that she was his fiancée. Holding her hand up, she shifted it left and right, much like Eric had, enjoying the sight of such a lovely thing on her hand.

"Oh, Eric. It's so very perfect. I love it."

"It does look perfect on your hand. So, you'll wear it? You'll wear my ring, Bev?"

"I'll never take it off."

Smiling, he lifted her hand, gazed at the ring on her finger, then pressed her hand to his chest. And before she could ask what he intended to do next, she got her answer.

Because he was kissing her.

Just as if she was everything to him. Everything that mattered, anyway.

Epilogue

Christmas Eve, one year later

"You are going to be late for your own wedding if you aren't careful, Aunt Beverly," Tricia said, walking into Beverly's room.

"I won't be late. I'm almost ready." Fussing with one of the sleeves of her wedding gown, she added, "I was, um, just doing a little bit of last-minute primping."

"I'm sure you look— Oh!" Tricia gasped as she rounded the corner and gazed at Beverly in wonder. "Oh, Aunt Bev, look at you."

Beverly turned back to the mirror she'd been staring blankly into for the last ten minutes. She was wearing a long, thick white satin gown. It was devoid of lace and bows and such. Instead, it featured a simple neckline, long sleeves, and had princess seams along the bodice. On her head was a silver comb with fresh orange blossoms threaded into it. It held a lovely white veil that flowed over her shoulders and down her back.

Walking to her side, Tricia said, "Aunt Beverly, you look beautiful. An absolutely beautiful Christmas bride."

"Thank you, dear. I, um, well, I *feel* beautiful today."

"You should. You've been waiting forever for this day."

"Not quite forever. I'm only thirty-four, you know."

"You know I didn't mean your age," she protested, blushing softly. "I meant that you've been engaged for a whole year."

"Most people don't consider a year engagement to be too long," Beverly pointed out. "It's only around here in Pinecraft that people seem in a rush to tie the knot."

"Ben and I didn't see any need to wait."

Beverly looked pointedly at Tricia's stomach. "I can't say why I ever thought you would want to wait. You do everything quickly. Even beginning your family," she teased. Tricia had discovered she was pregnant just five months ago.

Her sweet niece folded her arms around her middle. "As you've told me time and again, everything happens at the right time and for the right reason."

"That is true." Beverly had planned to get married outside the Orange Blossom Inn under a big white tent like Emma and Jay Hilty had done. Unfortunately, the Lord had other plans. About four days ago, the weather had turned unseasonably cool. And with the colder temperatures had come torrents of rain. It had been raining steadily for days.

Knowing there was nothing to do for it, Beverly and Eric had moved everything indoors. At first she'd been disappointed, but so many of her friends had stepped in to make things as wonderful as they could, it was impossible to not be excited now.

Her longtime friends Winnie and Sadie had fashioned a garland of red roses and threaded it through every banister and over every surface. Ginny Kaufmann had gotten her family to help move furniture and set up all the tables and chairs around the inn. Penny Knoxx and Emma Hilty had organized the food in the kitchen and so many others had stopped by, offering good wishes and their assistance. Beverly never could have made everything work out alone. Their help had been invaluable.

Beverly stepped away from the mirror and peeked at her closed bedroom door. "How is everything going downstairs?"

"Great."

"Really?"

"Well, it is pretty crowded down there," Tricia said. "A lot of people came. A whole lot of people. It feels like half of Pinecraft is here!"

"Yes, all we're missing is the rest of our family." A fierce winter storm had prevented most of her and Tricia's family from making the trip down to Florida.

Tricia nodded. "Everyone sounded so sad when they called. But at least they're planning to come in a few weeks, when you are back from your honeymoon."

"You're right. Their visit will be just as welcome then." She was about to tell Tricia how glad she was that she was there when a brisk knock sounded at the door. Before Tricia could reach the handle, it opened.

"Bev, you decent?" Jack asked, looking very dapper in a black suit with a red rose pinned to his lapel.

"I am," she said with a smile. "How did you manage to be the person to check on me?"

"I'm the best man," he said with, she thought, a look of pride. Tilting his head to one side, he grinned. "Just so you know, Eric is going crazy downstairs. He sent me up here to tell you that you're late." Looking over at Tricia, he added, "You were supposed to bring her downstairs, not sit up here chatting."

"We're not that late," Tricia protested.

Obviously not about to start debating the time, Jack carefully placed the veil over Beverly's face, taking the time to arrange it so it fell in perfect waves over her shoulders. Then he smiled. "You look beautiful."

"Thank you."

Tricia handed her a bouquet of red roses tied simply with a wide green velvet ribbon. "Now you're all set, Aunt Bev."

"*Danke*, Tricia."

Jack walked to the door and opened it wide. "You ready to go put my brother out of his misery?"

"I suppose I had better," she teased as she took his arm.

"She's a bride, Jack," Tricia pointed out as she followed them to the door. "You should be saying something more romantic!"

"I don't need to be romantic. That's my brother's job," he replied over his shoulder. "All I've got to do is get her to him. On time."

"Which I was already doing," Tricia muttered.

Beverly stifled a smile as Jack walked her to the top of the landing. Then she became aware that pretty much everyone she'd ever met was standing below them. Ready to watch their descent.

And right in front, standing directly at the foot of the stairs, was Eric. He, too, was wearing a black suit with a red rose on his lapel. He looked exceptionally handsome. But what caught her attention the most was the way he was staring up at her. He looked awestruck.

Tricia moved around her and slowly descended first. When she reached the main floor, Eric kissed her cheek and handed her off to Ben.

Then Eric looked back up at Beverly and grinned. And held out his hand.

Tears pricked her eyes. It was really happening. Years after a broken engagement and running an inn by herself and months after meeting the man who'd changed her life, she was getting married right here in Pinecraft, in front of so many people whom she now considered close friends and family. She was so blessed.

"Don't even think about crying, Bev," Jack warned under his breath. "Eric's going to kill me if you fall down these stairs."

His gruff warning was all she needed for her tears to become a chuckle. "I won't fall."

His hand tightened on her arm, and without another word, he guided her down the two flights of stairs. Jack needn't have worried. Even though she was wearing a long satin gown, holding a bouquet of red roses, and walking with several yards of netting covering her face, she'd never felt more sure-footed.

Down and down they went, each step confident.

Next thing she knew, Eric had her arm in his and he was walking her through the throng of people to the preacher at the front of the inn's gathering room.

While all of their guests took their seats, Eric leaned close and whispered in her ear. "You're my beautiful bride, Beverly. My beautiful Christmas bride. Right here in the Orange Blossom Inn. Right here in Pinecraft."

Beverly didn't even attempt to stifle her bright smile. While Tricia might think his words a bit less than romantic, she thought they were the most glorious ones she'd ever heard. Because they signified everything good in her life. Everything that was perfect and vibrant and special.

Because it seemed that she no longer merely dreamed in color. She lived it now. And her future had never seemed so bright.

Acknowledgments

Though I am sad to now say good-bye to Pinecraft after writing four full-length books and one novella, I am so grateful to have been given the opportunity to write this series. I also want to thank the many people who have worked so hard to make these books so much more than my dreams for them.

First and foremost, I am grateful to my editor, Chelsey Emmelhainz. From our first conversation about Pinecraft, she guided the direction of the series and helped me craft four books of which to be proud.

I'm also indebted to the whole team at HarperCollins for their support of these books. Thank you to the art department for designing the beautiful covers and to Laura Hartman Maestro for designing an adorable Pinecraft map. Thank you to Molly Birckhead for working so hard to spread the word about the series. I'm also in awe of the sales teams who work so hard with both bookstores and libraries to get these novels on shelves.

I am so thankful and appreciative to my publicist, Joanne Minutillo. Not only did she make our series launch and girlfriend getaway such a success down in Pinecraft, she joined me there! When I say she's amazing, she really is!

Thank you also goes out to photographer Katie Troyer for providing the lovely photos of Pinecraft, for author Sherry Gore for providing many of the recipes, and for Laurie and Lynne here in Cincinnati who do more things behind the scenes than I could ever list.

No acknowledgments like this would be complete without mentioning my husband, Tom. Thank you, Tom, for all the dinners you've cooked, the miles you've driven me to signings, and the hours you've listened to me talk about people who only exist in my imagination. You are one in a million, Tom. Really.

Thank you to my readers whose enthusiasm makes me want to write every day.

And finally, I would be remiss if I didn't mention how grateful I am for God's blessings and His presence when I write these novels. I know I don't write these books alone. He gives me the words.

Insights, Interviews & More . . .

About the author

About the book

Read on

Meet Shelley Shepard Gray

The New Studio

PEOPLE OFTEN ASK how I started writing. Some believe I've been a writer all my life; others ask if I've always felt I had a story I needed to tell. I'm afraid my reasons couldn't be more different. See, I started writing one day because I didn't have anything to read.

I've always loved to read. I was the girl in the back of the classroom with her nose in a book, the mom who kept a couple of novels in her car to read during soccer practice, the person who made weekly visits to the bookstore and the library.

Back when I taught elementary school, I used to read during my lunch breaks. One day, when I realized I'd forgotten to bring something to read, I turned on my computer and took a leap of faith. Feeling a little like I was doing something wrong, I typed those first words: *Chapter One*.

I didn't start writing with the intention of publishing a book. Actually, I just wrote for myself.

For the most part, I still write for myself, which is why, I think, I'm able to write so much. I write books that I'd like to read. Books that I would have liked to have in my old teacher tote bag. I'm always relieved and surprised and so happy when other people want to read my books, too!

Another question I'm often asked is why I choose to write inspirational fiction. Maybe at first glance, it does seem surprising. I'm not the type of person who usually talks about my faith in the line at the grocery store or when I'm out to lunch with friends. For me, my faith has always felt like more of a private thing. I feel that I'm still on my faith journey—still learning and studying God's word.

And that, I think, is why writing inspirational fiction is such a good fit for me. I enjoy writing about characters who happen to be in the middle of their faith journeys, too. They're not perfect, and they don't always make the right decisions. Sometimes they make mistakes, and sometimes they do something they're proud of. They're characters who are a lot like me.

Only God knows what else He has in store for me. He's given me the will and the ability to write stories to glorify Him. He's put many people in my life who are supportive and caring. I feel blessed and thankful . . . and excited to see what will happen next!

Letter from the Author

Dear Reader,

Last year we went to Denver for Christmas. My son had moved there about six months before and only got Christmas Eve and Christmas Day off. So, instead of having Arthur come home for Christmas, we went to him.

Like most people just starting out, his apartment was small. It was also filled with a bunch of our old furniture, skis, plastic bins filled with who-knows-what, and one sixty-five-pound furry white dog named Rudy. Our daughter Lesley opted to sleep on Arthur's floor on an air mattress. Tom and I opted to sleep at a hotel nearby.

To be honest, I have always liked hosting Christmas. I like putting up the tree. I love to bake. I like doing all the little "Christmasy" things that moms like to do for their kids, even when their kids are adults. Because of all that, I didn't exactly have real high expectations for this first Christmas where I wasn't the host. I shouldn't have worried, though. It turns out that our son loved hosting Christmas.

It also turned out that there are several advantages to four people and one furry dog hanging out together in a one-bedroom apartment. We spent lots of time together! We played Scrabble and Clue. Life and Hearts. Somehow, all four of us managed to make a standing rib roast with all the trimmings in a very tiny kitchen. We ate our Christmas meal around an old table with mismatched chairs and mismatched plates and silverware. It was perfect. Afterward, we all settled in and watched old James Bond movies. Rudy chewed on a bone.

Our time together was simple. We didn't do anything all that special. And because of that, I have to admit that it was the nicest

Christmas we'd had together in years. It turns out Arthur can host Christmas just fine.

We flew home on the morning of December twenty-sixth. I'd love to say it was an emotional good-bye, but it was hectic. It was snowing, Art was defrosting his car so he could go to work, and Lesley was trying to find something to put on that wasn't covered in white Rudy fur. It was only when we landed back in Cincinnati that I realized that our whirlwind trip was over and we wouldn't likely have another couple of days like that until, well, next Christmas.

Already I can't wait.

Thank you for reading this book. I hope you have a blessed Christmas, whether you're at home or in someone else's. Take time to give thanks, hug those who love you, and glory in the miracle of His birth.

Merry Christmas!
Shelley Shepard Gray

P.S. I love to hear from readers, either on Facebook, through my website, or through the postal system! If you'd care to write and tell me what you thought of the book, please do!

Shelley Shepard Gray
10663 Loveland Madeira Rd. #167
Loveland, OH 45140

Questions for Discussion

1. The book opens with Beverly being devastated by an unexpected event. How do you think she handles it?

2. After Eric reveals more of his past, Beverly is hurt that he'd kept much of it a secret. Who is right? Eric, for being cautious about revealing his past, or Beverly for wishing that he'd trusted her more from the beginning of their relationship?

3. Why do you think Josiah and Effie have become such good friends? How do they need each other?

4. Why do you think it was easier for Eric to ask Beverly's close friends for help than it was for her to reach out to them? Can you think of a situation in your life where it was hard to ask for help when you needed it?

5. What are your first impressions of Mark, Laura, and Peter?

6. One of the novel's themes is accepting and offering help, even when doing either is difficult to do. Can you think of a time when you've either accepted help that you didn't want to accept . . . or when you've offered to help someone without being asked?

7. How does Beverly become stronger during the novel? If you've read the series, how has she changed during the entire series?

8. What do you think will happen to Josiah and Peter?

9. What characters in the series did you connect with the most? Are there any that you would like to read more about?

Golatschen Christmas Cookies

Golatschen *is the German word for "pastry"*

⅔ cup sugar
1 cup butter, softened
½ teaspoon almond extract
2 cups flour
Any flavor jelly

Icing

1 cup powdered sugar
2–3 teaspoons water
1½ teaspoons almond extract

Preheat oven to 350°F. Cream sugar, butter, and ½ teaspoon of almond extract. Add flour and mix well. Shape into 1-inch balls and place on ungreased cookie sheets. Press thumb in centers and fill with 1 teaspoon jelly. Bake 10 to 12 minutes.

Mix icing ingredients, adding more water until icing is runny. Drizzle over warm cookies.

Shelley's Top Five Must-See Spots in Pinecraft

Honestly, I fell in love with everything about the tiny village of Pinecraft, nestled in the heart of Sarasota and nearby Siesta Key! Here are five places to start your journey:

1. *Yoder's Restaurant.* I've been to a lot of Amish restaurants. I've eaten a lot of coconut cream pie at each one. But nothing has compared to this well-known restaurant. The line to get in is always long, usually at least a thirty-minute wait. But the long lines allow everyone to chat and make friends.
2. *The Produce Market at Yoder's.* The market next to Yoder's is full of beautiful Florida-fresh produce. We couldn't resist picking up two pints of strawberries and five oranges. Just to snack on—in between servings of pie, of course!
3. *Pinecraft Park.* It's the social center of the community! The night we were there, kids were playing basketball, men and women were playing shuffleboard (women have their own lane), and there were at least another forty or fifty people standing around and visiting.
4. *The bus parking lot.* Behind the post office is a large parking lot where everyone meets to either board one of the Pioneer Trails buses or to watch who is arriving and leaving.
5. *Village Pizza.* It's located right behind Olaf's Creamery. You can order a pie and take it right over to one of the picnic tables outside. The pizza is delicious. Eating pizza outside in the sunshine in February in the Florida sun? Priceless.

Scenes from Pinecraft

Photographs courtesy of Katie Troyer, Sarasota, Florida

The Pioneer Trails bus arrives in Pinecraft.

Siblings and friends at Big Olaf in Pinecraft.

Scenes from Pinecraft *(continued)*

Enjoying a Song Fest at Pinecraft Park.

Playing bocce in Pinecraft Park.

A Sneak Peek from the First Book in Shelley's New Series, *A Charmed Amish Life*

A Son's Vow

Coming January 2016 from Avon Inspire

IT WAS ANOTHER picture-perfect day in Charm.

The sky was a pale blue, quietly complementing acres of green, vibrant farmland as far as the eye could see. Spring lambs had arrived. They were frolicking in the fields, their eager bleats echoing through the valley. The morning air was not too chilly or too damp. Instead, a hint of warmth teased the air, bringing with it as much hope as the tips of the crocus buds that peeked through the dark dirt filling the numerous clay pots decorating cleanly swept front porches.

It was the type of morning that encouraged a person to go out walking, to smile. The type of day that reminded one and all that God was present and did, indeed, bestow gifts.

In short, it was the type of day that used to give Darletta Kurtz hope. It used to spur her energy, revitalize her. It used to make her want to pull out a pencil and one of her many notebooks and record the images she saw and list activities she wanted to do.

It was the kind of day she used to love and maybe—just maybe—take for granted.

But now, as she rested her elbows on the worn wooden countertop that no doubt generations of postal workers before had rested on, too, Darla only silently acknowledged that another day had come. It was sure to feel as endless as the one before it, and would no doubt be exactly like the rest of the week. ▶

A Sneak Peek from the First Book in Shelley's New Series, *A Charmed Amish Life* *(continued)*

It was another day to get through. A way to pass ten hours of expected productivity before she could retreat to her bedroom and collapse on her bed. Only then would she feel any sense of peace. Because only then would she be able to wait for oblivion. She'd close her eyes, fall into a peaceful slumber, and, hopefully, forget her reality for eight hours.

Until nightfall, however, she had the day to survive.

It was the ninety-ninth day since her father had died. Tomorrow would bring the one hundredth. It was a benchmark she'd never intended to look forward to. Wearily, she wondered if anyone else in Charm was anticipating the milestone as well.

Undoubtedly some were.

After all, her father hadn't been the only man to die in the accident at the Kinsinger Lumber Mill. No, he was one of five. Though she'd never forget, there were many in Charm who took care to remind her of this constantly.

As Mary Weaver pushed open the door and strode forward, Darla braced herself.

"You have a lot of nerve, Darletta Kurtz, getting a job here like you did," Mary said as she slapped a ten-dollar bill on the counter. "It's bad enough that your family stayed in town, but here you are, thriving."

Each word hurt, as Mary no doubt intended for it to. Darla thought she would have been used to the verbal abuse by now, but it still felt like a slap in the face.

Just as she did two days before, Darla did her best to keep her voice even and her expression impassive. "What can I get ya?"

"One book of stamps. The flags."

After opening the thick wooden drawer that had served countless mail workers before her, Darla scanned the UPC code on the stamps and picked up the money. Quickly, she gave Mary the stamps and her change, taking care to set it on the counter so their fingers wouldn't have to touch. "Here you go, Mary. *Danke* for coming in."

Mary narrowed her eyes. "That's all you're gonna say?"

It was obvious that Mary was itching for a fight. But no way was Darla going to give it to her. She'd learned at least a couple of things in the ninety-nine days since the accident at the mill. It was always best to turn the other cheek. "There's nothing to say. Your mind is made up to be angry with me."

"My 'mind' has nothing to do with the facts. Everyone in Charm knows that your father caused the accident at the mill. He killed my Bryan, Clyde Fisher, Paul Beachy, and Stephen Kinsinger."

"You forgot to add one: John Kurtz, Mary. My father died, too, you know."

Mary's mouth flattened. "All of us are struggling with our losses. Struggling to make ends meet with our men gone. But here you are almost every morning, standing behind this counter with a smile on your face."

Though Mary wasn't the first person to say such a thing to her—she wasn't even the twenty-first—Darla still didn't understand why she should bear the weight of her father's guilt.

Especially since it had been proven that while her father's sleeve had gotten caught, and he had jerked and fallen into a stack of timber that had collapsed, he certainly hadn't intended to hurt a single person at the mill. Everyone who'd been there was marked by the terrible tragedy in December. Furthermore, when Stephen Kinsinger's son Lukas took over the mill, he'd publicly forgiven her father.

However, Lukas's speech had done little to change the general feeling of anger and hurt that pervaded their village. Somehow, it seemed that everyone needed someone to blame. And because John Kurtz wasn't there, many people felt his children would have to bear the brunt of the community's hurt and anger.

Now that it had been going on for ninety-nine days, Darla was getting pretty tired of it.

Which was why, even though she would likely not be heard, she stood up a little straighter and glared. "I'm merely doing my job, Mary."

Blue eyes flashed with anger. "What do you have to say about Aaron? He is still at the mill."

Clenching her hands, Darla fought to remain still. Her relationship with Aaron was both confusing and difficult. "I canna speak for my *bruder*," she said quietly.

"Everyone says he is becoming a problem. Men have heard him fault the mill for your father's poor judgment."

"Any problem Aaron might have at work is between him and Lukas and Levi Kinsinger," she said, staring directly at Mary and not the customers who'd just entered. "Now, do you need anything else?"

"I do not. You know I only came in here to give you a piece of my mind."

"And you've done that," a voice from the back of the room interrupted. It was one that Darla knew well. One that, until very recently, she used to hear on a daily basis.

Mary swerved around. "Lukas!" she exclaimed in a sickly sweet voice. "I didn't hear you come in." ▸

A Sneak Peek from the First Book in Shelley's New Series, *A Charmed Amish Life* *(continued)*

"I've only been here long enough to hear what you just said to Darla," Lukas Kinsinger replied. "I must say that I'm shocked to hear you are speaking to her in such a tone."

As Darla watched, Mary stepped away from the counter and toward Lukas, who was standing with his arms folded over his chest.

"How is your family, Lukas? My Thomas and I have been praying for you and your siblings."

"I appreciate your prayers, but I would be just as glad to know that you were praying for all the victims' families. Remember, forgiveness is a virtue."

"So is repentance," she replied as she looked over at Darla.

When Lukas said nothing, merely stared at her coolly, Mary darted outside.

Feeling his gaze now settle on her, Darla helped the two customers who were holding packages. Then, when the room was empty except for the two of them, she walked around the counter.

"Lukas."

"Hello, Darla." His light blue-gray eyes remained serious though his lips curved into the slightest of smiles. "How are you today?"

"I am well, *danke*," she lied. "What are you doing here?"

"Rebecca told me you got this job here two weeks ago. I wanted to see how it was going."

"I am learning a lot. It's a blessing, I think."

His eyes narrowed. "It didn't sound like it when I arrived. Does that happen a lot?"

"Does Mary come in to give me grief? *Jah*."

"I'll talk to her for you."

"*Danke*, but I'd rather you did not. She is upset and grieving. Sooner or later she'll let go of her anger." Well, she hoped so.

"What about you? Are you still grieving and upset?" he asked quietly.

She didn't know how to answer that. They'd once been good friends. Best friends. She should be able to converse with him by now. But ever since the accident, it felt like there was too much between them to ever speak to each other easily. Not only did they have their own grief to tackle but her brother was very angry. And, she heard, his brother was, too.

"I'm doing about as well as can be expected," she murmured, thinking of their preacher's last visit. He'd prayed with her and spoke of forgiveness. She hoped one day soon that advice would ease her heart. After gazing out the store's front window and seeing it devoid of prospective customers, she forced herself to continue their stilted conversation. "And you, Lukas? How are you today?"

"Almost *gut*."

"Why is that?"

The smile that had been playing on his lips transformed into a full grin. "The lambs are out."

"I heard them this morning. The Millers have a lively bunch this year." She almost smiled back at him. Even when he was a little boy, Lukas had loved the arrival of the spring lambs. Her *daed* used to ask him over just so Lukas could hold a newborn lamb from time to time. Just last year she'd teased Lukas, saying that it was a shame they no longer raised sheep because she would have enjoyed the sight of him in his plaid pajama bottoms and old undershirt, holding a day-old lamb like it was the most precious thing on earth.

He stuffed his hands in his back pockets. "We should stop by the Millers soon. You know they won't mind us visiting the lambs."

Just like they used to do.

Darla looked at the door longingly. Wished another customer would enter so Lukas would move on and not make her remember how close they used to be. And how welcome Lukas would be at the Millers' while her appearance would be barely tolerated.

"I don't have time to visit lambs. With my new job, I am pretty busy, you know. Now, how may I help you?"

"Shouldn't I be asking you that?" he said softly as he stepped toward her.

His softly spoken question, laced with just the slightest bit of affection, made her flinch. She raised her guard. If she didn't keep herself firmly in check she was liable to weaken and say something she would regret.

They'd been friends for a very long time. Lukas knew how close she'd been to her father. He'd meant the world to her. Surely he had to have known how difficult it was for her for his reputation to now be tainted? Couldn't he imagine how hard it was for her to even get through each day?